T0150109

An
Italian
Affair

AMANDA
BURNS

FiNGERPRINT!

Published by
FiNGERPRINT!
An imprint of Prakash Books India Pvt. Ltd

113/A, Darya Ganj,
New Delhi-110 002
Email: info@prakashbooks.com/sales@prakashbooks.com

 Fingerprint Publishing
 @FingerprintP
 @fingerprintpublishingbooks
www.fingerprintpublishing.com

ISBN: 978 93 5856 841 7

Dedication

To Fabio

Acknowledgment

Love always to *Stefano* for inspiring the story. And so much love and thanks to my friends. With extra special love to Mimi and Stella, Eleni, Hermione; friends are the longest love relationships we have; friendship lasts longer than husbands and lovers. Thanks to my lifelong friend Dijana Dawe, who speaks her mind with candor, who let me know there was something here.

A special mention to my dear friend Carolyn Burdet, an editor whose conversations encouraged my re-writes of the earliest drafts, and whose editing for the version sent to publishers, smoothed the possibility of a story that slips down like a summer spritz.

I am grateful to Sesh Subrahmanian who made the introduction to Fingerprint Publishing. As a new author my gratitude goes to Shantanu Duttagupta, executive publisher at Fingerprint Publishing, who believed in the story and agreed to publish the book. Many thanks to my editor at Fingerprint, Shilpa Mohan, who helped me shape the manuscript into what you hold now.

To my children, Renato, Bella, and Sophia, who are the lights in my life. They are the reason to keep growing in life, hopefully lighting the way for them to grow toward what might become reality in their lives if they want it enough.

Thanks to my first readers, Janet Gaze, Deb Greaves, Kate Hobson, Tania Horozides, Julie Kalman, and Kath Pelletti, whose early feedback offered me encouragement and support along the way. To Davide who always finds time to collect me from airports and train stations and take me out for pizza, his partner Deborah agrees that he is *buono come il pane*. To Manuela for her friendship that began the year I fell in love with life.

And to all of you who hold this book in your hands. I hope you enjoy the story. I hope it reminds you of that first love, the one that gave you sleepless nights for all the right and all the wrong reasons. That person who will always have a special place in your heart and soul and, in quiet moments and chaotic times, the memory of them reminds you that love is all there is.

Prologue

This story is about love and longing, but mostly it is about courage. Courage in the real meaning of following your heart. Of putting your heart out there, reaching toward what may be possible.

Sometimes you have to take a risk. Step forward into a space yet unformed, unknown, unsteady. Courage to say words that make you vulnerable. To be yourself in a way that strips you to the bone. Whether that takes you to far flung places or deep within yourself. Whether it is a journey of one step or a thousand miles. Your soul knows you should take it, no matter the outcome. We have one wild, amazing, enchanting moment on this earth. Embrace it.

PART
ONE

Girls' Weekends Are Dangerous

Julia held the keys to the small apartment. High on the rooftops of Verona, it was even more gorgeous than she'd imagined. Huge windows ran from floor to ceiling, blending the ancient with the modern and ensuring there was plenty of light and a sense of space. The large balcony, dressed in billowing curtains, was perfect for morning coffee. The bedroom nestled higher up on the mezzanine floor.

Looking at her phone, Julia thought about the message she needed to send. All the messages that had been sent. What would happen? After last week. After the walls between them had come crumbling down. Naked, exposed, together.

Would he come?

CHAPTER

1

The Winter AGM

Julia felt the wind moving her hair as she drove along the coast road. Sunny for June, she was taking advantage of the sunshine to put the roof down and let her hair down. A long weekend with the girls. Their annual general meeting, as they called it, where they would go over the year, celebrate, commiserate, drink, eat, dance, and then set goals for the next trip around the sun.

She was more than ready for this girls' weekend. Especially after a long overdue ending. Her nose wrinkled at the part the breakup was going to play in the conversation. Her closest friends, Mimi and Stella, hadn't liked Lars, but her friends knew her well, and they knew she would fall out of it, eventually.

Julia put it firmly out of her mind. Today was far too gorgeous to be dwelling on all that. Open-top car, loud music, and delicious things to eat and drink in the back seat. Turning up her favorite playlist, she flew down the highway.

The girls were already there, waiting. "Hey chicas!" she greeted them, turning off the music as she jumped out and was enveloped in four arms. "What were you playing?" Mimi demanded, "It was so loud!"

"Some Italian band I'm sure," Stella rolled her eyes with a smile. Julia's obsession with all things Italian had become part of who she was, though it was fun to tease her about it every now and again. Dancing around in a circle together, the excitement of the weekend was rising. Talking over each other, they led her inside to show her around.

"What a house!" Julia let out a low whistle. "This my room?" she poked her head through a doorway and looked enviously at the huge bed. Stella pointed down the corridor to another bedroom door.

"Thanks." Dumping her overnight bag on the bed, she threw her jacket over the armchair. With a glance at the marble tiles in the bathroom, she decided a bath was going to be her first treat, with a glass of prosecco in hand. Memories of long shared bubble baths, drunk on love, lay deep below her conscious mind. They stirred, awakened by the lightness in her heart.

She followed the voices back to the huge living room. Opening the fridge, she saw it was full of wine. "Girls, is this our entire menu?" she laughed, shaking her head.

Julia was a lightweight at the girls' weekends, falling into bed hours before the other two. It was astonishing that they had put up with her for all these years. Still, this weekend would be different. This weekend she was simply going to say, "Yes!" Yes to the next glass of wine. Yes to everything. Resolved, she pulled out a bottle of sparkling wine.

"Time for bubbles?" There was a resounding, "Yes!"

Julia turned her attention to the bottle. "Stand back," she warned. It was a running joke that prosecco and Stella were a dangerous combination after one fateful party when Stella had opened a fizzy bottle and nearly blinded herself on the flying cork.

Mimi waved to them from the balcony, "Come out here."

The breeze was light and full of scents from the sea that lapped onto the sand below them. Mimi had moved the chairs back from the table so they could sit facing the magnificent view. Julia slipped into her seat with a sigh of happiness.

"Cheers! Here's to a great girls' weekend." They all clinked glasses while Stella held their pose for a photo.

"I love it when we get together," sighed Mimi, her glass still raised in cheers. "It's been too long." She took a long draw on a joint, the first joint of many she would roll this weekend, and exhaled. "I'm totally ready for it."

She reached past Julia to hand it to Stella. "Yes, to everything, right?" Julia reminded herself. Reaching out her hand, she took the joint from Mimi's outstretched hand. The other two looked at her in shock.

"What?" Julia said with an air of feigned innocence. "Can I remind you, Mimi, who was it that rolled your first joint?"

"Very true! Joints and pizza. Go for it, babe. You deserve it."

They had shared a house long ago. It was a friendship that was at times raw, revealing, and uncompromising, yet always accepting, supportive and uplifting.

"I love you guys," Mimi said, contentedly.

"We've only just started,' grumbled Stella. "Don't get all sentimental on us."

They all laughed.

Settling in, they began the slow meandering unpacking of the last year, listening intently, sometimes talking over each other. Food was made, and eaten and plenty more food was prepared. They moved inside as night fell.

Stella put on some music and Julia went to get more wine from the kitchen. She topped up their glasses, swaying to the music. She had always loved to dance. They somehow always got into nightclubs, no matter their real age. Recently it was at parties or to the occasional band at a pub. Or she would turn up the speakers, open a music playlist, and dance at home when her children weren't around. Early adulthood was only slightly better than early adolescence in that their disapproval was less vocal but there were still looks of barely concealed horror.

"So," started Mimi, and a look passed between her and Stella, which meant they had planned something to say.

"I can feel this is going to be not so fun." Julia had a pretty good idea it would be about her love life or non-existent one.

"You're right," said Mimi, looking intently at Stella, "but it might be time to talk about what happened with Lars?"

"Yes," Stella chimed in, "what happened? Not that I'm unhappy you gave him the boot. I wasn't a fan. I'll concede he was tall and handsome."

". . . and rich," added Mimi. "But let's face it, he was a bit of a bore."

"He was an arse," Stella said, more bluntly. "I could never understand what you saw in him."

Julia laughed a little uncomfortably. She knew there would be no peace until she had offered up this story. She also knew they were asking about it because they only wanted the best for her.

Lars, she sighed. Drawing in a breath, Julia recounted the last few months of the failed relationship with brutal honesty. It was hard, she would rather have minimized the destruction of something she had once held out such hope for.

"When we first met, there was such an attraction. It took me by surprise. I hadn't expected to feel like that again, to actually want someone. Physically, I mean," Julia laughed self-consciously.

"He was also, conveniently, about to leave the country. I thought, perfect. I can pretend to fall in love and just play with that feeling, you know. It had been such a long time." She paused, shrugging. Mimi slipped an arm around her shoulders. Mimi had been there, by Julia's side, as her husband Hugh let go of his last breath. There were some things that didn't need words.

"I guess I wanted to dive into that feeling, that unexpected feeling that love can still be as delicious as it once was. Well, I'm not sure we can ever fall into it as totally and ridiculously as we do the first time. You know, the very first time," Julia closed her eyes, remembering. A face, one she tried hard to forget, swam into her mind.

Mimi nodded. "Mmm hmmm," she agreed. "Know just what you mean."

"When he decided he was going to commit, I was hopeful. And for a few months it was . . ." Julia paused and pulled her wrap closer. "Well, it was just lovely. It got harder as he got closer. He became so, I don't know, critical and suspicious. I think I tried to pour love into a space that ultimately was not able to hold it. Like a broken dam."

Stella passed her the joint and Julia took a long pull. It helped loosen her tongue.

"Then it wasn't lovely anymore. And eventually I had to stop because I wasn't getting replenished. I did warn him, but I don't think he believed I would end it." She sighed deeply, "Hope is the thing that keeps love alive. Even when things are hard. Hope and the knowledge that whatever is currently in play, it will pass. I stopped believing it would pass. I stopped hoping."

The first inkling of her change of heart came in as a feeling of safety went out. His rages became more aggressive. She would notice him watching her. She took a photo without him realizing. Catching his face pulled into a shape that made her blood run cold. Whenever her resolve wavered, she would go back to look at that photo.

"Stop," said her heart. "There is no space for love here." But Julia's mind argued back, trying to point out all the good things. But it was too late and what was left was not enough. Hope went with it.

"Ultimately, I think I couldn't see myself with someone who lacked a generosity of spirit and a sense of forgiveness."

"For a Christian, he was very judgey," Mimi agreed.

"You mean, he was a hypocrite," said Stella, bluntly. "Wasn't he really jealous of some guy in your past?" Stella said, pointedly raising an eyebrow.

Julia felt a jolt as her heart missed a beat. "Oh yes, he was so jealous, but there was no reason to be. He even tried to forbid me from ever going to Verona again! As though somehow it would seduce me into doing something. Or as though someone would be waiting for me. Ridiculous. And anyway that was thirty years ago, for goodness' sake. I was a different person."

Wasn't she?

"Hmmm," said Mimi, "maybe we should see if we can find him for you."

"Who? No!" Julia snorted, "Let's not. Why don't we concentrate on Stella's goal of getting an online profile."

"No deflecting," said Mimi, waving any possible interruption away. "Just because one guy didn't work out, doesn't mean you can sneak back into your shell. You've done your work. Your kids are adults. Hugh's been gone a long time now. It's time to live for yourself."

Mimi was just hitting her stride, dancing to the tune she'd chosen from the playlist. Stella was nodding in agreement.

"Sure," Julia sighed, "just find me a tall dark handsome Italian-speaking billionaire, and I'm in." Though the prosecco and conversation were a reminder that there was only one. There had only ever been one.

"Psssh, what are you always saying? A man is not a financial plan," snorted Stella, "though the rest is fair enough. What about the one Lars was jealous of? Wasn't he Italian? Yes, I'm sure he was." Stella had the instinct of bloodhound, she couldn't let the idea go, and she was beginning to wonder if that Italian had something to do with Julia's obsession.

"What! No! No. I don't think so," Julia shook her head. "Italian, yes. But that's all in the past," she was laughing too much at Stella's raised eyebrow, which she waggled at her friend along with the half-full bottle. "That is so in the past. Come on, it was thirty years ago. Top me up, please! Anyway, Stella, it's your turn."

Mimi and Stella were finally diverted, and Julia let out a quiet sigh of relief as the spotlight shifted from her.

Stella had separated from her husband a year ago after they had been married for decades. She was ready to move on fast. No time to waste and too many men to be sampled. So many hilarious encounters, and the most recent account of a drunken night and a handsome young man who had been more than willing to help Stella move on! They had laughed until their cheeks hurt.

Julia wasn't so sure she was ready to enter that fray again. She was still recovering from the jealous rages that had punctuated the last months of her relationship with Lars. Julia had never encountered stifling jealousy before. Lars would fly into a rage over the smallest thing, anything that reminded him that she had had a life before meeting him. She had tried to be patient, reassuring, compassionate. But she found herself tied up in knots, not knowing what to say or what to share. Then she would be accused of lying because he was convinced she hadn't told him something or she had left something out.

The reality was that she left things out because he would jump on them as some sort of warped evidence that she was not capable of loving him, or he would use it as an excuse to start a row, slamming her integrity. Julia began to sort through her life, trying to anticipate what might trigger his rage. It was a Sisyphean task, as the triggers were completely random. A song in a shop, a scene in a movie, or an ad on TV. It was futile. When he started turning up at places unannounced and uninvited, she felt suffocated. Eventually, she had disentangled herself and stepped away. No. Julia was happy to be single again. She missed the intimacy. But the cost was too high, and peace was too sweet to resist.

The girls were busy preparing to launch Stella onto the dating scene. Gathering around the laptop, they drafted a profile for Stella that was honest and funny.

"Ok," Stella's finger hovered over the go live button, "shall I?"

"Do it, do it!" they cried in unison.

"Done!"

Not a minute passed before Stella exclaimed, "Oh, someone has liked me, oh and someone else. This is a bit full-on!" Then they were all laughing and checking out the possible suitors.

Mimi and Julia smiled conspiratorially at each other. Stella had come through a difficult time; it was great to see her open to the possibility of meeting someone new. She gave the appearance of being extremely tough and formidable which was a handy quality in her role running a large organisation. Yet, any threats to her family could crush her. Even if she didn't share it with many people, the break-up of her family had been devastating. Mimi and Julia were waiting for her to get to the anger part. It would come. And it would not be pretty. Stella was always forthright and at times, shocking in her observations and comments, but her heart was generous and kind.

Mimi sidled up to Julia. "Don't think we have forgotten about you, Ms Cancerian hiding in your shell!"

Julia laughed, knowing she had only sidestepped that issue for the moment. She had hoped they wouldn't return to that topic this weekend. It was a false hope. She could probably distract Mimi or at least appeal to her softer side. Stella was another thing altogether. It wasn't long before Stella, satisfied with the online attention her own profile had received but not ready to take it further, brought up the topic.

"Okay, so who was the Italian lover you lived with that year? Was he hot? I don't think I have ever seen a photo. Mimi, have you seen him?" Stella was all about men at the moment.

"Nope," Mimi shook her head, looking at Julia with a shrug of her shoulders. "See I told you there would be no escape."

"I don't have any pictures of him," Julia answered. "It was last century you know. Cameras on your phone weren't a thing. In fact, mobile phones weren't even a thing."

"Thank goodness!" said Mimi. They laughed, well aware of how grateful they were for a life lived with much less scrutiny and fewer records of youthful misadventure.

"Yes, but," there was no getting away from Stella when she had a path she wanted to follow. "What was the story, come on, spill the tea."

Julia laughed and Mimi looked puzzled. Stella had a way of finding things out and there was no doubt that there was no chance of not 'spilling the tea' or telling all.

"Okay," Julia resigned herself to the grilling. "You know I lived in Italy for a year when I was 23. I lived with a very handsome and sexy Italian man called Stefano, who truly showed me what love was. And then he broke my heart."

"Ahh things are making sense," prompted Stella. "How come Lars was so jealous of him. Is there something you're not sharing?

Are you still in contact with him? Come on, if you can't tell us, then who can you tell?"

That was true. Even though Julia was deeply private about many things, there was a small handful of people who knew her thoughts, maybe not the innermost thoughts, but most of her secrets.

"There really isn't anything to tell. I left when I was 24 when I found out that he had a long-term girlfriend from his village. Very Italian. I asked him to choose, and he couldn't commit to doing that. I wanted more from life than to hang around waiting for him to make a decision, so I left Italy, came back to Melbourne, and eventually I picked myself up and got on with my life."

It had become easier with time to tell that story. Truth was, it hadn't been easy at the time. Leaving him had shattered her. She had kept the real story hidden deep inside her. Unable to articulate the depth of the love and unwilling to have it dismissed as a foolish infatuation, the first love of youth.

Drawing a breath, she went on, "It's true, I've never completely forgotten him. I felt free that year in a way I never had before, and maybe never really have since. Even though it ended, and I was crushed." She made a nonchalant gesture with her hand to minimize the impact of that last sentence. Fooling no one.

"Well, you know, it's not as though I've sat in a darkened cobwebbed room like Miss Havisham, a jilted bride. But I guess when Lars asked me about great loves, Stefano was right there, immediately in my mind. I didn't realize Lars would try to weaponize that memory. In a funny way, his focus on it made me realize how important that relationship was to me, and how grateful I was to Stefano and to that time. I wouldn't have wanted to miss that experience, no matter the cost. You know the cliché . . . better to have lost in love . . ."

Stella's hunch was right though. Julia was leaving something out. She didn't tell them about the unexpected meeting seven years ago in Venice. She kept that secret close to her heart, not wanting it to be spoken of or analyzed. It had been beautiful, if fleeting.

"You know my loves," said Julia looking at her two friends, "We have all walked through a lot of shit in our lives. It's important to find those nuggets of joy and love and keep them close."

There was truth in those words. Whilst there had been tragedies and challenges, they would highlight what was good and encourage what was possible for each other. It held them together when times were hard. They were silent for a moment. Then Stella stood up and poured the wine. "Hmmmph, that is true, but no way am I ready to look back with any loving kindness at that shithead of a man I was unfortunately married to."

Mimi and Julia nodded in furious agreement. The breakdown of Stella's marriage to her teenage sweetheart was still raw. But she was doing so well, and this weekend, with the new online profile, was a clear indication that the door on the past was being firmly closed.

Mimi turned to Julia, looking at her speculatively. Mimi had a quiet way of sifting through things and finding the truth of the matter.

"What?" Julia said. "What mischievous thought is dancing around in your head?"

"Well," Mimi tilted her head in that way that Julia knew only too well meant whatever was about to happen was going to be challenging but likely worth hearing it. "I'm wondering what Stefano is doing right now?"

It wasn't as though this thought hadn't crossed her mind every now and again in the last thirty years. But she had never seriously followed through on it. Not even when she had seen him that time in Venice. She preferred to preserve the memory of all that was good. No that was an inadequate word. All that was wonderful about their time together.

She could still remember the first time she saw him.

2

The First Time

Julia had been traveling with her friend Jane, when they fell into the reception area of the youth hostel in Verona. Standing behind the desk, Stefano was patiently answering the questions of the girl in front of her at check-in, even though all the answers were written on a board right behind him. Julia watched him. Patient and charming. She imagined he had answered those questions a thousand times. Was he always so thoughtful? Present in the moment with each and every visitor? For the first time in some days, she wondered what she looked like. Certainly, she knew what she smelled like after the long train trip from Spain, through France and into Italy. Not to mention the very long steep walk of the Salita Fontana del Ferro which led to the hostel from the train station. She grimaced.

"It's ok, I can read," were Julia's first words to him, stepping closer to the desk. She could see his curly hair as he wrote something down. Cute, she had thought at the time. He had looked up and their eyes locked. Something shifted, as if the world had tilted. Then she blinked and things reverted to normal.

"Of course, sometimes it's just a little like that," he smiled, and Julia stood there grinning back. "Can I have your documents?" "Oh sure, here," she handed over the passports, dropping them as she did so. Stefano stepped out from behind the desk, as Julia knelt to pick them up. Her hand touched his and it happened again. Tilting, shifting. She felt unsteady and the touch of his hand on her elbow as he helped her stand was not helpful at all. She felt giddy. Stefano flicked quickly through the first one, giving a cursory glance at Jane before opening hers. "*Giulia,*" he whispered. Her name sounded like music in his mouth. "Giulia, you have come home, no?" Julia blushed and then laughed lightly, "Well I hope I don't meet quite the same end." Stefano suddenly realized what he had said, "*Scusa*! Sorry! No! I didn't mean that. I'm Stefano, welcome."

"Stefano," she repeated. He quickly stamped their hostel cards and handed back the documents. She stepped away from the desk. The people behind her were beginning to make impatient noises.

He watched her as she hoisted her bag on her back and walked upstairs with Jane to find their room. Exploring the villa, they often passed the main desk in reception. Jane kept nudging her, whispering that he was looking at her again. Julia would glance over; he would smile and look away. As they wandered through the gardens, he was there again, leaning in the doorway. Watching her.

Julia had just turned 22. Had she known then that he would be someone who would eventually hold a thread from past to the future? That all she had to do was think of him and she would follow that thread back to a moment in her life when all was yet to unfold, all was about to change. If she'd known, would she have accepted his invitation to go for ice cream? To get in the car and drive to Lake Garda? She had walked to the edge of the water, watching the sun set behind the mountains, creating sparkling rivers of light that seemed to come straight toward her.

She wasn't sure. Julia let the memory take her back.

She couldn't quite believe she was standing by an Italian lake. Water always drew her, whether the sea, a river, or a lake, there was something about the way it moved, it was mesmerizing. The rich colors of the buildings and the softness of the light were reminders that she was a long way from home. And this young Italian man. Julia wasn't sure what had happened earlier when she had first arrived, when the world had tilted. There was something about him that seemed to pull her. As though she knew him from somewhere else. Some other time. Some other life.

Stefano walked up to her. She could feel him standing beside her. There was something in his body that was in communication with hers. His hand slipped down along her forearm and his fingers entwined with hers. They didn't speak, though she saw he was watching her as she watched the sunset. She remembered a sensation of anticipation fluttering in her belly. Warming her as it sent pulses of energy from her core.

A gust of wind caught her hair and blew it into his face. She turned to him laughing and apologizing. He stood in front of her, a smile on his face, her hair billowing around them. "Don't worry about it," he had said, brushing her hair behind her ears with his free hand.

Julia looked at him. His eyes smiling at her as much as his mouth. She leaned toward him. There was a shift in his expression as he tilted his head forward. Something like longing in his eyes. Their lips touched, ever so lightly. To move quickly would take them to a place they were not yet ready to go. Julia felt him tremble and realized that she felt unsteady, as though her feet weren't planted on the ground. Very slowly he stepped closer. Julia could feel his body through the light fabric of her shirt. She didn't move as he rested his hand on the small of her back and pulled her closer. He reached out to touch her cheek, sliding his hand back into her hair. Their breath mingling in the space between. She wanted him to kiss her, kiss her properly, but she didn't want to break this spell he was weaving around them.

"Julia," he murmured against her mouth, "Julia." She felt her tongue slip out between her lips, touching his. Time slowed, suspended in the possibility. Sighing, he opened his mouth. She let her tongue gently trace his upper lip before retreating. This time it was his tongue that followed hers. Running around her top lip before tracing the bottom one. She felt like her knees were about to give way. She opened her mouth, bringing her tongue out to meet his and inviting him in. She could feel her breasts pushing against his chest. Their hips almost touching.

A noise behind startled them. "Stefano!" Luca called, "*arrivati i gelati*. The ice creams are here."

Stefano stepped back. Julia felt disoriented, as though she had been asleep, dreaming.

"Is everything okay?" he held her arms.

"Yes, I just . . ." she smiled. "I'm okay."

"Come on. Let's eat some *gelati*."

His grin was promising, something she wasn't sure, but there was a feeling in her stomach that said otherwise. Julia nodded as he took her hand and guided her to the cafe where Jane and Luca had already ordered scoops of ice cream. Jane threw her a glance that held a thousand questions. Julia smiled and slipped into a chair. Stefano sat beside her, pulling his chair in so their knees touched. As she dug the spoon into the creamy chocolate ice cream, Julia was acutely aware of feeling the heat of his body next to her. She could feel his eyes on her face and her face was burning under the gaze. She felt flushed and slightly self-conscious, but none of that could dissipate the sensation in her core, like bubbles or sparks that made her feel as though she could do anything.

Sitting on the smooth leather seats in the back of the car, feeling the wind in her hair and listening to the beautiful language in the mouths of those young men, stayed with her. Unable to take her eyes from his face as he turned to talk to her. What had he been thinking? Much later Julia would find out that on that drive to the lake, he had fallen into her eyes, fallen in love with the carefree exuberance she once thought only the young have.

Would Julia have changed her mind, had she known the echoes that would follow her all her life, when he asked her to come to his room? She had said no at first, but then she had taken his hand.

He led her through the garden until they reached the crumbling garden house. There was not much to it. A tiny bathroom, some stairs up to the room where he slept. Julia had felt strangely nervous, as though something was about to happen that would be different from anything she had experienced before.

Pulling her gently toward him, he began to murmur words about her beauty, her eyes. Julia giggled. "What is it?" he asked, his English almost perfect and definitely sexy.

"Nothing," Julia tried to reassure him, "I'm just not used to compliments."

"Well, you should be. You should get used to them." She felt herself blush.

"And your name, Julia," he breathed it into her mouth, and it sounded like the most beautiful thing she had ever heard. "Julia, you are beautiful, and I would like to kiss you."

His face was tilted down toward her, and suddenly Julia couldn't laugh because all the breath had left her body. "Give me your mouth," he whispered. Reaching up, she touched her lips to his. His arms tightened as he returned the kiss she offered. The moment their lips touched, something ignited deep within. He pulled her even closer, exploring her mouth with his tongue. Her body moulding into his. He ran his hands along her spine, pressing her closer. Julia leaned into him, feeling the heat of his body, and a slight trembling. His hands moved lower, sliding around her hips then up. Julia stepped back slightly, offering him a way to slide his hands inside her shirt. Raising her arms above her head in invitation. She wasn't wearing much underneath.

"*Dio, sei Bellissima.* God, you are beautiful," he breathed.

Julia tugged his shirt out of his jeans, running her hands over the smooth skin of his stomach and chest, then around his back as he pulled the shirt over his head. Pulling her close again, Julia felt her breasts brush across his chest.

His hands moved from her back and ran along her side, tracing the shape of her breasts. He kissed her again. Julia felt her head spin and her knees tremble. She stepped back and the back of her legs hit the edge of the bed. Smiling up at him, she sat down, as he knelt before her. He looked at her for a long time. It was intense. Julia sat, eyes closed, completely still. The air was charged. She felt it move as he reached for her. His hands touched her face, tracing her mouth. Parting her lips, catching his thumb in her mouth as he brushed it across her lower lip. Sucking it gently, she heard his breath sigh out. Releasing it, she felt him bring it to her breast, brushing the wet tip of his thumb around her nipple. The sensation expanding as he replaced his thumb with his mouth. Julia's head fell back as she pushed her breast toward his mouth. He spent time first on one and then the other, swapping hand and mouth.

She looked up at the ceiling through half closed eyes. The shadows from the candle danced across the frescoes. Her breath becoming shallow, fast, as the sensation from his mouth on her nipple seemed to trace a direct path down to her groin.

Moving her hands to the front of his jeans, she could feel him straining against the fabric. Slowly she undid the buttons. He leaned back, watching her as she touched him. He stood up reaching a hand to lift her from where she sat. Instead, Julia shifted forward, her mouth close to his thigh. Looking up she met his gaze, a quick smile on her face. Then his hands were in her hair, half directing, half holding himself upright. She felt as much as she heard his breathing become uneven. Releasing him, she stood, opening her own jeans and with a quick shimmy, they dropped to the floor. Stefano turned to sit on the bed, moving her to stand in front of him. He ran his hands around her back, down around her buttocks, bringing his fingers between her legs to meet his mouth. Julia's hands rested in his tight curls, holding herself still as the fire inside flamed higher. He moved the fabric of her underwear to the side. His fingers were exploring, feeling the heat. Julia's hands threaded through his hair as wave after wave of sensation rippled through her. She felt herself begin to dissolve. "Stop, stop, I need you."

He stood up, kissing her stomach, breasts, throat and mouth. She could taste herself on him. She lay back on the bed, unable to stand as the sensations rippled through her. He moved between her legs. Julia bent her knees and wrapped her legs around his back. Pulling him closer. They moved together. She could feel the heat pooling where they joined. Hot, slippery, divine. His breath quickened, as he kissed her neck, her face, her mouth. She held onto him, running her hands around his body. "*Vengo*, I'm coming. *Non posso* . . . I can't . . . stop."

"Yes," she answered, as she felt herself begin to let go, "Yes, yes."

The endless pull of desire had begun that night. In that large airy room, where candles danced in the corners. Where the frescoes were crumbling, and the bed was narrow. Italy, Stefano, it was all unbelievably romantic, seductive, irresistible. Julia had stepped into that room, knowing exactly what was about to happen. Unable, unwilling to stop it.

As she lay there curled in his arms, a cassette player, playing Leonard Cohen, and the music was making perfect sense, as if it had been written for them. From that moment on, that music would send her flying back to that room conjuring up Stefano's face as though real enough to touch him.

Life had made sense to Julia in that room. Hidden in the garden of an Italian villa masquerading as a youth hostel.

Love made sense. Sneaking in behind the more easily explained desire. As she slipped into his arms, full of longing, Julia didn't notice that love slipped in with it and nestled quietly in her heart.

She had stayed for a week. Longer than intended. The days were spent exploring the city, ending in long languorous nights of love making. If she hadn't been in love with Italy before then, by the time she left, Julia was totally in love with everything. The language. The food. The buildings. The art. And him.

Something had begun. Something awakened. Something that would burn throughout time.

She had returned, 18 months later, with no plans or intentions to stay. It was supposed to be a rescue trip to Switzerland, to help Jane who had been caught up in a difficult situation. Julia had taken her away to Verona, instinctively knowing Stefano would help. He would be there to welcome them. But it was more than just seeking help, she was drawn there. No idea that a year would pass and the thought of ever leaving would cause a wrenching pain. A soul's trick of the conscious mind.

Coming back to the present moment, the girls' weekend, Julia reached for her glass. Was the time right? she wondered. What would she say to him if a message were sent now? Those memories were precious, and she could let them play through her mind without feeling the pain that had accompanied them for a long time. Some of the memories, especially the endless love making in beautiful rooms, were memories she was happy to hold on to.

A smile playing on her lips, she looked up at the other two. What were they doing, she wondered.

"Okay," Mimi looked up a triumphant smile on her face. "We've found him!"

"What!" No!" Julia felt her heart start to race. "Oh my God!"

Stella took her hand and pulled Julia over to the computer. "Look, he's on Facebook. I must say, he is hot. Look at those eyes, smoulderingly delicious. If that is not a cheeky little come hither and play with me smile, I don't know what is!"

Julia almost didn't want to look. He'd looked so good when she had met him in Venice seven years ago that surely, he wouldn't have changed, but it felt weird to have him scrutinized by her friends. Covering her eyes with her hands, she came closer to the table.

Mimi grabbed her hands and pulled them away. "Look," she said, "is that him?"

Julia peeked at the Facebook page. She felt her breath heavy in her chest, as though the air had left the room. There was a roaring in her ears. It was him. Staring out at her from the screen. Staring into her soul and taking her breath away. Julia nodded slowly, not trusting herself to speak.

"Great," said Stella, "let's send him a message and see if he responds."

Julia looked at her, shaking her head. She stepped back, away from the screen, fighting to get her emotions under control. Julia had decided not to message him after seeing him in Venice. Afraid of what it might mean and unable to hold onto that dream, in the face of all the responsibilities of parenthood on the other side of the world from him. Afraid of what it would do to her heart.

Mimi handed her the wine. Julia took it gratefully, gulping it down. She steadied herself on the arm of the sofa. The other two looked at her.

"I have never seen you like this," Mimi said. "You've faced death with more composure. What did this guy do to you?"

Julia looked up at her and waved her arm vaguely spanning the room, as if to say so much and nothing at all.

"Give me a minute," Julia pleaded, "it's just a bit of a shock to see him again all these years later. I mean, I know he looks older, don't we all," she pulled a wry face. "But I guess I didn't expect the sight of him to . . ."

"Hit you in the guts?" said Stella directly, hitting the point head on.

"Yep," Julia agreed looking at her, "right here." She doubled over her fist that pushed into her stomach.

"Soooooo," said Mimi, "Shall we?"

"Ohh," said Stella, "we shall."

"Wait." Julia wasn't sure this was a good idea. She didn't want to tell them that she had met up with him again in the last decade. That she had left and tried very hard not to look back. Knowing that there was something between them that would never be finished, never be at peace until, unless . . . no that was not a place to go even in her secret dreams.

"Okay," said Mimi, a glint in her eyes and a stern look at Stella. "Let's go outside, look at the stars, smoke this lovely joint. And then we can decide."

Mimi knew that pushing was unlikely to get Julia where they wanted. Julia always needed time. Mimi knew her friend. She knew to let the idea settle. She knew that once Julia had decided, then rather than scuttle sideways, she would dart forward and surprise them all. That was definitely a habit Julia had tried to contain.

Spontaneous and carefree could just as easily be impulsive and careless.

They stepped outside. The air was still warm, but the sky had moved from red to the deepest blue. Not much light pollution over the sea meant the winter sky was embroidered with stars. Mimi looked at her, standing at the edge of the deck, looking upwards. Nudging Julia with her elbow, she raised her eyebrows, offering her the joint. Julia took it, and a smile of satisfaction appeared on Mimi's face.

"Good on you, babe, you need to relax. You do so much, and you never take time for yourself. You need more lessons from your Sagittarius bestie. We may do a lot for everyone else, but we remember to do things for ourselves too."

Julia smiled, "True. It's good to know you're here to help me look after myself," she was laughing again as she waggled the joint in Mimi's face.

They stood there quietly, enjoying the stars and the sound of the sea. Stella came out, handing them their wine glasses.

"Great choice, Stella," said Julia waving her glass to take in the house, the sea, the sky.

"Of course, my darlings, only the best for you."

"You know I love you girls," Mimi said with a smile. This time they let her.

It was true. They had been through a lot. They had cared for sick children, they had been through divorce, they had seen off cancer, the death of parents and, in Julia's case, her husband Hugh.

Time had burnished their friendship into something rich and deep. It was a connection that made Julia wonder if the concept of soulmates was something not just limited to love affairs but was just the tip of an interwoven web that connected people throughout time and space. Maybe Stefano fitted in there somewhere. It was a nice idea.

Julia turned to share it and then realized she didn't have to. They already knew that being together in this moment, and all the moments before and after was part of the essential ingredients for a life well lived and well loved. That thought decided her.

Julia took a deep breath. "Okay, let's do it."

"I knew you would! I knew you'd say yes." Mimi threw her arms in the air then flung them around her. Stella laughed, "Well I wasn't sure, but I was pretty sure I would persuade you if necessary."

They moved back into the house. Julia for fear she would change her mind. Her friends to make sure she didn't. Opening up her laptop, she quickly typed in his name in the Facebook search bar. There he was again. Her courage almost failed. But then she looked at her friends, looked back at the screen, looked in her heart and pressed send.

"It's done!" Mimi and Stella cheered and clapped. Shutting the laptop, Julia felt a surge of energy, of hopefulness that overcame the fear.

"Let's dance!" Mimi called as she lined up the music.

They began to swirl and twirl around the room. The music wrapped around them, all their favorites. The Girls Weekend playlist was perfect. "I'm your Venus, your desire . . ." Bananarama, classic. Laughing they moved around the improvised dance floor. Raising their glasses in the air, they circled around each other.

"Oh," Julia caught sight of their reflection in the window reflection, "we're the *Three of Cups*!" There would be time for tarot this weekend, and the *Three of Cups* was one of her favorite cards. Women dancing, joyous, and celebratory.

One song flew into another until much later they collapsed into bed. Tired, a little drunk, but happy, satisfied that the world was still a beautiful place, and they still had the privilege to enjoy it.

As she pulled the covers over her, Julia had a strange feeling. For the first time in decades, she would be truly alone. The day-to-day responsibilities of raising a family was done. Time began to stretch forward in a way that suddenly looked very different. Julia realized she was free for the first time since she was in her mid-twenties. Free to do as she pleased and not be required to do anything for anyone but herself.

Free to go to Italy. To close a circle that maybe had never been properly completed. She wondered where he was in life now. Seven years ago, the meeting had been brief and the pain of leaving him was as raw as it had been all those years ago.

Julia lay in bed looking at the moon as it fell behind the trees. She remembered leaving. Stefano had driven her to the airport. He had never once asked her to stay. Never once asked her to wait and see. Sobbing her way through the airport at Milan, inconsolable and incoherent, as though her heart had been ripped from her and her soul had retreated into a small place. She remembered the flight attendant asking her a question and she was unable to answer. They must have thought her a little unhinged. Though it was Italy so perhaps they had seen it all before. Perhaps it was okay to be destroyed by love, perhaps it is inevitable. She knew full well, in the physical world, all love has its own ending. Should she risk opening up that scar running through them both? Julia already knew the answer. She had to see if what she felt was just the fantasy of a young woman, or something more.

And if it were to be something more? Well, that was a bridge to be crossed or burned when she reached it.

The full story that Julia hadn't told them, hadn't allowed into the inner sanctum of wine and friendship. She didn't know why she hadn't wanted to say it, beyond a sense that it was something sacred, something she held deep within her. She hadn't shared much about Stefano with anyone. She hadn't spoken about how totally in love she had been with him and her utter devastation at its abrupt end.

Young. Without cares or responsibilities. They had loved and lived at full speed. Until it had crashed. Perhaps inevitably. But those feelings of longing. They were always there. Just below the surface. Ready to flow out of her soul and into her heart.

CHAPTER

3

Cartomancy

Stella was wrapped in a silk dressing gown that set off her auburn hair to perfection. Always stylish, Stella's presence in a room was easily felt. Mimi, dressed in her signature red, was making coffee as Stella scrolled through the overnight influx of messages from the dating site.

"Wow, I never realized how intense this would be."

"Careful!" Julia warned her, moving to the fridge, "Men lie just as much as women, about their age, their bodies, and their height. Which is just too funny, I mean you can explain away some things but your height. Nope. If he looks like he can't possibly be 50, then the chances are he's using old photos. It was one of the things that pissed me off about Lars. He'd go on and on about integrity, but he lied about his age."

"Oh honey," said Mimi, "there was much more not to like about him than that!"

The comment hung in the air. It was unusual for Mimi to be so outspoken. She was such a romantic optimist. Always looking for the best possible outcome, the highest motives. Though Julia remembered a previous comment Mimi had made about Lars and their relationship when she had suggested that Julia stayed with him because she liked the drama.

The comment had stung. Then the insight settled into her skin as she slowly but surely began to step away from the drama she had been caught up in. Every time he would fly into a jealous rage or begin to grill her about some long-forgotten lover or criticize a choice she had made or an action she had taken, or disparage anything Italian, she would take a deep breath and decide it wasn't her drama. It was his. In doing so she had reclaimed herself, and her freedom. It had been hard to let go of the impulse to please and appease. Hard to let go of someone she genuinely had feelings for. He was the first person she'd had feelings for in a long time, but she was clear about one thing. She was not interested in being known as a drama queen. Though it had been more than the drama which had driven her away. It had been the attempt to use her past against her as a way to shame her. The past was the past. Yes, she'd made some mistakes, sometimes she had made some dubious choices. But that was life. That was living. She had forgiven herself for those mistakes. She had learned to let things go. The past was no longer a place of shame or fear for her.

Like everyone, she had to navigate the occasional trigger, but she was a firm believer that by the time you headed into midlife, you had better be able to recognize the tendrils of the past and decide who was in charge of the present. The unrelenting onslaught of unjustified accusations and contempt had made her give up trying to understand his jealousy, give up trying to excuse his relentless questioning and accusations, give up trying to hold space for his fear. Fear was born from deep insecurity, from loss and from lack, but it had become too much to bear.

She knew Mimi and Stella thought she'd held on too long. But sometimes when love is at stake you have to make sure. She had tried to love him, but she loved herself more.

Julia stared into her empty coffee cup, before she looked up, "You're right, Mimi. There was so much more." They all laughed, any tension dissipating with it.

"Phew," said Stella, "We were just checking that it really was over. Because we were getting to intervention stage."

Julia put her hands up, open palmed showing she was giving up. "I know, I know. And while you were always careful not to say it, you sent clear unspoken messages that you didn't like him very much. Even though I struggled, it did give me the strength to face the truth, because I knew, no matter what or how long it took, you would be there for me."

Mimi put her arm around Julia's shoulders. "Absolutely babe, we're here every time."

"Coffee now please," Julia said, embarrassed.

"So," said Mimi, "When are we putting your profile together?"

"I don't think I'm in a hurry to do that, not after the Lars situation. I'm not really a 'get back on the horse' sort of person." Julia paused, "and aside from that disaster, no one else ever took my fancy," her tone was light, breezy.

"That's because you're too fussy," offered Mimi, "you never give them a chance. Though to be fair, Hugh is a difficult ghost to dispel and you know . . ." she tapered off.

"You know . . . what?" asked Stella. Julia's interest was piqued too. Hugh and Mimi had been good friends and work colleagues. Mimi had introduced them one night at Friday drinks.

"Oh nothing, all those conversations, books, and things." Mimi's tone was breezy. "Yes, that's true, he was always reading something interesting or provocative. It made for great conversation, at least until he got really sick. He would never talk about his illness. Anyway, coffee now please," Julia implored.

Mimi had a bit of a moral dilemma. Before he died, Hugh had made Mimi promise never to introduce Julia to someone else. Mimi didn't think encouraging Julia to go online was quite the same. But she didn't want to offer it up for debate. It had been difficult enough for Julia to get this far, that information would not help her move on.

"So," said Stella, looking up from her phone. "Any news from far-flung places?"

Julia felt her face redden. All that talk about Lars and the end of that relationship had almost let that indiscretion fall out of her head. Almost. "I haven't checked, I'll check later, you know time zones. He probably hasn't even seen it."

"Stop stalling," said Stella, "check now."

"Ok, Ok, so bossy!" said Julia, reaching for her phone.

There was a notification. Her mouth went dry, and the coffee suddenly tasted like sand. He had sent her a message.

She put her mug down.

"What, tell us. Did he accept the friend request. Did he reply. Tell us!"

Mimi and Stella crowded around the phone. Julia hugged the phone to her chest.

Stella reached for her phone, "Do we have to go beat him up?"

"He's sent a message. I just—"

"Show us."

"What did he say?" asked Mimi, not understanding a word of the Italian.

"Just that yesterday he was walking over the bridge where we used to meet, in the beginning. He was thinking of me, then this message appeared."

"Oohhhh!" exclaimed Mimi, "that's a good sign."

"Okay so I don't need to beat him up," added Stella.

"What are you going to do?" asked Mimi, "What are you going to say?"

"Wait before you reply," Stella was shaking her head, now. "I'm not so sure. He does look extremely hot in that photo. I think you might need to find out what he's up to before you get too deep in that rabbit hole. He did break your heart, after all."

"Sure, he did, but I'm not that person anymore." Julia almost convinced herself.

Mimi rubbed her back, "That's right, you're tough and, O.M.G. he's pretty gorgeous and clearly, he still thinks about you after all these years. Anyway, it's not like you're about to run off to Italy. Right?"

"Right?" Mimi repeated after the silence extended.

"No," Julia scoffed, "How could I? The kids would never let me go."

"Stuff the kids," said Stella, "Cat has finished school, Morgan and Orlando have moved out and are living their lives. What have you got to lose?"

"Apart from my peace of mind? My dignity?" Julia held up a hand to stop the protests. "Okay I will respond and then we'll see. Maybe he's married, maybe this is an old picture. Who knows." Julia nodded her head.

Maybe he had forgiven her after that night in Venice, but she wasn't ready to talk about that. She changed the subject.

"So, what are we doing today?"

Food and shopping featured strongly in the plans. Julia was happy to leave them to it. As a single parent since Hugh died, for as long as she could remember, all the decisions had rested with her. Julia was looking forward to having time for herself. And after the developments of the last 24 hours, maybe some time to explore other possibilities. She shook her head. "Stop it, Julia!" she admonished herself. "Don't start down a path where you know what the ending looks like."

"There's a farmers' market in the next town," said Mimi. "Let's all go have some fun, buy some food. Lots of antique stalls. Stella you are sure to find a million things for the house.

The decision was made.

The market was busy. "Coffee?" offered Mimi. Julia pulled a face at the first sip. Since spending time in Italy, and then living in Melbourne where they were all coffee snobs, she had got a taste for good coffee. It wasn't terrible, she thought, taking another sip, though she wasn't sure her old Italian lover would have agreed.

She remembered their morning coffee, poured into large ceramic bowls. Julia had taken two of the dishes from the hostel for her apartment. She still had them. They had followed her around from house share to house share. Then to London and back. Thick and heavy pottery, there was something comforting about holding them, as though their weight could stop the world moving so fast. They reminded her of simpler times. They were a reminder of love that nudged her heart.

Julia pushed that thought away. She had made her peace with that time. Stefano was safely tucked in a corner of her mind where she could gaze on him and feel all the feels, without having to crumple to the floor.

At the market there were rows of colorful stalls and stands. Stella was deep in conversation with a smallholder about ingredients, which was odd as Stella hated cooking and would rarely volunteer to make a meal. She brought different gifts to the table. Julia would always be grateful for her friend's protective lion heart. She had been a pillar of strength when Hugh died, while the children were still young. It was Stella, fiercely protective, that her daughter Morgan had chosen to have by her side at the funeral. It was as much as Morgan could do to face the day, but she could not cope with people's questions and comments about losing her father, however kindly or well meant. Stella was like a lioness, guarding the child's privacy to mourn her father without anyone intruding on her thoughts, she made sure no one could approach Morgan to console her, without Stella saying so.

Lots of people were out enjoying the sunshine. Julia stood with Mimi in the middle of the crowd.

"It's good coffee. But not as good as that guy over there looks good." Mimi nodded toward Stella. "He's your type." Mimi and Stella had been friends from the moment they met in high school. Julia had come later to the friendship, firstly through Mimi, they were roommates working together and sharing a house in their early twenties, and they knew most of each other's secrets. Julia thought Stella sometimes despaired of her, but Mimi always understood. Even if she didn't always agree.

"Yes," Julia nodded. "But I am not sure I can cope with too many more of her exploits. My stomach hurt from laughing for days after the last one!"

"I'm not sure I can cope with any more dating mishaps. God knows what she'll be like now she has an online smorgasbord to choose from!" Mimi was an incurable romantic, seeing the best in almost everyone. Stella, on the other hand, was a funny mix of directness that at times bordered on vulgar. Stella spoke a good game when it came to random sex and a variety of partners. But Julia knew it was all talk. Stella had married young and stayed faithfully married for a long time. "I wouldn't worry too much," she reassured Mimi. "She's more used to being married, even if it was horrid at the end. She'll settle down when she finds a partner."

Sometimes Julia had wondered how she would settle into a new relationship. She had been on her own after Hugh died, until she met Lars. Julia had begun to think that was a terrible waste of some of her best years. While she wasn't about to jump right back in to dating, she wasn't going to waste another ten years.

Stella returned from her haggling. Julia peered into one of the brown paper bags. "Oh God Stella! You're not actually going to cook are you?" Stella pulled a face that suggested she was offended. Then it crumpled into a wicked smile. "Ha, no. I'm not. But you are. I've just been choosing the ingredients for your famous risotto. If you are going to get all Italian on us, we might as well benefit from it." Julia brought her palms together in mock prayer. "Phew, I thought Mimi and I were in real trouble or you'd lost your freaking mind!"

Grabbing her arm, they began to wander toward the car.

Set back from the main stalls was a tent decorated in sparkling shawls thrown over a deep purple cloth. The fortune teller's tent.

"Let's go and see if she's free," Mimi urged. There was little hesitation, even from Stella. The woman inside would be dressed for the role. The whole atmosphere would add to the enjoyment. Who knew, she might even be good.

Julia found herself sitting across the fortune teller, whose headscarf was covered in suns and moons. The woman shuffled the cards, eyes closed, then spread the cards in a crescent moon shape. One by one the woman laid the cards out.

She looked up at Julia and smiled.

"You already know something about the symbols on the cards."

Julia nodded. That was true, she had a well-loved pack. On weekends like this one, a card spread with her friends was a good way to dig deeper into some issues and open up a conversation.

"Good, then you understand that they simply speak of what is possible."

Julia nodded again.

"So, you know something about the cards. But do you really know yourself?"

Julia laughed, though she felt a bit put out by that comment. "Well I hope I know something about myself after all the years of therapy I have done!"

The woman nodded, "Yes it's true that you know some things about yourself, and then again, maybe there are things you know about yourself that you are a little shy to admit."

Julia blushed as her mind flew back to her memories from the night before. Was that what she was referring to?

"I can see from your face that perhaps I am right," the fortune teller nodded.

"You have very strong friendships, and you treasure them, they are joyful, supportive and you all care for one another," pointing to the Three of Cups card. "And this is you," pointing to the Queen of Cups.

"When you walked in, I thought to myself, here is a woman who is ready to throw everything into the air and see what happens. Does that feel true?" She stared at her so intently, it felt as if the fortune teller had read her mind, not just the cards. Julia laughed again but a sense of unease settled in her stomach.

"There have been a lot of changes to deal with in your life. But you are resilient, you have grown through the hard times. See the Star card here, there are new possibilities arising. There is something you have set in motion, recently. Something that has long links into the past, perhaps karmic," she paused waiting for Julia to show a sign of recognition. But Julia had been turned to stone.

"Someone has been watching you for a long time. They're waiting for you. Until recently you have been unaware of it. Then something happened, something changed. You asked a question," she paused, looking intently at the cards. "Yes, the universe has answered," pointing at the Wheel of Fortune. "Yes, there is love. And hope. There is someone here who has been important to you, no, who is still important to you. They have reached out for you many times, they responded to your call each time. Even when you haven't been aware you made one. This person is here again. Perhaps they're here to stay. He loves you. He has loved you for a long time. There is marriage here. There are a lot of interpretations on what marriage might look like. But when I see marriage, I see the ring. I see the contract. The souls' contract."

She looked up and held Julia's gaze. "You should have stayed when you saw him seven years ago."

Julia felt lightheaded. How did she know about that? Julia leaned in closely.

"He wants to marry you," the fortune teller declared, her voice emphatic. "He has dreamed of you all his life. But there will be some difficult choices to make. There are choices for him as much as for you. His way may not be as clear or as simple." The woman looked at Julia intently. "You know the saying, be careful what you wish for?"

Julia nodded carefully.

"Be sure you are ready for the consequences of your wishes."

Julia felt her face redden.

Ducking out of the tent, the cool air felt refreshing. Closing her eyes, Julia raised her face to the weak winter sunshine.

"Be careful what you wish for." she thought. What if she wished for him, for them to find each other at this stage of their lives. Would it be wrong to wish for that? To hope for that? What were the consequences? She shivered.

Julia had been so careful. With sole responsibility for her three children, she had focused on building up her career, supporting them and ensuring they had everything they needed. Making sure they were looked after and safe. She had probably overcompensated, if that were even possible. How can you overcompensate for the loss of a parent? But now they were growing up, those responsibilities were no longer the same.

Julia had begun to think about what it might be like to be free. To travel alone and to make decisions to suit herself. To make choices. Choices that had consequences.

She knew, with every cell in her body, that something had come alive inside her. Something she had not dared truly look at. Would she go and see what was there and find out what might be? Regardless of the consequences. That was the question she kept asking herself. Was she ready to open herself up to love again, or risk everything again to give that one love another chance?

Julia had spent too long alone, happily, to be able to give that up for anything less than amazing. And despite a promising start, Lars had become much less than amazing. Another A word came to mind, and she was glad to be free of him. But was she setting a bar too high? What if there was no more amazing? Had she had her share of amazing?

CHAPTER

4

Seven Years Earlier. Venice

Pausing on the steps down to the tarmac, Julia took a deep breath and filled her lungs with the sweet warm air that made her feel she had landed and come home. Since touching down in Italy, she had hardly had time to think as they herded the students off the plane and into the coach. It wasn't the first time since the time she lived here that Julia had been back to Italy, but it was the first time she had come alone. Well, alone with two colleagues and twenty students in tow.

They had been on a grand tour, moving quickly through Italy from Milan, to Florence to Rome then back up to Venice. It was like re-reading a much-loved novel years later, when you brought a different perspective, a different kind of wisdom.

Julia embraced the museums, the historical walks, the pilgrim passageways, with as much glee as she had embraced the bars, the bustling piazza, in earlier times. This time Julia learned more about

Caravaggio and all the other artists than she ever had before. Even the churches came to life with her art teacher colleague as guide. She traced their journey on social media, posting updates on her itinerary as they moved northwards.

Venice was the last major stop on the journey. They would stay on the island of Lido in the lagoon, away from the hustle and bustle of the busy canals, for a different perspective on life in that unique Italian city.

The weather was perfect, and the students were excited. The water taxis, the canals, the faded grandeur, the carnival costumes. Their energy didn't flag as long as you fed them regularly and gave them some freedom. Julia and a colleague took the group toward the water ferry for Murano. She had never been to the smaller islands and was looking forward to seeing the glass making that happened there. Pausing near the ferry stop, the students were hassling for lunch. They filled some tables in a square and the students ordered food. "Let's get a pizza!" Taking their photo, she posted an update. "Lunch Break!"

That was when it happened. Julia's phone pinged. A message arrived from a name that called from her past. No greeting, just an address. Julia stood there unable to move. The people jostled her. She didn't notice. Her whole world narrowed onto the small screen. Him. Here?

Julia pressed the address and the link opened, sending it to the map. The directions appeared. It was a five-minute walk along the canal path, over the bridge, and a few steps along to a piazza. Julia looked at the students, they would be happy for half an hour, eating slices of pizza and chatting. She spoke quietly to her colleague. "Do you mind if I leave you for half an hour and take a walk."

Head bent over her phone, Julia followed the directions leading her to . . . to what? She wasn't sure and didn't want to think too hard about what was at the end of the line. Or rather who.

Nearing the piazza, she checked herself in a reflection. Thank goodness she was wearing a decent top. Though her jeans weren't the most flattering, they would have to do. Why was she even thinking that? "Well," her ego answered, "because you want to look as good as you can. Though are you sure you want to do this? Really? I mean, he broke your heart. Yep okay, you look pretty good all things considered. But I don't know. Should we? I'm not sure." "I'm not sure either," she thought.

"Let's just see," whispered her heart.

Her heart won.

There was a building where people were going in and out. Julia's feet took her toward the door, it slid back quietly, and she stepped inside. It was a hotel. Well, that made sense. Shaking her head. Nothing about this day was making sense anymore. She turned to face the reception desk.

"*Salve, C'e' un Stefano Ba* . . . Is there a Stefano here?" her voice stopped working. It was him, stepping out from an office behind the desk.

"*Ciao* Julia." A grin spread across his face. Light shining from his eyes.

His appearance sent a shot through her body. Her heart leapt, her stomach flipped and flipped again, followed by a familiar tingling sensation. He walked toward her, slipping out from behind the desk.

"Ciao Julia," he repeated softly, a softer smile now lighting up his face, "I wasn't sure if you would come. I have been watching you make your way around Italy and saw you coming closer every day. I was hoping you would come to Venice. When I saw you were just around the corner, well, I had to see if you would come."

"Ciao," she whispered softly.

Her heart took over. Her mouth was already returning his smile, beaming at him. He took her elbow, steering her toward the inner courtyard. The sensation of his touch made Julia tremble and she stumbled. Pull yourself together, she thought to herself. But her heart was singing a happy song and her body was leaning into his offer of support as he guided her out into the bright sunshine.

"So, how have you been? It's so amazing to see you." His English was as gloriously accented as before.

"Fine, well, mostly fine. My husband died a few years ago, that's been pretty hard on everyone. I have three children." Damn, why did she say that? Shut up Julia. "So how about you? How have you been?"

Stefano smiled at her. She noticed he was trembling too. Was he nervous? Nervous about seeing her. Julia couldn't quite believe that. He had always been so confident and in control.

"I know all that. Have you time to sit for a while? Time for a coffee? When do you need to be back?"

"I have about twenty minutes then I have to get back. Yes, I can have a coffee." Julia smiled weakly.

How did he know all that? Why did he know all that, was the more important question, whispered her heart. "Shut up heart," said her ego, but with little force and less effect.

Sitting at the small table, Julia felt his presence keenly. Her body leaned toward him and his body moved toward hers. They sat in silence for a few moments, not uncomfortably, just looking at each other. Julia noticed he had filled out. There were a few more lines when he smiled his easy smile, but he was still handsome. Damn it, he was still so handsome. And the energy, the energy between them leapt and shimmered as though it was alive. Julia was pretty sure he could feel it. He took her hand. The energy intensified. She met his gaze.

"It is so amazing to see you. I can't quite get my head around the fact that you are sitting here in front of me. I can touch you.

And see your eyes. Those amazing eyes that haunt . . . those eyes," he fell silent.

Julia wondered what he had been about to say, they haunted him? That she had haunted him?

"It is incredible to see you too. I can't actually believe it, either. I . . . I don't know what to say."

"Say nothing. It's enough that you are here. How long are you here? Can I see you? You're staying on Lido right?"

Julia nodded. Of course he knew where she was. He must have been tracing her route as she announced it on Facebook.

"Can I come see you? Tonight? I can come around 7. We can have dinner and talk then. Okay?"

Julia nodded again, unable to do anything else. Standing up, he took her hand and led her back to the front door. Leaning in, he kissed her on the cheek.

"*A dopo.* See you later."

Julia left in a daze. As she retraced her steps, her hand reached to touch her cheek where he had left a kiss. His face, his body, his smell, and his voice. His soft molten honeyed voice was vibrating through her. It was all she could do to not turn and run back. Run into his arms and feel them hold her close like they had so many years ago.

The clamoring of the students' voices broke through her reverie. Waving at them as she drew near.

"Okay, shall we get the ferry? Let's go." She moved in a trance. As the ferry pulled away from the dock, Julia turned to look back at the path she traced. A path that had taken her back twenty-five years to a time when she was young and free, and hopelessly in love with the man she had just seen. For the first time in twenty-five years.

"Hey Ms Hood, where did you go? Are you okay?" One of the students asked, slightly concerned. Julia smiled at her.

"Yes, I am okay. I just . . . never mind. I'm fine." Julia shook herself, bringing herself back to the present and the smiling faces of the three students in front of her.

"Tell us! You looked kind of different when you came back. What happened, where did you go?"

Julia looked at the girls smiling. The shock of seeing him had faded and been replaced by a sense of shivery deliciousness where you just wanted to hug yourself.

"I will tell you all about it, but I am going to say it in Italian so you can understand whatever you do." Hoping they might not understand too much and needing to say out loud what had just happened, to make it real.

Julia looked at the girls smiling.

They nodded enthusiastically.

"*Allora,*" she began, "*tanto tempo fa quando avevo 23 anni, ho abitato in Italia per un anno. Ho imparato a parlare l'italiano ed mi sono innamorata di un ragazzo bellissimo, che si chiama Stefano. Abitavamo insieme. E' stato un periodo veramente fantastico, pieno d'amore. Uscivamo insieme ogni sera, incontravamo amici, frequentavamo certi posti . . . E' stata veramente una storia di amore senza fine, almeno così pensavo al tempo. Poi, beh. Qualcosa e' successo, qualcosa che non andava per me. Così sono tornata in Australia. Ho continuato la mia vita e non ci siamo sentiti più. Ma sapevo, sapevo che lui era l'amore della mia vita. Non c'e stato nessuno, neanche mio marito, che mi ha fatto sentire, come me ha fatto sentire lui. Ma ho dovuto lasciarlo nel passato. Non c'era l'internet, costava telefonare all'estero.*

Non ci siamo più sentiti, più visiti. Fino ad oggi, fin' oggi quando lui mi ha mandato un messaggio. E così' sono andata a trovarlo."*

---

* So, a long time ago, when I was 23, I lived in Italy for a year. I learned Italian, and I fell in love with a handsome Italian called Stefano. We lived together. It was a really fantastic time, full of love. We went out every evening, meeting friends, and going to our favorite places. It was a story of endless love, at least that is what I thought then. Then, well, something happened that did work for me. So, I returned

Suddenly Julia noticed a woman staring at her, quietly translating Julia's story to her friend. The woman looked at her and smiled. "I'm so sorry for eavesdropping," her New York accent was strong, "I was just translating for my friend. You've just seen an old lover. After twenty-five years! Someone you lived with when you were twenty-three. It sounds so amazing! But he broke your heart. The love of your life. So what happened? What happened when you saw him? What a story! What a love story!"

The girls, who had been unable to follow most of her story, were all ears. Julia smiled. Unable to hide the feelings that were bubbling away inside her.

"A difficult story, what can I say? The heart wants what it wants."

The woman nodded in agreement. "The heart wants what the heart wants," she repeated, nodding. "You have to see him again. So will you stay? What will you do? This is so romantic."

Fortunately, the ferry pulled into the dock at Murano and as everyone pushed off the boat, the woman and her friend were shuffled away in the crowd. Julia didn't want to think about him too much or what had happened. Or what might happen.

"So Ms Hood, are you going to see him?" asked one of the girls.

"I don't know. Maybe," Julia guided them in front of her, "Go on, go and explore and we will meet back here in about an hour." Julia needed time. Time to process what had just happened.

Later that evening, Julia found herself standing at the ferry dock near the hotel. Her hands were twisting together as she stood there watching the ferry approach from the main island.

---

to Australia and got on with my life and never heard from him again. But I knew that he was the love of my life. No one, not even my husband, made me feel like he did. But I had to leave all that in the past. There was no internet, and international calls were expensive. We never saw each other again. Until today, when he sent me a message. So, I went to see him.

She smoothed her dress for the hundredth time. Hoping she looked okay. Wishing she had something more . . . More what? thought Julia. Flattering? Sexy? For heavens' sake, you're on a school trip. Just stop thinking like that. It's dinner. It's a catch up with an old boyfriend. Life has moved on. You have moved on. Look at what you have done since you left him. You've studied, traveled, got married, had a family, faced cancer, and lost a husband.

Julia took a deep breath and blew it out slowly. Trying desperately to counter the other part of her that was dancing around excitedly. Ecstatically.

The ferry had docked while Julia was arguing with herself, and suddenly he was there, in front of her. All thoughts of how she looked or what she was going to say dissolved in an instant.

"*Bella*," his gorgeous lazy smile lit up his face. Leaning forward he kissed her on both cheeks. She held his forearms to steady herself, returning the greeting.

"Ciao, it's so surreal to see you." She leaned forward as though to hug him before pulling herself upright. "Shall we walk?" she suggested, needing to soothe her agitation.

They set off along the long street that led from one side of the island to the other. At first there was a lot of silence. Sharing snippets of their lives from the time in between. It felt too big. They just chipped pieces off here and there. Married and divorced, no kids for him. Married and widowed, three children for Julia. Work here and there. She had studied Italian at university after leaving him. He whistled, impressed, but then he had always known she was smart. Smart, independent, and beautiful.

All their talk was punctuated with long silences. Long moments of just looking at each other and grinning. Julia could feel every inch of him beside her.

They were so polite and respectful. It felt awkward as though they were blindfolded, feeling their way around the shapes and shadows of their memories. Around the space between them. They stopped at a bar for a drink, where tables spilled out onto the pavement filling the air with voices. Sitting on a terrace in the fading light, the old ease between them, that had seen them create their own world full of laughter and silliness, full of desire, began to find its way back. Where they could be in the middle of a crowded bar, and everything would disappear in the presence of the other.

"Tell me about your children. I have seen pictures of course and I think there is Orlando, Morgan, and Cat, right?"

Julia was surprised and, if she were honest, a little startled. He must have been watching her more closely than she realized. "Yes, that's right. Orlando has just turned 21. He is so tall and handsome. Smart too."

Stefano laughed, "*Giusto*—It's right that a mother thinks like that of her son. It's the Italian way."

Julia laughed too, "But also my girls! They are beautiful people, and full of personality. Morgan is talented and can sing, but oh my, she is challenging at times," Julia's smile was strained. Of all her children, Morgan was perhaps the most like her father and she missed him. Stefano reached across the table, taking her hand. "I'm sure you're a great mother. It must be hard to do it alone." Tears pricked Julia's eyes and she blinked them back. "Thanks. It has its moments, but we're getting there."

More at ease now, they walked again. The road led to a beach. Not like those back home in Australia where the ocean rolled into an endless expanse of sand, but still, there was space. The wind whistled through the rigging of the sailing boats as if willing them out to sea.

The sun had started to set, and they stopped for a while, sitting on the back of one of the little fishing boats that had been dragged well up above the water line. Watching the sun slip away. It was ridiculously romantic, she thought. Sunset, beach, Italy. Him. Always him.

Julia felt his presence intensely. Energy rippled but there was still a barrier between them. Unspoken, unsure, full of questions that may never be answered. She wondered if he felt it. She wondered what might happen if she turned to him. Her eyes resolutely faced the sea, but her entire body vibrated.

Julia could feel her body listing toward him. Like he was some sort of ballast, and she was trying to right herself. She stood up. Deliberately breaking the spell to create space, to haul herself to a safe distance. They walked again. The prosecco singing in her veins.

He reached for her hand, like he always had. They were standing in the middle of a piazza, under a streetlamp. There was an imperceptible shift and suddenly she was in his arms, and he was kissing her. Deeply, urgently. Julia was consumed by the longing that rose within her. She felt him responding to her. Suddenly he pulled away and she shivered at the loss.

"Sorry, Sorry Julia, please excuse me. I promised myself I wouldn't do that. I just couldn't resist. I'm sorry."

"It's ok," Julia reassured him. "Really." But it wasn't, not at all.

Julia felt herself begin to fragment. She had loved him with the abandon of youth. The freedom of no responsibilities. No calls on her time. No care for anyone other than the person in front of you and the love you make together. And, she remembered, in one conversation, in just one meeting, that love had come falling in ashes around her. She could taste them again in her mouth.

He took her hand and they sat at a bar near the water. The conversation was different now. They sat close together, thighs touching, holding hands across the table like they used to do. Julia observed the feelings that flooded through her. She loved him still. She had known since the moment she had read that text. Every cell in her body yearned for his touch, his voice, his smell, his love.

Julia thought she had closed her heart to him. But one message, one meeting, one touch, one kiss and she could see love rippling outwards before her. Every part of her was in conflict, screaming danger, yet longing for love. The weight of care and responsibilities and the heavier weight of death and loss still felt almost unbearable. She was not free to live a life where only love mattered.

She wasn't ready even for this. This prosecco, this conversation. As delicious and thrilling as it was. It was sweet, it pierced her heart and she felt bathed in a sense of wonder. She was reluctant to dispel any of it. She would hold it in her heart as a talisman. As a reminder that there was more. It wasn't finished and she hadn't been wrong about the power of their love.

But she could not stay.

5

The Sacred and the Profane

Stefano pulled the phone from his pocket. He'd been checking it incessantly since her message. He had spent a lot of time over the last thirty years, thinking of her. Remembering her and, when internet made it possible, he'd looked for her online.

When he first knew her, his desire for her had taken him by surprise. Julia had got under his skin and he couldn't leave her alone. She had poured her love over him like honey. Inexperienced, a little naïve, unashamedly vulnerable. Whenever he thought about her, his mind was tangled up with images, sounds, and taste. Memories of her followed him. When they came, it was as though she was standing in front of him. The feeling in his stomach when he knew they would make love. He felt it now. Knowing it was a momentary release. Knowing she would come again and again into his dreams. Day and night. As he sat outside in the cool of the evening, he called up one of his favorite daydreams, closing his eyes, he let his mind take him there.

When her visa was nearing its end, he had taken her on a long drive to Switzerland, so she could step across the border and back again, to get her passport stamped again. So that he could have her for another six months. They ate in a small restaurant in the mountains. He remembered the meal, blueberry gnocchi, asking her whether she preferred this meal or something simpler. Julia had looked at him, her face so full of love that he wanted to hold her. Pull her onto his lap and kiss her until they were both breathless.

"I don't care. What we eat is immaterial to me. I only care about being with you."

And the drive back. His eyes closed at the memory. Desire stirring immediately. The drive back where she had looked at him with an impish grin. He remembered the car. A white Renault. Manual. The highway was fairly quiet.

"What?" he had asked her, unable to repress an answering smile, "What are you thinking about? What are you up to?" Glancing over at her, he watched as she put her index finger into her mouth. He felt a shot of desire hit him.

"Julia? What are you doing?"

She had smiled at him and taken the hand closest to her off the steering wheel. Bringing it to her mouth, she pulled in one of her fingers. Running her tongue around it before giving it a light suck.

"*Niente* . . . nothing." She lied. The truth sparkling in her eyes. "I was just thinking what it might be like if I touched you. How it might impact your driving." Julia had reached over, running her hand across the front of his trousers.

He shot a glance across at her, acutely aware of her hand making lazy circles in his groin and his immediate response.

"What exactly are you thinking about?" his voice strained.

"Well," Julia answered, "I can see. I can feel. That you might have something for me to do. While we go on this long, long drive back home."

Stefano felt his stomach flip. What was she thinking? Surely, she wasn't going to. But she was. He felt her fingers undo the buttons of his jeans. He could feel her watching him. Looking at his face. He tried not to close his eyes as they sped down the highway. He could feel himself tilting toward the edge. The unexpected. The wanting. He had fooled around in cars before. He was Italian after all. But this. This was different. There was an edge of danger that made it even more erotic.

"Julia, Julia," he moaned, "stop, stop."

Julia had pulled her hair back as she leant over him. His eyes squeezed shut before snapping open. "Driving, driving," he told himself. One hand off the wheel, he threaded his fingers through her hair. Feeling her begin a gentle insistent rhythm. Fuck, fuck he couldn't believe what was happening. Teasing him as she brought him close to the edge and then let the desire subside just enough. A truck passed them. He wondered if the driver could see. And then he didn't care. Didn't care if they crashed.

Slowing down, he pulled over to the side of the road, narrowly missing the fence that ran alongside the verge. He sat there breathing heavily. Julia leaned back against the passenger door, a smile playing at the corners of her mouth. Who was this woman who had stepped into his life with her smile that made him feel as though he was the only man in the world. A warmth suffused his whole body, centring in his chest.

"Julia," he said shaking his head, "Julia."

"Drive," she said.

And now that message. Of course, he had responded immediately. He knew why, but he wasn't ready to admit it to himself. She had appeared in Venice after all those years and disappeared again. He remembered the moment she stepped through the door. It was as though the intervening years had simply dissolved. Everything he had felt for her then came rushing back with a force that was unexpected and destabilising. On the ferry to Lido to meet her that evening, he had been transported to the times when he would leave work to head home to her. It felt as though all was right with the world. It had felt like that again that evening when he had held her again. Kissed her. And then watched her walk away. He had let her walk away again.

And now. And now, his soul whispered. What happens now? He didn't know. He couldn't let his mind go there. There was too much that would unravel. Too much that he would have to unravel. So now we wait. Let's wait and see if the time is right.

CHAPTER

6

Lost in Love

That night, after she had slipped into bed, Julia found herself thinking about the past. She didn't often let herself dwell on him, on them together, when she let her mind wander back to that time. It had been too painful at first, she would find herself gasping for air, curled up as if to hold the pieces of herself together. Over time the edges had softened. There were memories that would leave her feeling shaken and bereft. As though something deep and warm had been ripped away. Could she allow a memory to float up before her? 18 months after they had first met, she had returned to Italy.

With her stompy Blundstone boots, vintage skirts, and knitted jumpers, Julia was an anomaly in the elegant Italian city. The Italian women in their fur coats and high heeled boots, peddling along the cobbled streets, probably looked askance at her thrown-together vintage shop style of inner-city Melbourne. Though Julia was oblivious to their opinions.

She was lost in the crisp cold air of the northern European winter, the heartbreaking beauty of the snow, and completely in love.

Finding a small apartment, she used to marvel that people had lived in those rooms for more than 400 years. Every step was a feast for the eyes and a lesson for her tongue. How to order breakfast, gather lunch from the little grocery store and the fruit and vegetable shop at the end of the street. A lesson in independence as she began to create a new life, far away from all that she had experienced in her life before. For a girl from the suburbs of Australia, it was a crash course in life and in courage. It had been completely and utterly intoxicating.

When her savings began to run out, she had looked for work. The first few shifts at the local restaurant were a disaster. Her pitiful Italian had tripped her up and caused confusion. Even now she grimaced, though at the time she had flushed with embarrassment as she misheard orders, wrote down the wrong things. She remembered going home and telling Stefano he was not allowed to speak in English anymore. He had smiled and kissed her as he undressed her, made love to her, telling her at every step, what he was doing and planning to do. The memory made her shiver, and not with cold. Even now, it took so little for her body to remember how it felt to be in his arms. How he would peel off her clothes, following the exposed skin with small kisses. At other times, they would catch each other's gaze and the energy that pulled them together would take over. They would begin the night in one place, then wend their way home, the last stop at Gorky's, the small back street bar owned by Lorenzo and Paulo. She could see the colors, the shadows, the quiet of streets far from the busy centre. The area they liked. Their area. She remembered walking from one bar to another, down a dimly lit alleyway. Stefano had stopped. He pulled her against his body, kissing her until she was breathless.

Standing in a purple shadow, the orange light of the lamp post warming the sides of the houses that lined the way. Running his hands down her sides then slipping them up along the insides of her thighs, his breath sped up as he pushed himself against her. His hands moved higher, brushing against the light fabric of her panties. Her arms around his neck, holding on as the desire buckled her knees. For a moment, the world disappeared and all that mattered was the need for him. Wanting him inside her as though she was not complete without him. Sliding her hand down to wrestle with his belt buckle as she pushed against his hand, slick with the wanting that answered his. He turned her so her shoulders were against the wall, lifting her leg to wrap around his waist. She leaned against the wall, feeling the warm hard stone against her back. Tilting herself forward. Urgent need made them both oblivious to their surroundings.

"Julia," he murmured into her neck, "I want you. Need you."

"*Sì*, yes," her hips moved forward, arching her body so he could reach.

A noise at the top of the alleyway brought them to their senses. Had someone seen them? He stepped back, as she straightened herself. He buttoned his jeans with some difficulty. Holding each other, laughing, they left the alleyway and stepped into their favorite bar. It was busy, noisy, but did little to dampen the magic they had weaved around themselves.

Waving at Lorenzo, they slipped into seats at the bar. Stefano's hand unconsciously slid along her leg, up along her thigh.

Lorenzo, watched as he dried some glasses. Even he could feel it, the energy between them. There was something there, something that made every other man realize that this woman was not available. Even for those men who found that a particularly engaging challenge, a call to action. Even he felt that challenge and usually he was open to the chase. The futility of that pursuit was obvious. He had watched Stefano and Julia over the last few months. Even at the start, their attachment had been intense. Tonight, it was amplified, it was pulsing.

Strangely, that made him feel sad, bereft. As though he had glimpsed something secret. It diminished whatever he had experienced to merely childish games.

He mixed some drinks, and placed them on the counter. Julia turned her gaze to him, smiling. Her face lit up from deep within her. For Lorenzo it was as though a bolt of electricity ran through him. He could understand Stefano's obsession. She radiated.

Closing his eyes, he found the sadness had changed. As though he'd been given a gift, a possibility of whatever it was these two shared. If he dared. If he had the courage to step into life with his heart full. It felt possible and it filled him with terror. It takes courage, the intense vulnerability to open the heart. That possibility of finding the other person who could hold you in their soul was rare and the possibility of all things aligning, time, distance, and being free to follow your heart, was even rarer. Part of a soul stream where two people meet at the right moment. In the right bodies. That connection created something more than just the moment, it was something that lived on and could never be broken, even if they were broken. It was something which passes from soul to soul, eternal, karmic. Lorenzo shook his head and the spell was broken.

Returning home with a broken heart, Julia had held onto that year in the way someone holds onto the ground when the sky is spinning. She had taken the language with her. Even now she loved the feel of it in her mouth, the music of the words in her ears. Her senses had been brought to life, tuned into the centuries old spaces she had passed through. That was part of the love affair. The way the air felt when you stepped into it, the way the light was soft and golden rather than hard and glaring white. The hum of people that never completely quietened, the lights that never completely dimmed. Italy had seeped into her soul. She could no longer deny that he had stayed on in her heart as well. It was a love that transcended anything she had ever known or experienced. A love that had lasted across time and distance. It had remained curled in a corner of her mind, shifting like a light breeze, forever just at the edge of her consciousness. Even then, she had known there was something unique, something beyond herself, even beyond him. Stefano would one day tell Julia that love was not a big enough word to contain what they had been, what they were, to each other.

There was no point in regret. Three decades had passed and both of them had stepped into other lives, other relationships, other dreams. The relationship had ended but they had not forgotten it. The love they had conjured up, created, dived into, still lingered in the corners of her heart, in the nooks and crannies of her mind. Even when her heart was broken, Julia had not hated him. She had never once felt indifferent either. Perhaps that was why she stuffed down the memories, unable to erase them, unwilling to let them go.

She wondered how he felt now. What made him think of her. That is always the question of love. What is in the mind, and heart and soul of another. Do they feel the energy the same way you do? Did he then? Does he now?

That message had brought the year they spent together roaring back into her consciousness. Did she want to risk being crushed again? Crushed because he might be unwilling or unable to truly step in to loving her. Damn, she didn't know what to do. She was getting way too ahead of things. Better to start with a simple response to the message. One step at a time.

As the fortune teller had said. She had set things in motion, all that remained was to see what might be. And deal with the consequences.

CHAPTER

7

Flights of Fancy

It had started slowly. A message here and there. As though they were circling each other. Asking without asking, and reading, probably too much, between the lines. Julia tried not to think too far ahead. Each time a message notification pinged, it was like having a delicious secret. To be honest, she was struggling to keep it in check, to stop her flights of fancy and stay grounded, in the present. But there was something tantalizing about the what if and the why not. Two phrases that sent her spinning off onto pathways that had seemed perplexing. Though she had to admit, those impulsive, even careless choices, had always brought gifts of lessons learned. Right now, she could feel herself opening up to curiosity and possibility.

After some busy mornings had thwarted her walks along the beach, finding herself there again was bliss. Not so much an indulgence, to her walking on the beach was necessary. Whatever the weather, the beach was always there. She had begun to realize how much she needed it. She needed it to breathe. Feeling her feet in the wet sand, all the small adjustments through her legs as she walked the shoreline. Holding her in place as though without this reminder of her presence, she might just not be. She looked out over the bay, her feet disappearing as the waves moved the sand, something happened, it was as though her edges were blurry. As though she could vanish in a moment. Untethered, it felt new, strange and somehow slightly enticing. Would she just float away? Like a balloon that had slipped out of someone's hand. Would she float, higher and higher and like Icarus, come too close to the sun? Or could she somehow guide this feeling, this state of being? Direct it with a slight tilt here and a correction there and in some way find herself where she needed to be?

Shaking the sand from her feet, and her head for this foolishness, she started back toward home. Hugh had loved to travel and they had spent many family holidays driving through Europe. But he had left her here, far from the rest of the world. She sometimes wondered whether he had known, deep in his soul, to bring her here, to bring them all here. So that when he left, they would be surrounded by her friends and family. He had been gone twelve years now. Orlando was already a man making his way in the world, Morgan and Cat were beginning to find their way onto their life path. She would always be there for them, but they needed her less as they stepped into their own lives.

She wanted to be ready for the time when the skies would open again. To see where her untethered journey might lead, and who she might encounter along the way. Who indeed. Who was she kidding? Only herself. She knew who she wanted to encounter. Someone she knew had held a place in her heart. Who had called to her from another time, another place, another life. Someone who, otherwise inexplicably, was part of her soul.

She looked at her reflection. "Did she dare to eat a peach?"

"The juicier the better," answered her heart.

8

One Day Baby We'll Be Old

Checking her email, Julia's stomach fell to the floor. The hospital had sent a call back to the breast screening service, to check something in her left breast. The language was light and breezy. Just a check. Nothing to worry about. 95% of the time it's all good. With her history she'd be in the 5%. Was this some kind of punishment that she had dared to think of life opening up and being able to step into freedom? The color seeped from the day.

Julia's first instinct was to say nothing. She remembered the call with Mimi. Five years ago now. Sitting outside the cheery sunshine had seemed obscene in the face of that conversation. Multiple surgeries, chemo, ongoing bone pain. Things were okay now, but it was never far from their thoughts. Julia could list at least seven women, two who were no longer here. The first thing to do was to book the appointment. Then her fingers hovered over the girls' chat. Vulnerable, too right, Brené. This is when we know how vulnerable we are.

She sent a screenshot of the appointment with a simple word 'Fuck' below it.

Mimi was back within a minute. Julia breathed out.

Stella messaged her immediately. *WTF?*

Julia—*Had a routine breast screen a week ago, just got this email :(*

The messages flew back and forth. Mimi with a list of the best people to see. Stella with positive encouragement.

Not wanting to wait if there actually was something to be worried about, she managed to get the appointment brought forward. Who was she kidding, she was already worried.

Lying on the table, submitting to the ultrasound, she watched the clinician stop and click on what appeared to be an enormous dark spot in her left breast, taking measurements. Her heart was in her mouth.

"So," Julia was trying to be light, "is there anything to be worried about?"

Aside from what is clearly a huge tumor in her breast.

The clinician smiled at her reassuringly. "I think it's a cyst, nothing to worry about. I don't think we will need to do anything further."

"Look, I know you might think it's a cyst, but I have had two so called cysts in other parts of my body, and both of them ended up not being cysts. So as much as I hate needles, I would like you to run some more tests."

"I'll just confer with a colleague. I'll be back shortly." The radiographer left the room carrying her medical notes. Dismissive.

A couple of days later Julia found herself in the office of a breast surgeon. As she told her the story, she could feel the heat rising from her toes. She made it through her family history of cancer, her own brush with cancer, but it was when she started talking about Hugh that tipped her over. Tears fell down her cheeks as she tried to wave away the doctor's compassionate words. "It's not me I'm worried about, it's the impact on my children," she explained between deep breaths, to try to steady herself. "They can't lose two parents."

The surgeon pursed her lips. "I think we should do another scan to make sure."

She had been taken seriously, the breast surgeon agreed that more investigation was prudent and referred her for genetic testing. Julia felt relieved and also angry. She was fortunate, lucky to have the education and the means be able to take her health into her own hands. She knew how to say the right things to access this consultation and she could pay for the resources she needed. It was a level of privilege that she was not unaware of.

Stepping out of the doctor's office, she updated the group chat.

Julia— *"Happy to be taken seriously, but now I'm freaked out that I'm being taken seriously."*

The thought that kept pushing into her mind was "Please, please let it be okay. I promise I'm listening universe. Please. Just let me be in one piece." She was bargaining with something, someone, the Universe. That felt shallow but she was quite attached to her breasts. "Ha," the small voice in her head pipped up, "you also want something else, someone else to like them too."

"Shut up," Julia told herself. She didn't want to even think about the consequences of bad news.

Back home from the appointment, she stripped off and looked at herself in the mirror. She ran her hands over her breasts, hoping they were not traitors, about to betray her. Raising her arms and stretching on her toes, her breasts lifted and pushed out from her chest. She looked good all thing considered, even to her critical eye.

"Hmmm," she remembered the camera stand that had come with the light ring she used for Zoom meetings to stop her face from going bright red in the reflection of the last afternoon sun. Setting it up, she took some pictures, angling them so her face was not in the frame.

It felt strange to have naked pictures of herself on her photo roll. Somehow slightly illicit though it was only a naked body, her own naked body. It seemed reasonable to want a memento of how she looked intact, especially if she may soon face the knife.

Her phone pinged while she was busy looking at the images. She nearly dropped it.

Stefano— *"Bimba, are you there? How are you?"*

Julia— *"Yes, I'm here, I'm here."*

Stefano— *"Good? What's news?"*

Swiping over to the conversation with Stefano, she paused. The messages had been moving from flirty through suggestive to downright direct. At least from him. He had always been that way. The occasional messages he sent after she saw him in Venice that time on the school trip seven years ago were often almost suggestive. Julia had kept some space between them. Rarely responding. Keeping things light and casual. Stepping away when there was any sense of flirting. She did not respond at all in the time she was with Lars.

This time had been different. She had decided to meet him some way toward flirtatious. They had exchanged a few current photos, and she had found a few from when they were young. Still the suggestion of what might be shared had been in the air between them for some time. Did she dare? What was she even thinking. She had spent years counselling adolescents not to send naked images of themselves.

Julia bit her lip, her finger hovering over the phone. Could she trust him to understand the vulnerability she felt? That while they seemed to be playing a game, it was messing a bit with her head. On the one hand she didn't really know him at all. All the thoughts and ideas she had of him were not much more than projections of her own desires and fantasies. On the other, she had known him since time began, this she knew deep in her soul. And whether he felt that way was almost immaterial. He was that person for her. She blew a long breath through her mouth, her stomach and insides tightening with fear, excitement, desire, hope.

Looking at the image again, her face wasn't visible. Anything could happen once the results of the examinations and tests came back. Her breasts may not ever look like this again.

She couldn't actually believe she was even contemplating sending it. The long lines of her body were accentuated in the pose and her breasts held up okay. Her stomach was still reasonably flat and her hips and buttocks curved and dipped pleasingly enough. No, she wasn't unhappy with how she looked but sending it over the internet? That seemed like something a thoughtless adolescent would do, not a woman in midlife.

Be real she reminded herself, be present, be brave, be real.

Julia—*"They found something in one of my breasts. They don't think it's anything serious but I am going for some tests."*

Stefano—*"It's nothing, I'm sure."*

Julia smiled at his quick and easy reassurance.

Julia—*"Well in case they are mistaken, that you are mistaken, maybe I'll send you a photo for nostalgia."*

Stefano—*"Ma va! Don't tease me."*

Julia—*"I have one I like that I've just taken. If I find the courage I'll send it to you some day."*

Stefano—*"You don't need a lot of courage. You know I wouldn't share you."*

The anticipation was tingling through the messages. If she took this step, things would change. They would no longer be able to pretend that they were just old friends enjoying a conversation. Sending this photo was a flirtation that would set up some clear intentions.

"Oh well, one day baby we'll be old," she thought, and holding her breath, Julia pressed send.

The response was immediate.

Stefano—*"You are exactly as I remember. Excuse me but I am a bit overcome. You are beautiful."*

Julia let her breath out slowly, unaware how much she had tensed up.

Julia—*"Thanks, I also find you very sexy still. Not a bad situation given our age."*

Stefano—*"It's been a year that I haven't done much. I have to exercise."*

Julia smiled to herself. Stefano had never had a spare ounce of fat on him. But she liked the idea that he was concerned, and thinking about what might happen when they met. In for a penny, in for a pound, she thought as she crafted her response.

Julia—*"Yes because when I arrive, I will need a man in his best form, with a bit of stamina."*

Stefano—*"I promise!"*

Julia held fast to these dreams in the two tense weeks that followed. The first week held a series of appointments for ultrasounds and a biopsy. The hospital staff were reassuring and competent as they talked her through the procedures. One more day and she would see the surgeon. Then she would know if she faced a mountain of treatments.

The week held some reflection and a few decisions. Julia had been slowly setting up her three children, making sure they had what they needed if something happened to her. She had once heard a friend talk about how her mother had always said, "Better to give with warm hands than cold." It had become Julia's mantra too. Maybe now was the time to do some things for herself. But first, the appointment. Then she would see what next.

CHAPTER

9

Ciao Sexy Bimba

Stefano's messages continued with a regular stream of compliments. It didn't matter how old you were, Julia realized, desire was still something that pulled you forward, that kept you open and hopeful. Her mind shied away, but her body was right there. Desire. The need for someone to touch you, to hold you, to make love with you. It was still a driving force in midlife. It was like a return to herself in her early twenties, though with a little more wisdom and a little more confidence. Though Julia was not sure she could say that with any real certainty.

As she sat in the waiting room, she felt herself heat up. Three weeks off Hormone Replacement Therapy will do that to a woman, not to mention the anxiety of the next few minutes. Scrolling aimlessly through her phone, she waited for the heat to wash through her. She remembered the reason for going on HRT in the first place. Hot flushes every hour for weeks at a time.

Eleni, her friend since the first day of high school, said she had felt murderous in menopause until she started taking hormones.

"There's a design fault in women's bodies," thought Julia, and not for the first time.

Stepping into the surgeon's consulting rooms, she was greeted with a reassuring smile. Her test results were clear. The breast surgeon was upbeat. A follow up appointment in six months, otherwise go and enjoy life.

Julia felt the relief turn her bones to jelly. Beneath that, was something else. Julia wasn't sure exactly. But it felt more than relief. Something propelling to push her forward. Risk taking. Recklessness. She wasn't sure. But she felt alive.

The response from the girls was immediate.

Stella—*"Excellent, of course I knew it would be all clear! And now we can drink champagne to celebrate."*

Mimi—*"Ha great news babe. Stella—like we need an excuse to do that. By the way how much did you spend at the lingerie shop this time!"*

Julia laughed. There was a shared pact that retail therapy purchases were made in direct correlation to the seriousness of any medical news, and the expenditure was completely justified.

They made some quick arrangements to meet, and Julia jumped in the car to head home.

Her phone pinged as she pulled into the driveway.

Stefano.

Julia quickly typed—*"Ciao Bello. How are you?"*

Stefano—*"Good. Good. More importantly, what news?"*

She quickly filled him in on her good news. Messages went back and forth, and she asked him to send pictures of his life over there. Just everyday things that he did.

Stefano—*"Do you want me to go around taking selfies?"*

It made her smile to think that the word selfie had become ubiquitous, global.

Julia—*"Yes, or perhaps we could have a video call?"*

Stefano—*"Ah! that would be better."*

"But also, some selfies!" she added.

Stefano—*"I have to go now. There is a meeting about to start. We'll chat later."*

Julia—*"Have fun."*

What did he mean when he said a video call was a better idea? Did she want to do that? No! She didn't think so. It made her anxious. It was one thing to message each other, send a photo or two. But this made things real.

Later Stefano had sent a photo. A photo of himself looking at the camera with the tag line,

"Meeting finished. Time to think of other things."

There was no doubt in his smile, his gorgeous, stomach flipping grin. Trying for some nonchalance and scrambling to seem open and relaxed.

Julia—*"You are so handsome—but what are you thinking about?"* (her fingers paused; did she really want to know?)

Stefano—*"Indovina! Guess! So, Bimba, I am working until the afternoon. Let me know when I can call you."*

Her heart was racing. She did a quick calculation in her head.

Julia—*"There are nine hours of time difference. Your 3 p.m. will make it midnight for me."*

Stefano—*"Is that too late?"*

Julia—*"I don't think so, let's see?"*

"Let's not be too hasty," Julia thought. Though she knew she would be. She would be waiting until midnight to see if he called.

Until then she would be thinking about how to put herself together to not seem prepared for anything untoward, but at the same time to look as effortlessly sexy as possible. Laughing at herself at that. She could feel the anticipation or was it terror, zinging through her already. Cool and collected would be impossible to achieve.

Julia—*"Write to me around 2 p.m."*

Stefano—*"If I can call you straight away."*

Julia—*"Okay."*

Stefano—*"Ciao sexy Bimba."*

Julia—*"Ciao."*

Her phone pinged once more.

Stefano—*"I wanted to tell you that it's crazy that you still have breasts like that, the curve of your hips. You look exactly as I remembered you, as I have imagined you. Thank you, thank you for trusting me. You're beautiful. I would like to examine every inch of you again."*

Julia smiled. Damn it he was good. She got the music reference too, anchoring them to their shared past. She felt her stomach flip with the thought of speaking with him later. What was she doing. What was she thinking. Or rather, not thinking.

Her phone pinged an hour earlier than expected.

Stefano—*"Here I am, can I call you?"*

His face appeared on the screen as she tried to arrange herself to look casual and not full of expectations. What would they talk about? She wished she had been speaking Italian more regularly. She looked at him, looking at her.

His face was still the face she had loved thirty years ago. Her body softened and the spell that had woven around them all those years ago started to gently take its hold. Her worries vanished with the realization that this connection between them had always been there, waiting for life to be breathed into it whenever it was needed, whenever they wanted.

They stayed in the safe waters of a shared past. Asking after people. Julia laughed to hear that some of them were coming to visit him in a couple of weeks. Stefano recounted some stories which were full of misadventures and misfires. Some funny and some more serious. "But that's real, that is life," she thought.

"Joyous moments interspersed with sad and even tragic ones. No one was immune and we only have each other to pull us though."

They kept talking until she yawned. The time difference had sent the conversation in to the early hours.

Stefano—*"Bimba, you're tired, you should sleep, I should let you sleep."*

Julia—*"I am, but it is so amazing to talk to you, to see your face, to hear your voice. It's just amazing."*

He smiled at her as though she might disappear.

Stefano—*"What I would give to be able to touch you as well as see you."*

She felt his comment settle somewhere deep inside her.

Julia—*"I think I'd like that too."*

Julia shivered. She could imagine stepping into his arms. She imagined his touch. It wasn't difficult. They had spent a lot of time touching. A lot of time learning the way the other's body moved, felt, and responded.

The memory of him had helped her understand the infinite nature of love. The way love could endure, forgive, sustain, flourish, and simply be. She knew this love had been a gift. Had it been the gift of her life, she wondered, a gift of love with all its imperfect perfect messiness, all its wild and tender places. Perhaps it was just as well he had slipped below her consciousness for a time. Thinking about him was always a full-bodied experience. As though the world had been slightly knocked from its timeless rotation. Or she had.

She smiled to herself. It was so ridiculously romantic, like a movie where star-crossed lovers suddenly found themselves together, a moment in time. But unlike Hollywood, life still had other plans. Unexpected and unprepared, even now she kicked herself for not taking more from that time together in Venice. For not having enough courage and casting aside the weight of responsibility that pulled her back. The connection had been there, it was immediate and primal, coursing through her body, igniting her. Igniting him? The line that had been drawn between them when she had left Italy heartbroken and in pieces, had made her pause. She thought about the consequences. She knew only too well what might be on the other side and where that might leave her.

10

When the Witnesses Are Gone

Julia sent Stefano videos of her daily life in Australia, narrations about making meals, the misadventures of the dog, or the boat sheds that lined the beach where she walked in the early mornings. Deliberate in her communication, the pictures were un-posed, raw. She wanted him to see her as she was. In all the ways she was. No secrets. No attempt to adapt to meet some unknown or anticipated need he might have. She would be herself and that would just have to be enough. Every time, no matter state she was in, he would respond with appreciation. With desire.

In return he would share stories about the people in his local bars and restaurants. Julia watched his face start to lighten. His smiles become more frequent. Every story he shared, spoke to who he was, how he saw the world. She could see the young man she had known in this man who he had become. They laughed together often. She wanted to ask him how he felt about it all, beyond the present, beyond the immediate moment. Was it right to make plans beyond the possibility of seeing each other again in person one day? About what might happen when they were together, face to face. She was reasonably confident that the thrill that coursed through her body every time his face appeared on the screen would be there. What was it that pulled them together across time and distance?

For many years she had tried not to think of him at all. Except, she admitted to herself, that was not entirely true. He had slipped beneath her conscious thoughts during the time she was submerged in small children and married life. He had not bothered her then. Yet he was part of a time and space that held her when life was dark. The memory of him. Like a life jacket to keep her buoyant, alive, breathing. Holding her as she leaned away from love, leaned away from life. Holding her as she walked a dark path of grief and loss. For a long time, it hadn't been him in the flesh that had kept her moving toward the promise of the light. Rather the idea of him that was a fabrication of her mind. Part of a dreamscape which offered hope when there seemed nothing other than drudgery. A dreamscape which had enabled her to get up in the morning. To find the next step. And then the next.

Was he waiting for her or was that just some fantasy, one sided and unrequited? Had she breathed life into this relationship because of the girls' weekend? Was she making more of it than there was? What was she willing into existence? Did it matter? Maybe only if she made plans. Only if she forced an answer. Only if she took flight.

Stefano's voice melted the air,

Stefano—*"Ciao Bimba, are you already in bed? Have I called too late?"*

"No no, I am reading, and this is the most comfortable place. It's lovely, always, to speak with you," Julia smiled. Months had passed, she realized. Slowly unwinding the years in-between. The thrill of his face, his voice still as intense as the first time. She shifted on the bed and her shirt fell open slightly.

His gaze dropped then he looked up at her eyes. Had she noticed? He wondered. She was as beautiful as he remembered. She had wandered the corridors of his dreams, a spark of light that had kept him from, he wasn't sure, just existing? Perhaps. Perhaps she had unknowingly connected him to the parts of himself that yearned for greater things. He felt his heart pick up pace. He looked again. He could just see the outline of her breast. "Oh! to be able to touch her," he thought, and then immediately wished he hadn't. His body responded instantly to the imagining of touching her, of lightly running his fingers around the lines of her breasts. It always had. It had always been this way with her. She only had to walk into the room and his longing for her would begin. Sometimes, when they were out, she would press against him, a movement would reveal the curve of her breast or the top of her thigh or she could simply look at him in a certain way and he would take her hand and take her home.

Before he realized it, he told her. "Had you noticed how I was looking at your face and at your breast, Bimba?" he asked, looking intently into her eyes.

"Ah no," she laughed, "Shame on you!" But he could see she was not upset, even a little flattered by the comment. Maybe he hadn't been thinking straight, or rather he'd been thinking of himself and not of her. If he could feel this instant attraction, perhaps she could too. "Open another button?" a soft suggestion.

It hit her like a lightning bolt and settled somewhere in the pit of her stomach. But she wasn't afraid and they weren't butterflies of excitement. It was anticipation. Her mouth opened slightly, air passing quickly down her throat, and she felt a flush of desire. Unconsciously her hands went to the button. Opened it. Her breasts were exposed to his gaze. "You are beautiful."

"*Grazie*, thanks," Julia's voice was barely a whisper. A dialogue began in her head around what was happening, what might happen, what should she do, where should she stop? This was new territory for her. Part of her wanted to be wanton. Be open. But another part of her was slightly horrified. Exposed. Vulnerable.

"Bimba?"

"Yes?"

"Open one more. I would love to see you even if I cannot touch you."

Teasing him, Julia ran her hands around her breasts, slipping the fabric to the side. Wanton was definitely winning.

"Oh, but you are incredible."

"Thanks," she smiled.

Looking down, she realized her breasts were quite exposed. Instead of closing the shirt, she brought her hands to cup them.

"Oh I'm sorry, should I cover them?" looking up teasingly.

"No! Let them be. I would very much like to touch them, to lick them," he glanced at her face, checking to see if he'd gone too far. But her eyes were closed, as though imagining what his touch would be like.

Stefano imagined he was there with her. He surreptitiously moved one of his hands down to touch himself. He knew he would wouldn't stop. Thinking of her breasts. He slid down the zip on his jeans. He imagined that he could trace the outline of her breasts with his fingers. Bring his mouth down to lick them. Suck gently on her nipples. A deep feeling of pleasure expanded through his stomach and groin. He wondered what she would say if he asked to see more of her. He wondered what she would say if he asked her to touch herself. While he watched. Stefano could tell she was reluctant but perhaps not so reluctant that she would be offended.

The longing increased. He wanted to see her. He wanted to see her touch her breasts. Roll her fingers around her nipples.

To see her arse. God he would love to see that. To touch it. To imagine it bent over in front of him. Running his hands over her buttocks. Slipping them through her thighs to touch her. His hand moved up and down.

He mostly wanted to hold her.

To see her open herself to him. To watch as she touched herself. To see how she liked to be touched. How she brought herself to orgasm. Oh! he wanted to see that. Wanted to hear it. Hear the sounds she made. Imagining bring his mouth to her. His tongue licking at her and his mouth sucking her gently. He could feel the way she would push into his mouth. Seeking the pleasure that he would give her. Then she would take him. He knew. She would take him in her mouth and suck him. Lick him with long hard strokes that would finish with a swirl of her tongue around the tip. He couldn't decide what gave him more pleasure. The way she made him feel physically. The way she teased him and brought him to the edge.

He didn't speak of this. Not yet.

She had to go. The call ended with promises of another.

He imagined looking at her. Touching her.

It didn't take long.

CHAPTER

11

Guided by Venus

Julia preferred the blinds open, welcoming the moonlight and the sunlight. It allowed her to feel connected with the rhythm of the day, of the seasons, of life. She had spent a lot of time thinking about life in the last decade. Thoughts of life and thoughts of love. The need to lean out for love. To see where it might lead. It was as easy and as difficult as that. As Julia walked along the shoreline, she looked at the water, watching the waves moving in their endless rhythm as they appeared and disappeared back into the whole. The movement was always calming, slowing her heartbeat. Would the waves hold the answer.

It was the end of October. A time when much of the world marked the ending of summer and the start of the colder months. Day of the dead, Samhain, All Hallows eve. It was as good a time as any to reflect with ritual on letting go and creating space for the new. For the southern hemisphere, the days were noticeably longer.

Five weeks on from September's Spring Equinox, it was lighter in the morning. Beltane not Samhain. When the seeds planted in the winter, begin to find their way through the dark soil to the spring light. Julia wondered what seeds had she been planting with these conversations. What might push out through the soil into the light of the sun.

The living room was lit with flickering soft yellow candlelight. Julia filled a small bowl with sand she had collected from the beach. Placing a cone of incense in the centre, she touched a match to the tip. As the flame took hold, she watched it flare for a moment before puffing it out gently. The rich magic smoke of frankincense began to make its presence known as it wafted around the room. A goblet of wine. Paper and a pen. Julia sat there for a while. Letting thoughts run through her mind without structure. Just noticing what they were and where they were going. Where they might have been coming from.

Thoughts of him. Of them. Filled her mind. It was not difficult to find ones from the past. There were many where his smile stretched across his face. Lighting up his eyes as he looked at her. Her eyes closed and the images became more brilliant. A memory of the past floated before her eyes. It must have been winter.

The hostel was almost empty, and she had a room to herself. High ceilings and long tall windows. The four beds, all empty except for hers. Julia curled up asleep. The door opened and a quiet voice snuck into her dreams. A silhouette back lit by the weak dawn light. She reached a handout from under the covers and the shadow moved toward her.

Slipping into the bed, Stefano bought the chill of the morning. Shivering a little, she slipped her hands under his shirt.

"Mmmm, warm," he said, as his mouth found her ear. Nibbling at her neck. Uncurling herself Julia stretched along his body. The contrast of the fabric of his shirt, the cool metal of the belt buckle and the cool denim of his jeans rough against the soft fabric of her pyjamas.

"You have too many clothes on," she murmured. Tugging at his buckle. Her breasts pushed against his shirt, and she could feel her nipples harden.

"Are you cold?" he asked as his hands slid under her top and captured her breasts, his cold fingers softly brushing her nipples. Julia could feel the sensation run down to between her legs. Her mouth opened slightly, sucking in air, before a quiet moan exited with the breath. Stefano moved down in the bed, pulling the covers over his head, to take one of her breasts in his mouth. His cold lips were a delicious contrast with his hot mouth. Sucking gently through the soft silk. Julia tugged at his belt and undid the buttons, not interested in waiting or teasing. She could feel the desire pooling in her and the early morning seemed to make her skin, her nipples, every part of her exquisitely sensitive.

Stefano pushed down his jeans. Pushing aside the soft cotton of his trunks, moving his hips toward her, seeking the warm firm grip that would bring him to the point of release. Julia ran her hand around him, guiding him and brought her thumb to her mouth. He watched her as she stuck out her tongue and licked the first drops of his pleasure. Now it was his turn to moan. It was so sexy to watch.

No, it was more than sexy. There was something deeply intimate.

"Bimba," his voice yearning. A whisper. His hand slid along her side and hitched her leg over his hip, the other on her shoulder. Julia arched back, holding him as he thrust into her and she pushed down to meet him. Her breathing got faster and deeper with every thrust bringing the pleasure closer.

She held him as her whole body shuddered. Squeezing him tightly with the small inner muscles that rippled with pleasure. She felt herself dissolve as he shouted out in pleasure. The sensation sped outward. He held her tightly as waves of pleasure flooded through his body.

They lay there afterwards. On their sides. Face to face. Small smiles. His hand gently brushed the hair from her face. The blankets creating a cocoon of warmth of sex and sleep.

"Well good morning to you," she grinned.

He laughed softly. "Good morning, bella Bimba. I can't stay long. I have to go back down. But I will be free soon. Sleep a little longer. It's still early. Come and have some breakfast with me later."

She pushed out her bottom lip and snuggled in closer.

"Mmmm can't you stay a bit longer? You're warm now."

He answered by pulling her even closer and kissed her. It was a kiss that went on until her breath was spent. He felt himself stirring. She looked at him, her eyebrow rising.

"I have to go. I'll save it," he grinned, "come find me in a while."

Reluctantly he slid from the covers and stood before her. His capacity to recover was clear as he struggled to tuck himself away and button his fly. Julia gathered the blankets around her chin. Trying to keep the warmth. Her breath was now visible in the early morning light. Stefano looked down at her. He pulled the blankets back, exposing her nakedness to the cold air. Julia stretched in response to the shock. She watched him as he gazed at her. Feeling her heart swell. There was something about him. Something in his gaze that felt stripped as bare as she was now. His eyes flicked to hers. A crackle of energy shot between them. He ran his hand from her breast, along her flank, following the curves and dips down to her knee. He then pulled the covers up. Breaking the spell. A quick smile followed by a kiss, and he was gone. Julia listened to his footsteps echoing softly down the hallway.

Pulling back the covers, her feet touched the cold tiles as she strode over to the long windows and flung open the green shutters.

The room flooded with light. The green of the garden and soft sand colors of the buildings filled her eyes. The courtyard spread out below her. The tall iron gates that secured it were still closed. Steps led to the garden, where she had first taken his hand. There was something. Something happening that she hadn't experienced before. Julia wasn't sure where it might go. But she was sure of one thing. She would stay to find out.

Sitting crossed legged in front of the candles, Julia returned to the present. That feeling was pulsing in her again. The connection that had begun all those years ago. Julia wasn't sure it was time to take a step that would see her take flight. She was, however, ready to make some changes. To throw open the windows like she had that morning many years ago.

She would stop hiding in her house, using the excuse of her children's needs as a reason to stay single, focused on her career. Not a resolution as such. Rather a statement of intention. She would let her heart be open to love. To live and to love. Julia wrote them on the paper. That would be her intention.

She passed the paper through the incense smoke. Let the words fly freely. Lifting the paper to the candle flame, she watched it curl and begin to burn. Bringing the passion and possibilities to manifestation. As the flames began to lick her fingers, Julia dropped the paper onto the sand and watched it curl and disintegrate. There. Be held by the ground so that they may be made real. Julia picked up the goblet of wine and sprinkled a few drops on the cooling paper. May the heart recognize all that comes truly. She sipped the rest. The intentions had been sent.

12

Speak My Name

"I don't know. I might go to Italy next year," Julia was offhand in her comment, sipping the coffee. She was hoping Eleni would let it slide and at the same time she was hoping her friend would ask her more about it.

They no longer said how long they had known one another, just how old they were when they met. The first day of secondary school. From then on, all the way through until the end of their final year, they would meet at the school gate. Julia was usually there waiting when the big yellow station wagon which held her friend pulled up. One of those gifts, thought Julia, serendipitous or karmic, either way a gift that she had been forever grateful for. Their friendship had weathered some rough spots but time had burnished it to a golden shine. Julia treasured it and she knew Eleni did as well. Smart and thoughtful, Eleni was her integrity commissioner. She would always remind Julia that this was a lens worth looking through. Whenever decisions were hard, or complex or teetering on something morally ambiguous.

"To see Stefano?"

"How the heck do you do that," Julia said out loud. Was it written on her face?

Eleni laughed, "I have known you for way too long. I don't really know much about Stefano, but I have witnessed how that year shaped the rest of your life. You returned a different person."

Julia choked on her coffee. Eleni waited, smiling.

"I watched as you came back, lost and sad. Then you threw yourself into your studies, your year in Italy built a foundation for so much of what happened after that. It's almost like you kept a part of that year alive by weaving it into the fabric of your life. So, I am going to assume this trip, your first on your own since you came back that time, might lead you back there. Back to him?"

Julia nodded. "Yes, I think I will possibly drop by and see him."

"Mimi and Stella told me you had a message from him. I never understood what happened, why you left? Though if I think about it, you were both very young," Eleni offered a way out and one forward.

"I was very young. Naïve. I think I was impatient and everything seems more black and white at that age. You know me, I won't compete for a man, ever. But really, when I think about it from this perspective, I think maybe our love was too big for us. We were too immature, too self-centred, to honor what it was we had between us. We have talked about it. I think we both recognize that there was something like that at play," Julia stopped, realizing that she had perhaps said too much, revealed too much.

Eleni was looking at her, grinning from ear to ear.

"Ahh so you are in quite a lot of contact then?"

Julia couldn't stop herself grinning.

"Yes, the odd text, how are you, that kind of thing." But her smile, her tone, her face revealed otherwise, and Eleni had known her for a long time. There had been a lot more conversation, if she read her friend's face clearly. Julia was lit up from within. It had been a long time since she had looked like that, flushed with joy and sparkling with her usual energy.

"You love Stefano," Eleni teased in the way she had done so for all the decades of their friendship.

Julia threw a cushion at her. Not wanting to say that out loud. She couldn't allow that thought to be too present. Julia certainly didn't want to say it.

"I do think there might be something there but I am not so foolish to believe it's . . ." Julia stopped and started, not wanting to say that word, "but I feel as though maybe there is a circle to close or another to open. Anyway, it feels like the time is right."

"Hmm, I think so too. I have a feeling about this. I feel it's going to be good."

Julia rolled her eyes at Eleni. "Stop it, stop your premonitions!" I have had quite enough of that, Julia thought to herself. The fortune teller's words played on her mind.

Eleni laughed again. "Well, I have been right about a few things."

Julia secretly hoped Eleni was right about these feelings as well. But it felt like a lot could happen, a lot there was no way she could be in control of.

"Come on," Eleni pulled her out of her reverie, "the movie is about to start."

13

Dreaming of Him

Plans. The thought of travel. She called her friend Hermione. They had met at Olympia exhibition centre in London where Hermione was organising a series of talks and events. Their friendship was sparked by immediate recognition and cemented by their shared interests, philosophies, and views of the world.

"I'm thinking of coming over to England, as soon as the skies are open," Julia began.

"Yes! That would be wonderful! When? Of course, you must stay with me."

"I will, I will!" matching Hermione's enthusiasm. "Then I might pop over to Italy," she dropped it in to the conversation, casually.

"Oh Italy! Oh! I want to go. Let's see where things are at when you arrive, but we can go to the seaside while you're in England, let's go to the coast."

The call finished with arrangements starting to take shape and dates written in diaries. Stefano's name was on her tongue. Waiting to be spoken, waiting to be shared. But not yet.

"It's funny," Julia thought, the desire to speak about the one you love. To hear their name in your ears, to feel the words in your mouth. As though in speaking their name you invoke their presence.

Words have power. Power to heal. Power to find your way back to something, to someone, perhaps even to yourself. If she spoke his name, would it make him real?

It was early morning for her, late night for him when he called.

"What are you thinking Bimba?" Stefano asked.

Julia smiled back at him. Shaking her head. "About us. Because even if we are apart at the moment. I am imagining what it might be like when I am there with you."

"Tell me a little about what you think it will be like?" a suggestive grin played around his mouth.

Julia's smile widened responding to the tone in his voice.

"How would it be?" she raised her eyebrows a little, "Okay close your eyes, listen carefully to my voice. I will tell you how it will be."

He closed his eyes, though he would open them soon enough. Not wanting to miss her face.

"I want you to imagine this scene," Julia began, "I have just arrived in Italy. I'm not sure where I am, but it doesn't matter because when I step through the arrival doors at the airport, all I can see is your face. My whole body is suddenly tingling. You walk up to me. We are standing in front of each other. Almost touching, but not quite touching. We can feel the energy between us. We have spent the last few months wondering what it might be like to be face-to-face again. That energy that has been building up between us explodes. It's almost as though it's something living. Perhaps it is. You bring your hand to my face and I take hold of your wrist as you cup my cheek. The touch is like a lightning strike . . ."

Her words weaved a scene and they fell into it as though it were real. They were silent for a long while afterwards. Just looking at each other. He smiled and her face broke into a smile that lit up her eyes. She nodded, embarrassed, but also feeling freer.

"I cannot wait to do that with you," he said.

She looked at him, "You have to tell me if you really want me to come. At least for a month," she added quickly, not wanting to raise the stakes too high and not wanting to overcommit either, said that inner voice. But her heart was in her throat and her face burned.

"A month is okay . . . to begin with," he replied.

They were both grinning now. "Like a pair of idiots, beautiful idiots," he thought.

14

Burn That Bridge

Something had shifted. Intensified. A line had been crossed and she knew she could no longer step back over it. They spoke every day. Sometimes just an exchange of messages. Sometimes long rambling conversations. And every now and then, something more. Julia began to get to know him again. But he said it wasn't getting to know each other, because they already knew each other so well, it was just that thirty years were missing but he didn't believe they had changed that much.

She'd been thinking about that. It made her wonder about whether she had created a narrative about him in her mind. He was an Italian lover, with all the stereotypical behavior that goes with that. Handsome, charming, and not to be trusted. It had kept her safe. Hidden deep in her subconscious was a knowing. A knowing that to entertain more than a little whimsy, more than thinking of their story as a twinkle in her eye in her later years, to hope for anything more than that, would undo her. It was so much easier to think of him as someone who sought simple pleasure and easy company. That was the story she had told herself to protect herself. But now she didn't know if that was true.

Julia started to fall in love with this Stefano. Not with the memories of him. This Stefano who spoke so freely, so beautifully, so openly. Julia watched his face become animated and his smile broader. Making her realize that when they had first started talking, he had been different. Closed. Sadder. Now he laughed. Perhaps he dreamed of her too?

Julia knew she had begun to dream. To see him. To be held by him. To make love with him. To maybe, maybe stay this time. What would her friends think about it? Her friends were encouraging her forward. Then every now and again one of them would ask, seriously, but you will come back, right? She would smile and nod. Not daring to believe that he would want her to stay. Julia wondered how she would be able to leave him after a month. Would he let her go? She hoped not. Secretly in her heart, she hoped not. She booked the ticket. In four months, she would be there.

Just as she began to let the dreams carry her away, there was news. The hotel Stefano managed was to close. He would be going home until he found something else. The words fall on her like stones. Home? Suddenly she realized that his life was much more than the story they have been weaving together these last months. "Home?" She asked, not wanting to ask the next question. The important question. The question she already knows the answer to. "Yes. But don't worry. We will still speak. It will be okay."

And for a few days, it was.

Then he disappeared completely.

Julia sighed as she looked at Hermione through the screen.

"I don't know what is happening or rather not happening. Everything was moving along and," Julia stopped herself, not really wanting to talk about how intimate things had become. "And now he has disappeared. I haven't heard from him for weeks."

Hermione looked back at her. Her eyes soft and her face carefully arranged into a neutral expression. If there was one thing about Hermione, she would be honest. Julia always knew Hermione would let her explore what she feared and bring into the open thoughts she didn't want to acknowledge. That's when she would be honest. She sometimes stated the uncomfortable truth, but always with love and kindness. Right now, Julia wished she would not do that, but at the same time she knew it was inevitable.

"What are you feeling?" Hermione asked.

"Like a fool, like a stupid fool. What am I doing? What am I doing getting bound up in a situation that simply may be a figment of my imagination. I feel like some stupid lovesick teenager. It's embarrassing," Julia half laughed at herself. It was embarrassing. She just didn't expect to be in her fifties and still feeling this way.

"Seriously," Julia went on, "what the hell am I doing. I don't want these feelings of longing, despair, and uncertainty. I feel like I should have all this sorted out by now. I should be able to make rational, thoughtful, wise decisions. Not base the next stage of my life on something fanciful."

"Why do you think it's fanciful?" Hermione smiled but she was serious.

The question hung in the air. Julia didn't want to answer it. She didn't want to voice her deepest fears. That somehow all those words of love, of attraction, of desire, were just lines. Just things he'd say to anyone.

This possibility of opening to love had brought with it a sense of vulnerability that she had deliberately avoided. It seemed unfair that the one thing she knew that would give her life color and meaning, was the very thing that could pull down the hard earned and carefully won tranquillity of her life right now.

Julia shook her head. Closing her eyes to stop the dampness getting worse. Taking in a lungful of air. She exhaled and opened her eyes.

"I don't know. I think I've been dreaming and maybe I have created some castles in the clouds," Julia admitted ruefully. "I know there is something between us. Something that has kept us connected or that reconnected us after decades. It doesn't feel one way. I don't think it is. But I don't really know what it is, especially now he's gone quiet," Julia shrugged, indicating her inner sense of helplessness.

She felt adrift, not untethered in the way she had months ago, before they had started talking. But definitely adrift. As though the little boat that she had thought they were building together had suddenly headed out to sea with just her in it.

Hermione nodded. She could see that pain in her friend, and it surprised her. Julia's willingness to look on the bright side was an asset when the world seemed to get dark. Hermione had drawn on that strength herself at times. The capacity to manage life's challenges with a level of equilibrium was a feature of Julia's character. She had managed so many ups and downs in her life and she was one of the most resilient, cheerful, and optimistic people Hermione knew. But then she also knew that Julia had been alone for a very long time, putting her children first, carrying all the responsibility for the household, she had avoided being in a relationship, until that rather unfortunate one with Lars. This love story with Stefano, Hermione could see it was different, it had always been different. It was getting harder to enthuse about Julia going to see him in Italy, if he was making it clear just how unclear his intentions were.

"What is really the problem?" Hermione asked, "Is it that he seems to have disappeared or that you are feeling so adrift because of it?"

As always, Hermione was shining a searchlight and heading right for the core of the problem. Julia thought about her question.

"It's definitely both. But I think the bigger thing is this feeling of vulnerability. That I have been foolish enough to want something and I was taking a chance, I was open to wanting it, I'd booked my ticket. Then suddenly it was all stripped away. I feel like I've been a fool."

"You're not a fool," said Hermione softly. "It's not foolish to open up for love. It's not easy to take that risk. It takes courage and vulnerability. And sometimes, even when you take that risk, it doesn't work out," she said it gently but it hit to the core.

Julia looked up at her stricken and the look on her face made Hermione add hastily, "Not that I think this is not going to work out. I feel like it will, though it seems almost unfair to say that while he is saying nothing. I am not sure why there is this bump in the road, but it feels as though there might be a very important reason, and I'm sensing it's not how he feels about you. I think something has happened there; something is going on for him. I don't get a sense that he has just lost interest in you and wandered off to do something else. Anyway, you have that ticket and I have a lovely big house full of cats and *prosecco*. Come stay with me instead."

They finished their call with promises to see each other soon. Julia would use the ticket to fly to England. Then she would find her way to Italy.

"You can come and stay with me, in Verona," she offered, but Hermione laughed and shook her head. "Nice and cosy, with the three of us. No, I don't think you're going to need me in Italy. But you must come and stay with me for a few days. It will be so good to see you, and you can go off and explore and come back any time." She wanted Julia to feel free to go to Italy if he called, without leaving her feeling too forlorn if he didn't. "We'll have fun."

And they would. It wasn't quite the way Julia imagined when she planned the trip. She had booked a couple of places to stay in Italy, near where she used to live. Near him, she thought, though she pushed that thought away. It would be good to be back in Italy. And who knows, maybe he would be in touch. There were still several weeks before she left.

Julia thought of when the fortune teller had told her she had set something in motion and to be careful what she wished for. No, it wasn't quite that. She had said to be prepared for the consequences of her wishes.

What if she wished for Stefano? What if she wished for love and adventure? What if the consequences of those wishes weren't the realization of those things, but the disappointment of wanting something you can never have.

CHAPTER

15

Falling Behind Me

The silence went on and on. Julia didn't want to admit to herself that she was waiting. But she was. It annoyed her that someone could so easily take up space in her thoughts. That she could miss someone who she didn't even really know. Who was she missing? Or what was she missing? Was it the attention? The compliments, the conversations. The desire he expressed so poetically? Was it the idea that someone somewhere was thinking of her? Someone who knew her from the before times. When she was still mostly just herself. Not yet occupied by the needs of others. Not yet subsumed into the expectations of what she should be as a wife or a mother. The time when her life stretched ahead of her with possibilities.

Why was that so important to her? A love story that could sweeten her nights as time took her beyond such things? Or had something else been awakened. Had she been asleep all this time.

Determinedly holding up the weight of a life when Hugh was ill and since he died.

What had awakened her? Or maybe a more interesting question was why. Why had she found herself untethered. What did it mean to be untethered in midlife. Why was she contemplating letting go of family, of friends, of work, of career. Julia had some idea of what she might like to do, but no idea as to whether it could sustain more than her spirit.

Untethered.

Julia pushed the food around her plate. She had come for dinner with Eleni, her oldest friend who was now looking at her quizzically.

"Not hungry? You don't like my cooking?" Eleni played up her Greek accent to lighten the accusation.

Julia smiled at her. "Of course I do! Are you crazy! I'm just not really hungry," her breath blew out of her mouth as she finished her sentence.

"Tell me," Eleni said.

Julia looked at her. "I'm okay. I'm just annoyed at myself really. Annoyed at myself for being disappointed. And also," Julia trailed off.

"I think it's normal to be disappointed. But I don't think it's all over just yet," Eleni reached across the table. Always on my team, thought Julia. She squeezed Eleni's hand in thanks. "Anyway, I'm going to go to Italy," she said, "I'll go see my friends in London first."

"It will be good to get away. We have all been stuck for so long," Eleni was sidestepping the real reason Julia wanted to travel to the other side of the world.

Julia nodded. She was tired. Tired of wondering what she was doing with her life. Tired of feeling so responsible, tired of being responsible and carrying all the responsibility.

She looked back at Eleni. "I just don't understand why I feel this way. I mean in some ways it's interesting. How is it that I feel like I'm some sort of lovelorn teenager. All the feels! Yet at the same time, I am looking at myself thinking what the actual fuck. Can you not be a grown up? Surely a grown up would be more logical? You know—self regulate better."

Eleni laughed, "Yes but self-regulation doesn't mean you don't feel things. It just means you don't emote over everyone. And you're not emoting over everyone, at least not too much," she smiled to take the sting out of the last comment.

"Thanks," Julia laughed back, "though it is weird. Well maybe not weird, but it's certainly strange to have these feeling of despair and loss over something that was really, I don't know, maybe just made up. Maybe just made up in my head because it was . . . familiar," Julia shrugged, biting her lip.

"Hmmm familiar, yes in that you knew him. But that was more than just a catch up. You were speaking for months not just weeks."

Julia's cheeks felt red, and she couldn't quite meet Eleni's eye. "Hmmm well yes it did get intense." And how, Julia thought, but there were some things that were not to be shared.

"Do I think he has feelings for me?" She sipped the delicious Italian Soave Eleni had poured, "Yes, yes he does. We spoke practically every day."

The constant contact they had couldn't practically go on in the same way without transforming into something. In her mind it had been leading to a physical meeting. Maybe that's why he stopped. Perhaps the reality was that Stefano was a coward. He had said as much himself when she had asked him why he hadn't followed her all those years ago. It wasn't because he didn't love her. He had made that clear, again and again. Julia knew love could be scary. Terrifying. Especially one as intense and as enduring as theirs.

Could she blame him? Whatever it was between them, was it too much for him?

Julia had thought Stefano felt the same way. "I'm thinking of coming to Italy," she'd said. "I'm coming for a month. Tell me now if you really want that to happen because you know I will come if you want me to."

"A month," he had said, "a month would do for a start." Perhaps he hadn't believed her. Then he didn't know her. Or maybe he did, hence the disappearance. The withdrawal. The retreat. Julia sighed as she pulled the car into the garage. There was nothing she could do about it. She certainly wasn't going to keep sending messages into an abyss. What might have happened after that month she hadn't let herself imagine in any great detail. Would she have left her family, her children her friends and her work, her security? Would she leave all that? What would be enough to leave that for?

"Love," whispered her soul to her heart. "Love would be enough."

She just had to let it fall behind her, feel the shadow creep into the places where she had dared to dream. She had done it before. It just felt like something elemental had broken in her. Stefano had been that one light in the darkness that had helped pull her forward. A sweet memory whose very existence had been reason to dream of better times. But now. Now she was drowning. And she was tired. Tired of trying. Tired of swimming only to be washed up on the shore alone. Again.

"Shut up, Heart." Julia said to herself. "You are not in charge anymore."

16

Irony and Resolution

It was ironic. Ironic that in her intention to step out from behind her roles as mother, teacher, friend, to reclaim the role of lover and perhaps partner, she had found her way back to the past while thinking she was looking to the future. Not so much a moving forward, as a mining of the past. Perhaps that was what life was all about. A constant circle looping back to the past as a way of guiding the future. What lesson had been learned. What could be left.

Sitting outside on the deck at Mimi's place in the countryside was peaceful, nestled in nature. The shadows of the sun turning them sepia. Gathering as women have since the start of time. To honor the turning of the year. The points of stillness at solstice and equinox. The rhythms of the moon that pulled and pushed as it did the waves on the shore. "This is our place of worship," thought Julia. "In the gathering. In the being together where words are spoken and silence is shared."

They would laugh and dance, eat and drink. There would be ease and tension, and always acceptance even when the challenges went to the core. It was good to be a part of this circle, which expanded and contracted to embrace whoever stepped in. Sometimes they would mark the time with a ritual, at others, it was freeform and flowing into the crevices of hearts and minds.

Julia reached forward to fill her glass. Her prosecco sloshed as Stella nudged her in the ribs. "What is it about you and men from overseas?" asked Stella, "It's a bit insulting to those of us who have Australian partners. Do you really think that Australian men aren't good enough for you?" She was only half joking.

"No!" Julia laughed, licking the wine from her hand as she righted the glass. "I'd be happy to date an Australian."

"Ha it would have to be an Australian who wanted to take you off to live in Europe," chimed in Mimi.

Julia nodded her head, "Yes exactly." They all laughed. "I promise I'll come back. No reason to stay. Though you never know who I might meet on the plane."

Mimi leaned forward, topping up her glass.

"Well, I don't understand it. Though at least you are consistent in your choice of foreigners."

"Exactly," agreed Stella, "It's like the United Nations, your love life."

"Well, look I am just doing my part for inclusion and diversity!" Julia nearly spat out her drink, putting her hands up, her eyes danced. "But come on—to be fair, I haven't dated anyone other than Lars since Hugh died. Let's not forget I met Hugh twenty-five years ago. So, it has been a long time since all that." She finished with a wicked grin.

"Well yes, but Hugh took you to live in London," Stella countered.

"But I came back."

Stella rolled her eyes, "Ten years later! Okay so Lars was German, that's not Australian."

She pronounced as though she were a judge and Julia's romantic tendencies and preferences were on trial.

Julia nodded, holding her hands up in submission. "Guilty, your honor."

"It's funny, Lars was so weird about your thing with Italy," offered Mimi, "yet here you are about to get on a plane and go to Italy."

"Yes, in a way I have him to thank for all this," said Julia, raising her glass. "I realized that he couldn't possibly love me, definitely not the way I want to be loved. But he did remind me, briefly, that love is something to be treasured. Perhaps it is the holy grail we are all seeking, to meet someone, something imagined, to seek it though perhaps to never really find it. Maybe we just get to hold it for a moment. Reminding us of why we are here."

Mimi nodded empathically. It gladdened her heart to hear her friend be so clear. There was so much love between them. Soul sisters.

"He was obsessed with trying to disentangle me from my memories. I don't even understand how you can reconcile wanting to deny someone a part of themselves, with that being love. Well, it's not love, is it, because if you truly love someone, then you love them just the way they are."

"Hmmmph," said Stella, "come on, he wanted you to empty yourself of any color. I should know all about that. I think I have spent the last 30 years slowly draining of color. But no more! Maybe I'll pick up where you left off, and find myself an Italian lover."

Julia was thoughtful. "It's so many things that chip away at a relationship. If you are brave enough you can speak up. I don't think I did enough of that with Hugh. Especially toward the end. It's so easy to slip into roles that feel safe and familiar, yet they hold you tight and don't let you grow. I tried not to do that with Lars. Wanting to be as authentic and honest as I could be. I can't imagine how it must have been like for you, Stella. To be honest I am not sure that anything I did could have changed things for Lars. But it did change things for me."

Julia gave Mimi a quick smile, "Venus in Leo. My relationship with Lars helped me understand that planetary placement!"

Mimi smiled at her friend. "Generosity in love."

"Now to find someone who is worthy of receiving it."

Julia laughed to deflect the seriousness of her words.

Mimi jumped in. "Yes, babe. Someone who is worthy of you and your beautiful heart."

"Exactly true," chimed in Stella. "And if it means we have to visit you in Italy or anywhere else in the world, then I guess that is a sacrifice we'll make for your happiness."

Stella was quick to start making plans. Narrowing her focus on where might be the best place to meet Italian men. "They're everywhere," Julia was droll, "It is Italy after all." Mimi's daughter wandered through at that moment.

"What is Stella going on about?" she whispered to her mother.

"Julia's obsession with Italy and her Italian lover from the past."

"Oh, Julia I'll come with you to Italy. Maybe I'll take an Italian lover too."

"Oh you should!" Mimi was first to reply.

Julia laughed. "Sure, come with me. If I have to find a lover for Stella, I might as well find one for you too. Though, I don't think either of you will need my help."

Julia looked at her friends, thinking about how fragile and fleeting life was. That midlife shake on the shoulder was about as real as it got. When you began to look forward and realize that there might just be an end coming into view. Julia knew that life's wheel could suddenly spin too fast, and you could no longer hold on. It could happen at any age. But there was something about hitting your midlife. Slipping over fifty and sliding toward sixty, all of a sudden life seemed to speed up just as you wanted it to slow down.

"Perhaps we are all trying to live some sort of hero's journey," she thought to herself, "waiting for the message from the mystic. The supernatural creature who will send us on our quest." Much better to go out and seek your own adventure. Julia was prepared to admit it, and it had been a while since she had been brave like that.

Peace and quiet, they were dead people's goals. They had been Lars's goals. Retired at fifty, he wanted to spend the rest of his life playing golf and fishing. One evening he had asked her about past loves. Julia had looked at him. Love. Yes. Not many true loves. Hugh, her husband. And one more. Julia hadn't been aware of her face. She hadn't noticed how she lit up at the memory. But Lars had. He returned to that conversation again and again, chipping away insistently at that memory. Honing in on what and who lay behind that love which had crossed her face. Trying to destroy something that had been so enduring and now she realized the absolute futility of all he had tried to do. Every time he had rained scorn down on her choices, she had gathered them to her more closely. It's how she had realized that Stefano had been her light in the darkness. A small still light that always drew her forward. Onward.

Julia shivered, as though the memory of Lars had cast a shadow. She would rather be alone than have to live without her memories, than have to deny love. Julia knew her view of life was not so black and white. Perhaps that was one of the small gifts of loss. Even her marriage to Hugh. She looked back with tenderness, shaped by the knowing that Hugh's life had been short. There was no place for recriminations for him or herself. She knew she was here because of love. Love for him, love for their children, love for herself. The sort of love that came with life's experiences. A way of loving that loved because of the scars, not despite them, that accepted the flaws. Because that is what being human is all about.

And this love. Her love for Italy, for Stefano and for herself, her foolish, young, intoxicated with life and all that love promised, self. This love was unbreakable. Julia knew that now.

And so here she was, suitcases packed, passport and travel documents in order. No matter what happened. If nothing happened. She would, at least, know.

Mimi and Stella drove her to the airport.

"Are you ready?" Mimi asked.

"Yes, I have packed what I need, I can buy whatever I have forgotten," deliberately being obtuse.

"That's not what I meant."

"I know, I think I'm either excited or terrified, it all feels the same in the body."

Julia felt sick. But was she ready to step into whatever awaited her.

She looked across at Stella and back at Mimi.

"It's going to be okay, and if it doesn't work out, if I don't see him at all or if I do see him and my heart gets broken again, then that's okay. We can't live a wholehearted life if we won't heed the call for adventure every now and again."

"You're right," Stella glanced at her, "but damn you're brave."

Julia took a deep breath and nodded her thanks. Mimi's hand stretched forward and she took it.

"You'll be okay," Mimi offered.

"If I come back in pieces then I know just who has the right glue to put me back together again," Julia grinned.

"You bet," Mimi's hand squeezed hard. "Okay here we are."

"Just drop me, there is no need to come in, find somewhere to park, all that palaver."

"No way, how long have we all been waiting for an airport farewell! For years. We are getting out and drinking a cocktail in the bar before you go through the big doors." "Then," added Stella, "we'll drink another."

They sat at the airport bar. "Such weird places, airports," said Julia.

"What do you mean?" asked Stella. "I like all the coming and goings, the people watching." "Sure," said Mimi, nudging Julia, "all the men in suits watching."

"Mimi! How can you say that?" Stella lifted her chin in the air as though to dismiss such nonsense. "I've been so restrained. Anyway, it's not the right time of day, or rather night, for the men in suits to be around."

"Plenty of men in uniform," offered Julia, "and women of course."

Stella looked at her, a glint in her eye, "We know that's much more Mimi's thing than mine."

Mimi pursed her lips in agreement, "True, you know I just love beauty in all her forms. It's the Venusian aesthetic for me every day."

"So," said Stella rounding on Julia. "Are you really ready? And don't give me the 'I can buy what I need there' bullshit. Are you ready for whatever happens or doesn't happen?"

Julia put her head in her hands. "I don't know," she looked up at them from between her fingers, "I mean, what on earth am I doing? Heading to the other side of the world for who knows what. I think I have lost my mind."

"Oh definitely that," agreed Stella. "Just don't be a cliché. You know the whole Eat, Pray, Love bullshit. And if you see him, jump him, like straight away." "What Stella means," interrupted Mimi, "is don't waste this opportunity. Whatever happens, whether you see Stefano or not. Enjoy yourself and," she said looking sideways at Stella, "fall in love or at least . . . you know . . . take Stella's advice."

The flight was mercifully empty and the seat beside her was free. Now that she was on the plane, her nerves had dissipated. She would soon be there. Soon enough anyway. She would land in England and go to stay with Hermione. There was still no contact from Stefano. She didn't know if she would see him. A tiny part of her wondered why she was going at all. Was it hopeless? Somewhere nestled in her heart was the belief, or at least a hope, that she would see him. Even if it wasn't looking likely. A hope that no matter how hard she tried to dislodge it, stubbornly refused to move. Maybe she was crazy. Maybe there was truth to the madness of a midlife crisis. Or maybe it was more real than anything else. Maybe it was love, not just for him, but for herself too.

Self-love, reflected Julia, is probably the hardest love of all. One that required constant nurturing, tending, not because it was greedy and grandiose. No that was ego, full of bluff and bluster, for some arrogance and denial. Self-love was a quieter, steadier flame, it was vulnerable to shame and contempt. It was not arrived at in the bright light of the day. Finding it called for inner journeys that were, sometimes, dark, the end point unknown, or resisted until it was impossible not to fall. Fall in, fall out, fall.

The unknown lay out in front of her. Julia had spun the wheel.

PART
TWO

The Lake

CHAPTER

17

Taking Flight

D ubai to London, the last leg of the flight. Julia's drowsy
mind drifted back to what she had imagined would
happen. Through the long months of contact over the
last year, Julia had created a fantasy. A fantasy where she would
arrive in Venice. He would be waiting for her. What would he think
of her now? What would she think of him? A lot of time had
passed and she was no longer the woman she'd been when they had
first met, thirty years ago. Young and unformed, almost translucent
as she passed through those years designed to fill us with color. She
remembered his eyes, and his grin. That grin that would light up
his face when he looked at her. A mischievous glint in his eye, as
though in any moment something could happen.

Remembering how she loved to wake to his face in the
morning. The way he would draw her close, make love with her

before slipping out of bed. Keeping the warmth tucked around her as he dressed. Only to pull the covers off as she lay there, to run his hand along her body. Every time. There was something both appreciative and possessive in that gesture. As though he was claiming her. Or that the last thing he would see of her, was a moment of beauty, of longing.

The memory made her shiver. Her heart ached at the knowledge that right now, the likelihood of seeing him at all was minimal. But she remembered the story she had told him, it filled her dreams as she slept.

The next time

Crossing the room to the door felt like a marathon. He was there. He was standing in front of her. In flesh and blood, *carne e ossa*. He had come to her.

"Ciao Julia," he said softly, "May I?"

Julia stepped back and he was in the room. It seemed smaller, hotter. A rivulet of water ran down her spine and she shivered.

"Ciao," her voice was a whisper.

He smiled. That grin that she remembered, that went all the way to his eyes. His eyes. Could she look at them?

"Bimba," he said, reaching out to cup her chin and tilting her head up. "You came," he said.

"Yes," she replied, "I wasn't sure if you'd come."

He looked at her, "But of course. You came all the way from Australia. Of course I am here."

He was close, so close. Julia began to feel the energy from his body surround her, drawing her closer, like it always had. Quickly steeping back, she smiled, feeling awkward.

"*Vino?* Wine?"

He nodded. "Sure, why not."

His voice, his accent, it was different having him here in the flesh. *Carne e ossa*—flesh and bone. She felt herself tremble as she moved to the cabinet, willing the shaking in her hands to stop. Fumbling the glasses, she became aware of him next to her.

His hand reached out to take the bottle.

"Shall I pour? You seem . . . shaky," his voice was soft next to her ear. But she noticed his hands were trembling too as he poured the wine. Her breath came faster, her lips parted as she looked at his face. At his mouth.

Mistake.

"Julia," he sighed as he moved his mouth toward hers.

His kiss was like lighting a fire that rippled through her, ripped through her more accurately. Any words, any thoughts, any sadness or regrets melted away. She couldn't think at all. *Spensierata.* Was that the word? Why was she even trying to find it? All her senses began to focus on her mouth, his mouth. The feeling of desire grew hotter. His hands slipped down her back. Pulling her closer, her body arched toward his. Feeling him pressing hard in return. Feeling his desire pushing at her. She moaned. He buried his face in her neck. She took a breath, steadying herself.

"*Vino?*" she tried again, wanting to slow things down, not wanting to. She couldn't think. He pulled back, looking at her. His face betrayed his thoughts. He shook his head.

"No," he said, touching her, "I don't really want wine."

Julia smiled and placed her hands on his shoulders. Leaning away she smiled up at him. Trying to gather herself

"Slowly slowly . . . no need to rush," she stepped back from him.

"No," he said, "let's not wait, it's not wine I want. I want to kiss you and feel you. Touch you so I know you are here."

He pulled her to him again. His face was close. She could feel his breath on her skin, imaging his mouth on her body. Her breath was ragged, she shivered.

"Cold," he queried. "I'll warm you."

Julia watched as he slid his hands down from her waist to her thighs. His fingers heading to the hem of her dress. Her breath came quicker. He bent his head and began to kiss her again. His hands teasing her, sliding the skirt of her dress up and down. Looking deep into her eyes, his mouth began to move down toward her neck.

He moved his mouth toward her breasts, pushing through the thin cotton of the dress. Aching for his touch, aching for his mouth. He removed one of his hands from her thighs and slid it up to the top of the dress, pushing aside the cotton he released them. Bending his head toward them, his mouth sought the small pink tips. Her body softened. Moulding against him like it used to. She could feel his desire getting harder.

Her hands slid from his shoulders and began to pull at the buckle on his belt.

"No!" he said more forcefully than intended. "We will start with you." He pushed her hands gently away and pulled her closer to him. She could feel the coolness of the buckle through her clothes and the hardness of him, insistent.

"But I want you," she whispered.

"I know Bimba, I know but we have time. You're right about that, it's just that I don't want to waste it drinking wine. I want to drink you instead, taste every part of you again as though for the first time."

It took all his strength not to push her back on the bed right away. Instead, he pushed himself away and cupped her face in his hands.

"You're right, we have time," he said finally.

He turned her so he could sit on the bed. She stood in front of him. He buried his head in her stomach and breathed in her scent, fresh and clean from the bath. Julia's hands found his curls, grey, almost white now, but still abundant. Just as she'd imagined, twisting her fingers through them as though to never let go. Tilting back slightly he grinned up at her. The top buttons of her light summer dress were opened. He could see her breasts; the tips of her nipples were hard and swollen. His hands returned to the hem of her dress. She felt him begin to slide the dress upwards, over her thighs. He touched her buttocks before sliding his hands back down her thighs.

She was glad she had spent the last few years walking for hours every day. The uneven sand on the beach had forced her muscles to stay firm. Coming from the southern summer, they had a light tan, smoothing the skin. She knew he had always liked her legs, the scoop of her hips, her buttocks.

He was sliding his hands around the tops of her thighs, across her buttocks. The pit of her stomach clenched as the aching for his touch grew stronger. It was all she could to hold still, knowing he was teasing. Loving it and wishing it would stop and move on, at the same time. Softly, imperceptibly, she felt his fingers brush between her thighs. She couldn't help the moan that escaped her lips.

He pulled the hem of her dress up to her hips, exposing her from the waist down. His hands were still as he bent his head and began to lay a line of kisses from her belly to the top of her underwear.

"Mmmmmm," he murmured.

Julia's legs began to tremble. She felt lightheaded. The wanting coursing through her. Her fingers were still in his hair and it was almost impossible not to push him lower. It was as though her body wanted to curl in around his mouth. One hand slipped down and began to slide around the edges of her panties, then sliding further underneath to slip along the skin where she was wet, waiting. She was lost in the sensations. Ripples after ripples of pleasure moved through her. Julia's hands were tight, trying to hold on, trying to stay upright. His mouth, his tongue began to follow his hands. She felt him move the wispy lace aside. Her knees began to buckle as his mouth moved to her core. She felt something soft and warm replace the circular movement of his fingers. Just the tip of his tongue, slow circles. Then he moved and pushed her onto the bed. She felt the bed take her weight as she began to dissolve. The sheets felt cool against her back in contrast to the heat pouring through her center. Her legs were open, knees bent, his hands cupped her buttocks. The movement of his tongue still slow and light. It was all she could do to stop herself from disappearing into the sensation.

Lifting to her elbows, she looked at his face, heavy with desire, his eyes hooded. He looked up, and that impish grin she remembered so well, lit his face.

Falling backwards, she arched her hips toward him. They were still for a moment, as though standing on the edge of the abyss, then the rhythm overtook them, instinctual, eternal. Like a ceremony, honoring all that was sacred, a primal infinite dance that took them in a spiral beyond all knowing.

But that wasn't how it happened. Not at all

CHAPTER

18

Tea, Toast and Tarot

Touching down in London, Julia headed to Hermione's home. Tea and toast by the fire, Julia was longing for that. Longing to sit in Hermione's tall and genteelly ageing Victorian house, where time seemed to slow down.

She settled into the kitchen chair, watching Hermione bring one dish after another of deliciousness out of the fridge and pantry. Like a fairy godmother, Hermione had this beautiful ability to create magic out of nothing. An atmosphere of possibility and bliss seemed to follow her wherever she went. Julia felt her body starting to unravel and let go of the journey.

There was an absolute privilege to friendships which stretched back in time, and she was grateful for it. And the delight of knowing someone like Hermione. Delicate, seemingly fragile but with an inner strength that held her up when needed.

She reminded Julia to look through the lens of a kaleidoscope when thinking about life. That life was much more nuanced and incredible than it's sometimes portrayed. Julia deeply appreciated Hermione for this. It helped her pull up out of the weeds of life when things became too mundane or when she herself lost her way into the structures and restrictions that society can impose. "Be like the willow tree," Hermione would say, "rather than stand against the inevitable storm like an oak tree." Mimi could do this too, Julia reflected. Maybe it was the willingness to be connected to the magic of life that shaped them in this way.

Much later they found themselves sitting by the fire sipping tea and nibbling on toast.

"You know," said Hermione, pouring another cup of tea, "you and I both have a sense of autonomy, 'a room of my own', alongside our occasional glimpse of a romantic nature. And however much we like to travel, we also know how make a home base that is our own. It's our foundation."

Julia thought about that for a moment. She wasn't quite sure she agreed with a romantic nature only arrived in glimpses. "I'm not sure. My romantic nature seems to have been consuming my waking thoughts for the past year. It's a bit exhausting. I've tried not to think about him, I've wanted to fill my head with other things, but the thought of him is stubbornly present." Julia shook her head. "I wasn't expecting it. I wasn't expecting to be so," she paused, "so consumed by it. It's perplexing. Aren't we supposed to not care about those things anymore?"

Julia smiled at Hermione and then they both laughed. While Hermione had a point, they were both very independent women, it seemed love and all those feelings was not done with either of them yet.

"You're right in a sense. I do like having the autonomy to do as I please. But the flip side is that sometimes we may seem so capable that we forget to let others know how much we need them."

Hermione nodded slowly, "It's difficult to do that, isn't it," it was almost a question. "That is the price you pay for freedom. I want to sustain a relationship that has commitment and freedom, freedom to travel, to see friends, to own my own time. Is that too much to ask?"

"It's only possible if you resist the call of social expectations. They can easily drag you into thinking your life has to follow a certain pattern, certain rules."

Julia ran her hand through her hair. This was the reason she was here and not yet in Italy. Why she had chosen to take a moment to collect herself. It was her first trip to the other side of the world, alone after thirty years. She had been called across the world for love. For the possibility of love. And she had come with no promises. Right now, all she had was faith. Faith that the call had not been false hope. Julia could still feel its echo. Its vibrations, ringing quietly in her soul. But she was also pretty sure she knew the reasons why Stefano had gone silent. Because there was something in the way. Or rather someone.

"Though of course there is also this stupid thing called integrity, you know when you have to stop lying to yourself that somehow your actions have integrity. When integrity is the thing that will help you look at yourself in the mirror. Not what anyone else thinks of you. Maybe it's even harder to decide what is the difference between social expectations and a deeper personal sense of what is right and wrong."

Julia was thinking about Stefano. Thinking about whether she would ask if he was with someone else, or if she would even care, if she had the chance to see him. She shuddered at the thought. It went against her personal sense of integrity to even contemplate the thought of betrayal. Because it would be hers as much as his.

"I think Virginia Woolf was right about needing a room of one's own," Hermione mused. "I need my own time and space. Just to be quiet and think in."

"Hmmm. Sometimes I can't decide if I want to merge with someone in that cosmic way or be like Artemis and live alone," Julia trailed off.

"What's in that tea, oh Greek goddess," enquired Hermione, raising an eyebrow.

"You brewed it winter fairy queen, you tell me!" Julia retorted laughing.

"What are we really talking about here?" asked Hermione shifting the tone back to the current dilemma. "What's going on with Stefano? Have you heard from him?"

Julia looked across the table. Not quite waiting to meet Hermione's eyes. Filling her lungs, she exhaled slowly.

"I think we can guess why he stopped speaking with me every day. Why he disappeared. The hotel where he worked is now closed, and I suppose he must have . . . I don't know . . . gone home. I guess I deluded myself into thinking that because he was alone in the hotel, he was alone or at least not otherwise engaged with someone. But when the hotel closed at the end of the season, he had to return to wherever home actually is, and the reality of what he was doing was staring him in the face. And all my fantasies. All our fantasies," Julia's fingers clicked.

Hermione looked at her pensively. "So, if you suspected he was living with someone . . ."

Julia grimaced, "How did I end up on the other side of the world with him in my heart?"

"It's not like you," Hermione agreed.

Julia nodded. It was true, she had to admit it now, she had deluded herself. She had let herself be swept up in a dream. Because he had always been there for her. Not in real life, but as an idea. A memory. He held a place in her heart and a piece of her soul.

Julia knew she could say this to Hermione and be understood. But she also knew that she had wilfully been avoiding engaging her brain, though not her heart. It had been easier to imagine that because he was alone in the hotel room, he was alone in his life. But now it was starting to look like there was more to the story than that. It was not just about that.

"If I'm being truthful, by showing up ready for a new courageous adventure, I could pretend I am ready to throw my life up in the air to follow love across the world like some heroine in a romantic story. All the while knowing that it was impossible."

That was an equally hard truth to hold. She could feel it like a pebble in her stomach.

"An impossible dream," Hermione said quietly.

"Maybe the real truth is I don't have to truly consider the possibility of leaving everything behind because part of me knows there probably isn't something here. Something real that requires me to make a change. What if his unavailability was subconsciously a safety net, stopping me from launching myself headfirst out of my life on the other side of the world."

Hermione nodded, listening silently.

"I could go to Italy, fill myself up with the idea of love and then leave again. Satisfied. No harm done and no real change is required."

"Hmmm I do know this," offered Hermione, interrupting her thoughts, "that look in that photo. The one he sent you. He loves you. The way he is looking at you. You can see it in every photo, from the ones you have of thirty years ago, to these ones, from the present. This is a man in love. I can feel it. I don't believe it is over. It just doesn't make sense that he has just disappeared. Shall we see what the cards say?" she was already pulling them out of the drawer.

The cards said what they always had, love, longing, possibility, and hope. But there was someone else appearing too. A woman, sharp and angular, a sword in hand and frown on her face. Julia looked at Hermione and shrugged. "So, there she is, because that is not me," said Julia defiantly.

Hermione nodded her agreement. "At least it's clearer now. You know it's complicated." There was an awkward silence. After a moment she added, "When is love ever not complicated?"

"It's rare to find peace and quiet when love is in the room," Julia tried to make light of it. "But I've always said, peace and quiet are dead people's goals!"

Walking up the stairs to bed, Julia reflected on the conversation. It was true she did like to have her own space and do her own thing. But she wasn't sure about living without love. Then there was the need to reconcile her own deception too. If she had not expected him to be free, then her own motivations were less clear and maybe less honorable.

Yet it was love that pulled her still, like a North star. To where, she was not yet sure. But she was sure about one thing. Julia had faith in her love for him and she had faith that they had something sacred. She would step into the unknown with all her heart, mind, body, and soul. If she ever got the chance.

Resolved, she slipped into bed. Sleep washed over her and she let the conversation unravel in her dreams.

19

The Healing Hare

The next morning they tumbled into the car and headed off to the holiday cottage in Devon. On the way they took a detour into the countryside. There was a surprise. Hermione had booked them a session of sound healing with gongs.

On the drive down, Julia told Hermione about the reading with the fortune teller at the marketplace. The one who had seemed to know exactly what was about to happen.

"It all was going exactly as she predicted until Stefano disappeared," said Julia. "It went from daily contact to a few paltry emails in the last couple of months," Julia's sigh was heavy with disappointment and tinged with loss.

Hermione looked across at her friend as they drove along country lanes. "Well the Healing Hare might be able to shed some light on that," she said thoughtfully.

Julia nodded, "I think the reality is he has got caught up in his life and he just put me to one side when things got complicated."

Julia offered this observation in a light tone. But Hermione wasn't as easily fooled. Hermione turned down a farm track and stopped the car outside a barn. "We're here. You can go first." Knowing her friend was impatient for any news and having to wait another two hours for her turn might be unbearable.

"I'll sit in the garden under these wind chimes," said Hermione lightly. Then, thinking to herself, "I'll tune in myself to see what's what." She blew some kisses as Julia disappeared inside.

Julia found herself in a room full of an incredible array of gongs. The Healing Hare was a friendly faced woman about the same age who exuded a quiet warmth and welcome. Julia felt immediately comfortable and relaxed, and curious about the way the session worked. They chatted for a while, and she was left with no doubt that the Healing Hare was insightful and psychic. Julia felt immensely encouraged by her and felt brave enough to ask about the thing that was on her mind.

The Healing Hare shook her head. "Why do you want to dig up the past, and open yourself up to hurt?"

The response was not entirely what Julia had hoped for and it didn't mirror the predictions of the fortune teller in the marketplace. But there was a possibility that things were not yet closed. If he were willing to step forward, this time. Another chance.

"You will know by tomorrow how it all pans out," said the Healing Hare. And with that Julia found herself lying on the bed in the middle of the gongs. Losing herself to the vibrations that rippled through the air and her body. The rich cadence, the diverse timbres all coming together as though she were a tuning fork. It was glorious.

She woke early the next day to the view of sunrise over the sea. They were in Devon. After breakfast, Hermione and Julia found themselves walking along the coastal path down to the cove. The view was spectacular. They sat for a while looking out over the sea. Marvelling at the sunshine and the river of sparkles that danced across the water directly to them.

"Bliss," offered Julia. The sound healing had begun a slow unwinding of all the tightly sprung stress. Each moment gently undoing years of what she'd been holding tightly inside her.

Hermione smiled and silently nodded in agreement. That was another thing about Hermione, she had quiet moments when she only spoke when it was necessary. Unless they had settled in for a deep chat or just consumed a bottle of bubbles, in which case, she began to personify her light fairy looks. Flitting around the spaces and speaking of esoteric and magical things. Julia loved her in all her guises.

That evening, Julia cooked a rich and tasty risotto and they curled up in the cosy front room of the cottage. A couple of comfortable sofas piled with cushions and throws faced the windows which overlooked the tiny town. They had piled logs into the woodburner and lit the fire.

Balancing dishes on their knees, with a glass of prosecco by their sides, they talked into the evening to catch up on years of distance, and it felt good to be so nourished in good company. The conversation fell quiet for a moment, and Hermione was suddenly serious after an evening of reminiscing, and laughter. Now Hermione was focused on Julia and the tricky situation of the missing Stefano.

"Let's see what's going on," said Hermione lighting more candles with intention. "Shall we see if there's any insight?"

Taking out her cards, Hermione began to shuffle. The cards began to fall out, jump out. Hermione placed them carefully before her. "It's an affair, or rather there is a triangle. Look, this card jumped out of the pack three times. He feels responsible to someone else. He does love you but he has responsibilities and he's worrying about the implications of that."

This was tough news. It wasn't what either of them hoped to hear. Hermione was not to be trifled with when it came to pulling back the curtains on what might be hidden, she was fearless and fierce about matters of the heart and soul. And she felt after months of silence, just when Julia was on the brink of coming across the world to see him, her friend needed to know the truth of what was going on.

Julia nodded, acknowledging the truth in her words.

"Yes. That feels right. I know he loves me. I can feel it. What I don't know is whether it's enough to change things." She trailed off hugging her knees. Hermione began placing cards in front of her.

Julia heard a ping from her phone. It was after 11 p.m. She immediately knew who it was from. She waited for Hermione to pause, not wanting to break her flow. She stopped talking and Julia stood up and left the room. "What is it?" Hermione called after her.

Julia returned and looked at her.

Stefano—*"I've found a job on the Lakes. I'll see you when you come to Torri."*

"Stefano has just sent a message." Her heart was in her throat.

"Healing Hare said I'd know what was going on by the end of today. It's him. He's got a new job in a hotel on the lake. That's near where I'm staying. He started the job yesterday. And he's coming to see me when I get to Lake Garda." She hugged the phone as though it was him.

20

Laughing at Plans

There is a saying that when people make plans, God laughs. It felt a bit like that at the moment. Julia had thought she would be in Venice. The whole scene of meeting again in a small hotel, well she'd let that dissolve some time ago. Now she found herself in a small town on Lake Garda, Torri del Benaco, in the north of Italy. Dragging her suitcase up two flights of stairs, inwardly cursing her choice, though when she reached the top, it was worth it. The owners clearly loved Klimt and the soft yellows of the walls with the bright oranges splashes of color graced the room with light. It was perfect.

Perfectly located, right in the middle of the town, just a few steps from the water. Pushing her empty suitcase into a corner and placing the final things in the bathroom cabinet, it would be good to feel settled for a while.

Settled. No Julia didn't feel settled at all. She felt like her body was full of electricity. She was finally here. Landing at the airport near Verona had been just the first step. The drive to the lake had done nothing to quieten her growing anticipation. Agitation. It was eight years since that time in Venice, thirty years since they were together. They had been in constant contact since the night he had messaged her when she was staying at the cottage in Devon. Flirty, sure there had been plenty of suggestive banter, but there was something running underneath it. Something that spoke to the magnitude of what was about to happen. What might happen, she reminded herself. Nothing was certain. She had prepared as well as she could, without wanting to seem too eager. Who was she kidding. She had just flown half way around the world at the tail end of a pandemic and in the early days of what might be World War III. For hope. For love. For him.

The tension in her body betrayed nerves and excitement, fear and anticipation. Sometimes she couldn't tell which was the cause. She was probably terrified if she was honest with herself. What was she doing here? Aside from the obvious. As she walked along the lake, the doubts began to creep in. Should she have just let sleeping dogs lie? Did she want to unearth this fully and potentially fall back into the pain of heart break? What about what the Healing Hare had said? The warning was clear, even if the outcome was uncertain. If she was truly honest with herself, she wasn't sure. There was a war going on between her heart and her head. At the moment, despite the fact she was here, her head had the upper hand. It had refused to indulge her heart's fantasy too much. "Sure, we can come here," said her head. "You love Italy. It will be restorative after all those years of work and caring for your family alone. But it's not about love okay?"

And that was also true. There was always something that nourished her when she was in Italy. Whatever happened, she had made it. That in itself was an achievement worth celebrating. Julia also, not so secretly, loved the fact that she was alone. There was something about the freedom of midlife when everything is possible again. She was reminded of her friend Wendy, a musician, a singer, weaving new stories of ancient tales. Making a decision decades ago to not live the life expected. Artists, creatives, all of them carefully curating and protecting a life of freedom. At times their choices, their behaviors seemed selfish or thoughtless, but that was to not understand the importance of protecting time. Time to let the mind wander, to let the heart open and the soul to fly. Too easily pinned down by all the things others wanted of you, if you weren't careful. Julia wondered what might be created in this time. This moment when she had nothing but herself. She felt a hollowness inside, not sure if it were a space to be filled or an emptiness to be avoided.

She headed to the supermarket for some distraction. A few things for the fridge, some bread and a bottle of wine. Lugging it back up the stairs was as bad as she had anticipated, but it was soon put away. Julia looked around with a sense of satisfaction. It was a few years since she had been in Italy, she felt pleased that she had been able to navigate with relative ease.

The bed looked inviting and despite the fact it was mid-afternoon, she wondered about the benefit of a nap. The shadows through the window were long when Julia woke. There was no sense of disorientation. She knew exactly where she was. Italy. Slipping out of bed, she padded to the bathroom. Looking at her reflection she pulled some faces. Some amazed. Some eyeballing, eyebrows raised. She laughed as she stepped into the shower. The water felt wonderful after the morning's travel. Feeling the water run from her hair, along her spine and down to her toes. Closing her eyes, she wondered what might happen. What would happen tomorrow when he comes. Her hands ran along her breasts and down across the dips and curves of her stomach and hips. Brushing the soft hair that framed the tops of her thighs.

Stepping out into the small street, Julia turned toward the lake. *La passeggiata*—the early evening stroll had begun and there were people out in the late afternoon sun. Joining them, Julia was taken aback by the stares. Her clothes might not be obviously out of fashion but she didn't think she looked too outlandish. But then she realized where she was. Here it was normal, expected, to be given the once over by anyone who passed by. Walking along by the edge of the lake, the warmth of the sun felt like honey after the cooler morning. She had come here seeking something. Answers? Questions? But Julia realized she had also come here seeking peace. Whatever happened or didn't happen with Stefano, she could find peace here.

The clouds hugged the top of the mountain. Finding a seat at one of the outside tables, Julia ordered a Campari spritz. The waiter brought her drink and some snacks. That lovely extra touch to support lingering and long conversations. There was something empowering about being alone. Julia let the feelings of self-consciousness rise and fall away. No one cared or made any comment. Her kindle was beside her if she needed it. But the view over the lake as the sun began to set was enough to hold her attention. Sipping her spritz, this moment felt peaceful and Julia wanted to be present in it.

Had she been foolish? she wondered. Foolish in the way that made eye rolling fun of women in midlife. She had been mostly driven by hope. By love or the possibility of love. She reflected wryly that on the one hand hope helped her keep moving from dark times, knowing things would change. On the other, it could blind her to the dangers. Like now. Despite the careful warnings of her mind, her heart was committed to finding out whether there was something here. Something that had the power to strip back the carefully constructed layers of a life. Her mind had learned the checks and balances. Her heart, however, was always colluding with hope.

That night their conversation had been brief. The briefest for a while. Julia had asked him how he was feeling and Stefano had answered honestly. "Conflicted."

There was a pause before she responded, "Conflicted? Oh."

Julia began to realize that all her secret fears, ones she had hardly wanted to admit to herself, had not been without merit. He was entangled in something, with someone. The impact, the implication of seeing her tomorrow had derailed him. The sentences felt sharp. It was as though he finally understood what he was doing. What he had done.

He was going to come and see her, but she should not hold any hope for what might be. He was not going to change his life. He was certain about that. At least this time she knew, from the start. It was one thing to imagine a romantic reunion, quite another to expect the object of your heart to be exactly where you needed them to.

She woke early, giving herself time to prepare. At least physically. She was less sure about her thoughts and her emotions. The meeting was not going to be anything like she anticipated.

Her mind admonishing her heart was still no match for hope. No matter what happened. Hope had wriggled in and was nestled there. Whether some of the fantasies she had had become real or not. Julia knew she could not take one step forward toward him without hope holding her. It held her tightly and whispered in her ear to trust in her soul and open her heart.

A long breath escaped her. It was all very well for her heart to be reckless. Unlike the first time when heartbreak of this magnitude came unexpectedly, she knew there would be a reckoning. The first time she had fled, pulling the shreds of her dignity around her.

Flown home to hide the pain from him, from everyone and even from herself. "And now?" whispered her heart, "What if this time is different. If this time he makes a different choice." Julia shushed her mind, which was about to take a stand about the notion of being chosen.

CHAPTER

21

The Hope of Tomorrow

The phone rang. He was at the door. Julia raced down the stairs, her heart thumping, her long skirt tangling around her legs. Slowing, her breath noisy in her throat, she paused, trying to quieten it. Her hand flicked the switch and the door opened. He was there. Any attempt to slow her heart was futile now. Her skin felt electric. Her mouth was dry. "Ciao." Her voice was a whisper.

"Here I am," he smiled. The usual greeting now in his mouth rather than on the screen.

"Come in," she waved.

He ducked his head in a shy greeting and followed her up the stairs.

Stefano felt his resolve ebb away. Now that he was here, he felt awkward. He didn't know what to say. All the words seemed to be stuck in his throat. Opening the door to the apartment, he stepped inside. Julia was looking at him, smiling. He returned the smile, but the sense of dissonance remained.

Long months of texting and talking when they were safely on different sides of the world now seemed unreal. This was reality. He knew she had come to Italy on the basis of those conversations. She'd come to see what there was between them. And he didn't know, despite what he'd said last night. She brought light into his life. Awakened him from a slumber he hadn't realized he'd fallen into. He had leaned toward that, toward that light and the hope that shone from her eyes. But he didn't know if he could give her anything real. There was an ache, a pull. But he didn't know.

Julia didn't know what to do either. They had both imagined this meeting for months. Now it was here, she felt awkward. Her hands reached for him, though she stopped them before the movement happened.

Moving around the small kitchen, she made him a coffee.

"Sugar?" he called.

"I don't have any." She felt bad. She had been to the grocery store three times the day before. He shrugged and asked for some milk. But she could tell he didn't like it.

They sat together on the sofa. She tucked her feet under his leg as they sipped their coffee. Julia looked at his face. He was as handsome as she remembered. Sure, he was greyer and there were a few lines. She could see he was tense. Her heart was skipping beats. There seemed to be an invisible barrier between them. All the intimacy and all the longing and the dreaming, hidden, inaccessible.

A desire to break through the moment overtook her.

"It's really lovely to see you," a small smile played on her lips.

"You too. Look, ummm, what if it's not like we imagined? What if it's . . ." he trailed off.

Julia was quiet for a moment. "I don't think it can be like we imagined. We have pretty vivid imaginations," her cheeks flushed pink at the memory. "We don't have to do anything. We can just be here."

"I have to tell you something. I don't know if I can do this. It's not you. You're beautiful Julia, you know I think so. *Bellissima.* But I'm not sure I can do this. There is a lot on my mind and perhaps I have realized that I am more conflicted than I thought. Now we are here together, this is how I am feeling about it."

Julia nodded. "It's okay. We don't have to do anything. I don't want you to feel that way," she was surprised and somewhat relieved.

"I'm sorry," he said. They were silent for a while.

"Are you disappointed?" he asked.

Julia searched her feelings.

"It's ok," she said. "I think I like you a little more because of it."

Now it was his turn to feel surprised and ashamed. This last year. The frequent conversations. The occasional video chat. It had been easy to slip into a flirtatious, suggestive space. He had looked forward to the times after work when he would be alone in his quarters at the hotel, able to call her. No, not just looked forward, something else had stirred, a need, a yearning. It was not just company, not just reminiscing.

Sometimes those moments with Julia seemed more real than his actual life. He hadn't thought about the impact of these conversations, about the effect this connection was having on her. Until now. She had intimated that he had held a special place in her heart and mind. That the occasional connection over the previous years had been a form of solace and support for her.

Julia leaned against him. They sat in silence. She glanced at him and saw his eyes full of tears. Gently her hand stroked his cheek. "Don't worry," she said softly. "It's ok, really."

His tears surprised her and she gave him time to blink them away.

"Perhaps we went too fast. We need some time," he offered.

"We also placed some high expectations on ourselves," she followed with a smile.

"True. It's very different in real life than via the computer."

She moved her head in agreement. "Would you like to go out for a coffee?"

"With sugar!" he laughed lightly. "Yes okay."

Julia slipped into the bathroom. Her reflection stared back at her. "It is what it is." She told herself sternly. "You took a risk, you took a chance. But you can't plan for everything." Julia lifted her shoulders philosophically. It was all she could do right now and it cloaked her, protecting her heart from the reality. As she came out of the bathroom, he was waiting to go in. She leaned into him, kissing him on the mouth. He responded, but it was soft, yearning, not passionate.

A heaviness had returned to her heart centre. It had lifted when she had left Lars and it had dissipated completely when she had started to respond to Stefano in the past year.

"I probably need a good cry," thought Julia. "And a good conversation with the girls." Though she dreaded telling them that she had known beforehand that there might be complications, rather than just hinting at the possibility and saying she didn't know any details. And now those complications had disrupted the romance they were all expecting her to find.

Putting on her shoes, grabbing a jacket and sunglasses, she followed him down the stairs. They walked along the lake, past the empty restaurants. Julia slipped her hand through his arm. The urge to touch him had not gone away, despite the awkward moment. He pulled her closer. Good, she thought, perhaps there is something here that time can soften and open.

"Everything okay?" he asked her. There was a lilt of anxiety in his tone. "I'm sorry," he apologized again.

Julia turned to him and placed her fingers on his mouth.

"I wanted to come here. I wanted to see if you could make a different choice this time. I hoped you might choose me." Julia shrugged. "But the fact that it was too much for you. Seeing me in person. Touching me in the flesh. The fact that you couldn't go through with it, even in the face of everything that's happened between us in the last year, it's okay. My old image of you was wrong, it was a bit one dimensional. I'm happy to find out I was wrong about it." Her shoulders moved again. "Well mostly happy, if I'm being completely honest," she smiled at him and dropped her hands. "I've loved you since the moment you asked me for my documents when I checked into the hostel the first time we met. I think I would rather know that love like ours was possible, than to never have known it. Whatever happened then. Whatever happens now."

Stefano was silent in the face of this statement. He wasn't sure if he could recognize himself in what she said. "We were so young Julia. You were so independent and full of life I think I was a little in awe of you. I was just a young man from a village. Not really even sure who I was or what I wanted. You made me feel as though I could do anything. Be anything. It was a bit overwhelming if I'm honest." They had loved one another with an intensity that had disarmed and scared him. She was like a flame, something so beautiful, full of movement and warmth. Hard to hold, he had thought at the time but irresistible.

"Really?" she replied. Unable to see herself in the vision he had of her. "Whereas I thought you were so cool. Sophisticated and worldly. I was just some Aussie girl from the suburbs," she smiled. "We were so young. Young and crazy. At least I was crazy. Crazy in love with you." She looked at him, her grin widening as he returned her smile and instinctively pulled her closer to him. They stood there, connected to the past.

She had made him feel something he had never felt again. He had felt that possibility grow over the last year as they had moved closer and closer together. But now she was here in front of him and he wasn't sure he had the courage to change his life. What had seemed easy via text had run aground in person. The reality of putting himself in conflict with his life rather than just talking or dreaming about it, was an unexpected complication.

Julia could sense that Stefano was discomforted. She understood now where things were with him. She was free of obligations to another adult. She had talked herself into believing he was alone. He lived alone at the hotel and the few times he was not there, she had not thought too deeply about that. She had been wrong, wilfully so, she realized now. Stefano was not free. She had been unwilling to face that fact. She could see the choice that confronted him. Layered with the pressure of living up to the fantasies they had shared.

Now she was here, he was not willing to take the next step toward her. Faced with the significance of it, he had chosen to remain with the way things were. Julia knew she would have to accept that. But it didn't change the fact that she still wanted him. There was something about him that drew her. She could feel the response in her body when he was in the room with her, when he was here beside her.

Perhaps that was all she would have to hold onto. Whether they made love or not was almost immaterial. What mattered was being in his presence one more time. That was a feeling she would hold onto. Knowing that he had come to see her was almost enough. She knew there was something eternal between them. That it could no longer be something they would live out, was a sadness she would have to carry, but it was no heavier than it had been thirty years ago. Perhaps it was sprinkled with longing, and wisdom. But the sense of loss of what they would never have was worth the moments they had together.

She watched him as he prepared to leave. Scarf, helmet, jacket. The Vespa was modern, practical, though not fast. Julia thought of him driving along the coast road around the lake in the cold early morning. How would he feel on the drive home? Relieved? Confused? How did she feel? Sad, definitely. But not all that surprised. His long silence had prepared her for this.

As she sat at a lakeside table that evening, feelings overwhelmed her and tears filled her eyes started to fall down her cheeks. Facing the water, she realized the deep melancholy of the sunset. Sunsets, full of awesome beauty and bone deep sadness that another day was done. All the sadness she had held close from the morning began to bubble up. The tightness that had held her together as she walked along the lake began to unravel. Loss and love and longing. Feelings from long ago and feelings from just this morning. Still present, still tangible. Still full of the beauty and the sadness reflected in the sinking sun.

Taking one last evening walk around the town, Julia realized she needed to get back to the apartment. Tears were flowing down her face. While they didn't bother her, in fact she was strangely welcoming the release, she realized the people she passed were looking at her with some concern. Seeking privacy, Julia slipped the key into the lock and made her way upstairs to her sanctuary. Switching on some lights, and shivering slightly, Julia hunted for the AC remote and switched on the heating. Moving to the kettle, she noticed the two coffee cups on the bench. A reminder of the morning. A reminder of him.

The tears began to flow even faster. She slumped onto the sofa, holding herself around her middle. No longer just tears, the sobs ripped through her, as her heart, so carefully protected, with the pragmatic philosophy born of necessity, so carefully mended, shattered again into tiny shards of light.

Sometime later Julia picked herself up and made the cup of tea. The room had warmed up and she felt calmer. The hot tea helped too. The evening spent looking at the water hadn't brought her any relief or resolve.

She knew he would send her a message soon. Usually around 9:30 p.m. once his shift had started and the guests had checked in.

It came early. And annoyingly that pleased her enormously.

Stefano—*"Ciao, Is everything okay?"*

Julia—*"Ciao, so so. I am full of sadness, regrets, love and hope. Also pizza and gelato. How are you?"*

Stefano—*"At work. All the rest is okay but no! Not sadness. Increase the dose of ice cream."*

She stopped her fingers from replying. Why not the sadness, thought Julia. The sadness is as real as the love and just as potent. She didn't think more *gelato* would help, though she appreciated his attempt to lighten the mood, her mood.

Julia—*"Err no—I have already eaten a tonne. Though that's usually good advice . . . it was really wonderful to see you."*

Stefano—*"Yes, it was."*

Julia—*"But tell me. How are you feeling?"*

Why can't you let sleeping dogs lie? she thought to herself, but then it felt important to keep the conversation honest. Real. Not lost in fantasy and temptation. She breathed out as he replied quickly.

Stefano—*"I don't know. I hope I will be calmer next time."*

There was so much in that sentence that she wanted to hold onto.

"What next time? When?" she wanted to shout.

What would happen if he was more serene? Should she ask? Was there any way to prepare herself for whatever would come? Would his answer even matter? If he built a carefully constructed frame for them to step through, would it help how she felt? Would it stop how she was feeling? Was it even worth asking how he might like to set the scene, set the tone of the next time? No matter how they set their expectations, Julia knew she would step into his arms if he opened them. She would kiss his mouth if he offered it. She would run her hands along his back and down his arms. She knew she would let him undress her and touch her. Julia knew this as deeply as she knew her own self.

How to respond to that. Easy. Easy enough. Vulnerability was the only answer. They were too far gone for anything less and there was too much at stake to do less.

Julia—*"The longing. The desire. I feel all of them. Next time. I like this phrase."*

She found herself crying again. Crying for the morning. Crying for the loss of love that stretched out beyond this moment. This moment of connection with the past before all the cares and worries of adult life. All that had happened in the time in between, all the loss. There was something bittersweet about it. Like the sunset that held both sadness and hope, loss and longing. Julia blew out a long breath. She began to feel her centre begin to balance. Though the pain in her chest, her heart centre, remained. At least this time, she thought, it was there at the right time.

After this morning she felt more confused than before. Though she noted that he had kept things carefully neutral and had not spoken of the desire that he had expressed from the safety of the opposite side of the world.

Listening to music, she wondered what the next steps might bring. And whether her heart would let her head do the leading. Her mouth pushed into a wry smile. Julia wondered if there would come an age when these feelings would dampen down. She hoped not. And that hope, the hope to feel into the very depths of her soul. That was worth the pain of today. The loss of yesterday. For the hope of tomorrow.

22

Dreaming of Her

He had dreamed of her that afternoon. Julia. He knew she had watched him leave and it was all he could do to not turn around. But he didn't turn back. He felt unable to betray the people he cared for. But she stood there and he saw her. Lit by the morning sun and lit from within. He knew he would love her for the rest of his life. And that knowing was tinged with joy and sadness.

She came to him in his sleep. Coming home had been challenging. There were problems. He was tired. Bone tired. The bed was inviting, calling to him and it was not long before his eyes closed. Oblivion welcomed. But his mind took him straight back to the morning. Retracing every step of his drive along the lake road. His steps to her door. He saw her again and felt the hit in his stomach as she opened the door and ushered him up the stairs. The conversation replaying in his dream. This time he could stare at her face. Marvel at the way she laughed and her smile which he felt enter his body. In his dream he took her in his arms. She stepped into his arms willingly. No unasked question on her face this time.

The kiss. Their tongues. He could feel her breasts against his chest. The thin material of her shirt, the hard nubs of her nipples. Opening the buttons with fevered fingers. He had longed for the possibility of touching them, touching her. His hands cupped them, fuller and softer than his fingers remembered. He watched her nipples harden. He could feel them aching for his mouth. Bending forward he licked first one then the other. Feeling her reaction as he was touching her, as if shocking her with something. She reached for his belt, pushing his jeans down over his hips. With a wriggle he slipped them off. His desire was obvious. She looked at him before she bent her head to kiss him there. His hands found her hair and his eyes closed. His body mirrored the dreamscape and he moaned in his sleep.

This time he didn't stop. They didn't stop. He lifted her head kissing her. "To bed," he said softly.

She lay on the bed. He stood there for a moment. Holding himself. Her shirt was open and he gazed at her body. Her breasts firm and the nipples hard. Her stomach flat and a light covering of hair between her legs. He had dreamed of this moment. Together they had used words to conjure it in their bodies.

"Open a little," his request was soft. Julia acquiesced. He knelt between her legs, moving the flimsy covering. She moaned, her hands moving in his hair.

His sleeping body responded. In his sleep his hands curved as if holding her thighs.

She implored in his dream, telling him she wanted him.

Lifting his head, he moved above her. She arched her hips to meet him. Sending him back through time to all the moments he had been here with her. Connected. Together they moved as one.

He could feel her breath in at his ear. Her teeth nipping at his lobe. Her mouth reaching his neck. They turned, so she was on top, placed her hands on his chest, she rocked back and forth above him. He could hear her small gasps of pleasure and felt himself nearing his own climax.

Stefano's body convulsed in the bed. It woke him with a start. Laying there, the late afternoon sun drifting over the bed, he wondered at the feelings. Some guilt, some regret. But mostly he felt a longing. A longing for himself, for his life. It was as though this moment in time had a message for him. He wasn't sure what it was, but he knew it had arrived with her. He had an overwhelming need to be with her again. To be in her presence and to touch her. With reverence. With awe. With hope.

CHAPTER

23

Dinner With a Friend

Julia spent the morning in bed. It felt like an indulgence. Taking it slow seemed like a good idea. Once she had decided that sleep was not returning, she slipped out of bed and made a ginger and lemon tea. It had been a while since she had started the day with that and it felt good to get back into the habit. Though it would soon be followed by a coffee. The day was cloudy so there was no rush to get moving. She dozed and read for most of the morning. Letting her feelings percolate inside her.

The middle of the day brought a quick call with her friend Marco. He was coming for dinner around 7:30 p.m. It made her smile. Theirs had been a long friendship. He made her laugh and think, two very attractive qualities in a friend, but she had never seen him as a boyfriend. She had spent time with him in Rome before she married, and then every time she came to Italy after

Hugh's death they would catch up. Julia felt a deep appreciation for the friendship. And it was reciprocated. It didn't matter when she arrived or what was happening, Marco was always there. Always generous with his time.

She waited for him at the petrol station. The advantage of having an apartment in the centre of town was the parking space that came with it. She arrived early and stood watching each car that pulled up, checking to recognize the driver, trying to ignore the stares from the patrons of the nearby bar. Julia wondered if they thought she was a prostitute, waiting on the curb side. She was relieved when Marco pulled in. Jumping into the car beside him, she told him about the stares, she wasn't sure whether to be offended or relieved that none of them had asked her. He laughed and she felt pleased that she had managed to make the joke work in Italian. Speaking in Italian was a joy for her but it was still hard work. It felt like a small victory even if it was at her own expense.

They walked toward a restaurant, away from the main strip. It was good to spend some time with an old friend. She did enjoy her own company and today had been time to her to sort her feelings, but a few hours chatting with Marco would take her mind off things. Off Stefano.

"Shall we start with an *aperitivo*?" he suggested.

"Sounds good to me," she nodded.

They found a table on the edge of the lake. Aperitifs, wine and pizza followed, along with laughter, memories and philosophies. She told him about the book she was reading and how sunsets were melancholic. They spent some time defining the word with examples and experiences.

Marco was easy company and patient with her stumbles in the language. She laughed even harder at his choice of Australian rules football teams.

"I had to choose them, they matched Hellas Verona."

"I can't believe you didn't consult me on this important decision! I mean football teams are for life. It's not a decision you can make simply on the color of the jersey."

Taken aback, Marco began to justify his choice, before he realized that her interest in Australian Rules football was lacklustre at best and her offence was pretended. Julia laughed and promised to send him some merchandise when she got home. "But you can have a second team," she said, "I will send you that scarf as well. At least then you'll have some hope of having a team in the finals!"

Putting the napkin over her head as she playacted walking into the shop to buy things for that team. *Incognito*, too embarrassed to let people know she was buying West Coast Eagles merchandise. He laughed even harder.

Julia loved his curious nature and entrepreneurial spirit. She was glad he spoke freely of his partner and she was looking forward to meeting her. Glad too she had never given in to his requests that they could be something more. She had always laughed it off as something to consider another time. She would dismiss him with the comment that who knows what might happen in future, they weren't dead yet. It was much more valuable to be his friend and part of his life. With Stefano, she could never be friends. With Marco they would be friends forever.

"And what about you," he asked as they sat there sipping coffee, empty plates in front of them.

"Me? No, there is no one in my life." It didn't exactly feel like a lie.

Marco looked at her speculatively. "You can't be alone forever. Consider my mum, after dad died, she has had a few 'friends'." His hands making air quotes. "If they got too close, started to expect her to look after them, she would . . ." he brushed his hands down his front, then flicked his fingers. The imagery clear. "You could at least do that. It's been a long time Julia. We are not meant to live on just pizza and prosecco!"

She smiled, about to tell him that maybe there was someone, when he went on.

"I didn't like that fellow you were with all those years ago. He was not good for you. Not good at all. At least you didn't hang around waiting on him." Marco's face reflected exactly what he thought of Stefano.

Julia shut her mouth fast.

Despite that shadow, the evening filled her with laughter and lifted her mood. Later getting ready for bed, she checked her phone. There was a message and a missed call from earlier. Even with a moment of pause, Julia knew she would respond. She wasn't interested in playing any games. The time for that was long gone. If it had ever existed.

Julia—*"I'm here. Safe and sound. I was at dinner. Perhaps I have had a little to drink."*

Julia smiled at herself. The prosecco had been delicious and she had sipped it with pleasure. Her head felt light.

Stefano—*Where? Where were you? Were you in Torri?*

Julia—*"Yes I am still here. Why did you call. Has something happened?"*

She was surprised by his sense of urgency.

Stefano—*"I wanted you to answer the phone and see that I had written to you."*

Julia—*"Do you miss me?"*

Stefano—*"You can't ask that, you know."*

Julia—*"Why?"*

Stefano—*"Because you expect something that I can't give you . . . for now."*

168

For now. For now! Hope, further embolden by several glasses of prosecco, took over her fingers.

Julia—*"According to you, life is so black and white? Perhaps it's true that I want things you can't give me, yet you write 'for now' so we are a long way from never."*

She could see him typing and stopping and typing again. After some time, he sent another message.

Stefano—*"Things change and anything could happen, but please don't ask me these questions."*

Julia—*"Ok. But why do these words make you feel bad? I'm not afraid to love you. But I understand that the situation is as it is. I like you even more now. I always thought I was just one of your girls. Last year I began to realize maybe I'd been mistaken. And now I think I understand."*

Stefano—*"What do you mean? What way mistaken?"*

Julia—*"In my heart I really hoped that you are not a superficial man. That you are a man full of emotions, thoughts and dreams. And I hoped there was a dream about me. I don't know if this dream will be hidden forever. But now I know it exists.*

Stefano—*"Julia, you know that what we have is not something small without meaning. It was never like that."*

Julia—*"I know, I have shared everything with you, things I could never say to anyone else. Despite your situation, that's how we are."*

There was a pause before he replied.

Stefano—*"If you want, I could come early tomorrow, I can stay at little longer."*

Oh, he is coming tomorrow! Julia could feel the bubbles of anticipation in her stomach. She hadn't been sure he would come. Though she had hoped and hoped with all her heart that he would. She'd sent a million messages out to the universe.

Julia—*"Of course I want to see you. I promise I will be awake and dressed as a nun, whatever time you arrive."*

Stefano—*Okay. We'll see each other tomorrow; I should be there around 8. Now go to bed, I have to close up. Until tomorrow. Good night."*

As Julia got ready for bed, she wondered at the power of love and desire. It would take him an hour to get here. Yet he was coming for a brief moment to sit on her sofa. Drink a coffee. To be in her presence. She would see him again. She hugged herself with happiness. From tears to joy. All in all, it had been a very good day.

CHAPTER

24

Take Two

Julia woke early and felt the effects of the prosecco from the night before. A shower and coffee were needed immediately. Once her hair was washed and freshly dried, she looked at herself critically.

"You might need a few days without wine," she admonished her reflection. "Who knows what might happen today. You need to have your wits about you." Then she smiled. A big grin lit up her face. He was coming. He would be here soon. She felt it through her body like a shiver, a vibration that attuned her to his.

Her phone pinged.

Stefano—*"I'm here."*

She buzzed the main door and stepped out to wait for him at the top of the stairs. "I have some sugar for your coffee." They smiled at each other. Julia felt the pull begin to tug at her. She wondered how he felt. If he felt it. It was strange. He was not the same as she remembered but in some ways, he was exactly as she remembered him. Perhaps this is what love is really like, she pondered. When the outer packaging is almost irrelevant to the recognition that this is the one you love.

She moved to the sofa, needing to keep some space between them as the desire to touch him grew stronger. It was as if she were a magnet and he was her true north.

Sipping her coffee, she asked how the job hunting was going.

"It's going well. There is an interview for a director's role, but I'm not sure if I want to do it. The responsibilities are endless and there is constant dealing with the owners, and the guests, it is exhausting. It will be a headache."

She understood what he meant. She knew the pressures of leadership. Julia much preferred the freedom of her life now. No clocks, not even an office. She was responsible to herself.

He moved to the sofa. She tucked her toes under his thigh. They talked for a while about work, and what he might do when work was no longer the most important thing.

All the while she could feel it. More than a spark, not quite a fire. It was present in the air. His hand reached out to rest on her knee. She placed her hand on his, gently moving her thumb in small circles. Laughing softly at his words. They began to talk of the past again. Julia knew it was the small flames that had taken them there. She could feel them slowly growing brighter as they walked together through the memories.

"Remind me again how much Lorenzo would charge us at Gorky's."

Stefano laughed, instinctively pulling her closer.

"*Dieci mila lire, 10,000 lire,* every time, regardless of how much we drank."

Julia smiled. "Well sometimes we just had one drink. Why do you think he did that?"

"He liked us."

"Well we were always happy, always laughing, always full of love. What's not to like," her smile grew wider.

"True," he said, "more often than not, we had more than a little alcohol already on board! Remember, we would start at Tre Santi, then head to Gorky's. Lorenzo and I liked each other, we could always talk. And he liked you too," Stefano paused. "Gianni liked you, but me not so much. I always found him a bit fake." Gianni was Lorenzo's partner in the bar. Less gregarious and always in the shadow of Lorenzo's easy charm. Lorenzo had the rakish looks of a pirate from the romantic novels who made women swoon. It would take a very confident man to not feel overshadowed.

"You probably didn't like him because he liked me," Julia said with a dig in his ribs. They were closer now. His arm curved around her. Her head rested on his chest.

"Yes perhaps that's true, and then there's Luca," he smiled at her. "Do you remember how I told you about meeting up with Luca, Alessandro and Federico?"

Julia nodded. It had been a funny conversation. He had got back late and called her. She had asked where the others were and he had laughed and said he told them he would sleep alone because they farted and snored. And then he'd said, actually it was so he could call her and talk to her in peace.

Julia had enjoyed hearing about the evening. She remembered the call. He said they had laughed so hard his cheeks and stomach hurt. He looked relaxed and happy. Maybe because of the company, or what the company represented. The past. A time when life was simpler. A time when she had been in his life. She had laughed with him, happy to share his joy.

He had seemed slightly drunk. Relaxed on his bed, smiling and looking at her.

"You know that Luca was in love with you?" he said.

"What!" she responded, "That is not true."

He nodded, all serious now. "Yes, it is true. Gianni too. You remember Gianni from the bar?"

"Of course I remember them. But they weren't in love with me."

She had never noticed any attention from anyone else. She only ever had eyes for Stefano. When they were together it was as though the world shifted focus.

"They were," Stefano insisted, "You were so sexy and the room would light up when you stepped into it."

He was reminiscing but this brought him into the present.

"I told Luca we are in contact again."

Julia nodded, "Well it would be good to see all of them again."

Julia listened to his heart beating under her ear. She let out a long slow breath.

"It doesn't matter what happens. It's enough to be here, to have you here, after the last year." She felt her eyes fill with tears, and blinked rapidly, not wanting to break the spell.

His hand ran along her back. It was getting harder to concentrate. She could feel her body responding to the nearness of him. The flames beginning to lick her desire. He shifted and she realized that the effect was not one-sided. His answering desire was clear. Julia looked up at him. He closed his eyes for a moment.

"Shall I move?" she whispered. They were quiet. Letting the feeling, the energy between them build.

"No."

Perhaps he had known it was there from the moment he saw her. Which is why, inexplicably to him, he couldn't just let himself take her. He knew he wanted to. The number of times he had fantasised about her from afar, over the years. But it was more than desire which moved him, as he realized now. It was longing. Longing for something. Something that until now he didn't know he lacked. It was the only way to explain why he was here now. And why he wanted her so badly and couldn't show her how much he longed for her. He had tried to say this one night last year when the messages had flown back and forth between them.

"Is there something greater than poetry? If there is, then it's you," he had written. *"Your shoulders, your breasts, your legs, your hair, your face, hold the beauty of the world. To caress them is like a moment of happiness that takes you in the stomach. I want to explain to you how I can sense you from your feet to your hair, but I do not know how to say it, I don't know how to articulate it. But you know it's like this."*

She knew. *"I understand because I feel it as well. I feel you in my soul."*

The longing that pulled her toward him. Something that endured, that belonged to the soul, yes also the body, the desire, and the heart, the feelings and the mind. She couldn't explain it any other way. *"Yes, it is the soul, which is perhaps the only thing higher than poetry,"* he had replied

A gentle question brought him out of his reverie. He inhaled deeply filling his lungs with the scent of her.

"And you, are you well?"

"Yes, I feel . . ." she paused, trying to find the sensation, "I feel lighter, happy."

"Before you go, we will make love." He heard himself speaking these words. "When you are in Verona."

Julia felt the thrill of his words ripple through her. Or right now would be okay too, she thought to herself. But she didn't say those words out loud. She wanted to breathe color into the love that connected them, and cup her hands around the flickering flame until it could resist any wind that might extinguish it. She had been right to wait until she was here in front of him before that unasked question could find its way to the space between them. Where they could ask it of each other and let their souls respond. For now, this was enough.

"When we are in Verona it would be wonderful to walk by the places we used to go," Julia suggested. "Though I don't think Gorky's exists anymore."

He nodded. "The last I heard, Lorenzo had sold Gorky's and bought Tre Santi."

They talked of the parties they had at their old apartment, of the times they were at Veccia Veronetta and he laughed at her recounting the first few nights she worked in the restaurant. Her Italian so bad she had just written anything that might approximate an order.

Her hands covered her face with embarrassment at the mistakes she had made. But she was laughing too. Her hand slid under his top, tugging it free from his jeans. Without thinking, she leaned over and kissed his stomach. Letting her tongue swirl in his navel. She heard him take a sharp intake of breath, but he didn't move away. Realising what she was doing, she sat up again.

"Would you like to see the apartment where I'll be staying?" she asked in an attempt to bring things back to some sort of safety. They sat and flicked through the images. He lingered over pictures of the bedroom.

"I didn't know if I would see you when I booked the apartment," said Julia, "but when I saw this room, I thought of you. It's a bit grand but it was too beautiful to pass up. Then I thought, maybe the stars will align and something will happen and you'll come."

"It's a beautiful room," he said. They both knew they would make love on that bed. He would take her in his arms and they would do all the things they had spoken about, written about in messages back and forth for the last year. It would be with the tenderness and the longing that had held their love through time.

Something had shifted imperceptibly. The door to another possibility had opened. All that was needed was to take the next step.

"It would it be great to go in to Tre Santi and see Lorenzo," said Julia.

"Yes, but I don't know if it's open during the day," those words bumped them gently back to the present. He checked the time.

"Bimba. I have to go."

"Okay I'll come with you to the bike."

They walked arm in arm. This time he leaned in for a kiss at every point of preparing to leave. His jacket, a kiss, his scarf, a kiss, his helmet, a kiss. One last kiss as he was sitting on the Vespa. "I'll see you on Monday," he lingered over a kiss, holding the key, reluctant to start the engine. "I'll write to you later."

She nodded. She watched him ride away, remembering the times he would leave their apartment after they had made love in the afternoon, always looking back at her, an impish grin on his face.

Returning along the street to her apartment this time felt monumentally different. Julia could feel herself beaming, she wondered if she was actually sending out sparks of light.

Across the road she saw a dress in the shop window. "That's the dress," she thought to herself, "that's the dress I'll be wearing when he makes love to me." Julia marched over and asked to try it on. Julia stepped out of the shop, swinging the bag, heading back toward her apartment.

Her phone vibrated in her pocket. Pulling it out, she looked at the screen. Lars. Her body tensed and she felt the heaviness land in her chest. He was definitely not someone she wanted intruding on this time. "That can go straight to voice mail," she thought, tucking the phone back in her pocket. It rang again, and again. Each time it hit the voice mail greeting, he would hang up and try again. Julia remembered how she felt toward the end when he would hound her with questions, demands. It had become exhausting and futile, impossible to satisfy whatever fears and suspicions had filled his mind. Resolved she let the phone vibrate away in her pocket.

Later that evening curiosity got the better of her. They hadn't been in contact since he had left Melbourne for Germany. She pressed the messages. Lars' voice filled the small flat.

"Julia! Where are you? Are you in Europe? The phone ring tone is different. Oh God don't tell me you are in Italy."

Then the next message. "You are in Italy aren't you. Are you with him? Julia you can't do that to us. You can't."

She felt her stomach rise to her throat. Lars always thought the worst. The worst of people and the worst of situations. He saw the world as a dangerous place and that he was some sort of protector. And then another message, his voice dominant.

"I'm coming to find you. I know where you will be. I'm coming to stop you. Don't do this, you can't do this. Don't do anything stupid before I get there."

"Shit!" she thought. "Shit, shit, shit." Though surely, he wouldn't really come to find her? How would he know where she was?

CHAPTER

25

Feels Like Home

The decision to head out for a day trip was weighing on her. On the one hand Julia knew she should get out and do something. Explore. The weekend loomed ahead. He wasn't coming until Monday. She would be alone during the day until she had a chance to speak with Stefano in the evening. Julia looked up the bus and ferry timetable. It would be a bit of a nightmare to figure out the journey, as the buses were not very regular, starting late and stopping early. And then there was Lars. Would he really come to Italy? It was just the sort of thing he would do, imagining he was on some sort of crusade. What if he turned up here? Imagine if she bumped into him as she walked around the little lake towns. She gave herself a little shake. "You know what you will say if he does." That was true. Her feelings certainly hadn't changed since the last time she had seen him.

A call from her daughter made up her mind.

"Mum, I have something to tell you. Some bad news. Some sad news," her daughter's voice faltered.

"What? What's happened?" Julia was not too concerned. Her youngest daughter, Cat, could turn something minor into a major stress. Julia had tried to navigate her children's teenage years with a dollop of philosophy. Friendship strife, heart break, a bad grade. All of it in reality was fleeting, a small part of all the things that made up the ups and downs of growing up.

"Joan died."

Julia nearly dropped the phone. "What? Oh my God."

Joan was the owner of the stables where her daughter kept her beloved horse, Teddy. She had been unfailingly kind and generous when they had arrived, offering to collect Cat's horse for her, helping them out with all the things they needed to do to settle him in. Julia was shocked. Joan was in her early 70s. Fit and healthy, full of energy. She was always at her happiest when she was out with the horses. And she loved talking to people. When they had first come to visit, Joan had been very clear about the type of people she wanted to be there. "Only good people, who are kind." Julia's misgivings about the move had dissipated at that moment.

"How did you find out?"

"Lesley told me."

"How are you feeling about it Cat?" Julia checked in on her daughter.

"I'm okay."

Julia knew that Cat wouldn't be at all okay. She was being brave. Joan had been such a warm and encouraging presence. Cat had felt safe and welcomed there and Joan had taken care of Cat, feeling a great deal of empathy with the loss of her dad at such a young age.

She remembered talking with Joan of her hopes for this trip just before she left. Joan had been delighted for her, speaking of her first husband who had died and then the joy at finding a second soulmate in Gregor. Julia remembered the tone and the love in Joan's voice as she spoke of feeling blessed. Even in a moment of loss. Blessed that she had been so fortunate to have experienced such a great love twice in her life. It had felt like a sign.

They had talked about some of the adventurous things Joan experienced in her early life. Traveling to Europe on a boat as a young woman, Joan earning her way by cutting hair for the passengers. Then a crazy time in London. Julia had laughed and told her she should write her memoirs. "Get all that down, Joan. It would make a great story." Joan had looked pleased. "When you get back, I'll tell it all to you. You can write it down."

Now that would never happen. Those memories, experiences, were gone forever.

There was a light wind as they crossed the lake. Julia watched the mountains from her vantage point. There was something about the lake that called to her. Something about the contrasts and the colors that seemed to tell her a story about life. The stillness of the mountains as they hugged the body of the water which was always in movement. Both were in an eternal relationship. The water always calling the mountains into her depths. Showing them their reflection. Holding their majesty in her stillness and her ripples. And the constant merging. The mountains slowly softening into her. The water embracing them with her endless movement. The shores hardly a line of separation, more a place where the two could flow together and become one.

"It is only our human need to define that keeps them apart. Our need to name things, to place some sort of permanence to help us manage our uncertainty," she thought. "The knowledge that one day we too will return to the earth. To the water."

Perhaps it was this knowing that had called her here, to Italy and to Stefano. They were like the mountain and the lake. The earth and the water. Julia smiled at the thought. Capricorn and Cancer. Could it be any more perfect as a metaphor? Then it struck her. That was all she needed to be. The lake. The lake with its stillness and depth. Its wildness and power. Constant, yet constantly changing. Understanding that while the mountains may hold it, they also embrace it.

Perhaps that was what pulled Stefano to her. Even as he tried to hold the boundaries of his life. He could see his true self reflected in her blue eyes. He knew that with every moment of an embrace, his edges were softening. Opening him to the endless beauty that was life and love entwined.

If she had not understood the consequences, the magnitude of what she was asking, and offering him, she did now. It was love. Love at a level that would shift from gentle reflections in calm waters to dark storms where her clouds might shroud his mind as often as his stones and rocks could cut through her wildest waves. Was she up for that sort of love? One that would ask of them to climb to the summit as well as plunge to the depths.

As the ferry docked at Sirmione, Julia slipped through the crowds and climbed the stairs to the battlements of the castle. The town was already busy, full of groups of tourists moving around in mindless patterns. It was the first time she had seen so many people in one place. Torri was quiet.

She was pleased she had come out. Movement helped to remind her that life would flow, with or without her influence. It felt like she was honoring the adventurous spirit in Joan as well. The spirit of all the women who had come before and would follow afterwards. Who had chosen courage over comfort and reached out for a wild precious and imperfect life. It had been right to be vulnerable and show him the possibility of another life, with her. Whatever he might chose to do.

Walking along the side of the small peninsula, Julia climbed through the gardens to the edge. It was one of her deepest pleasures, to walk the paths that people had walked for centuries. To touch the stones and the walls that had offered shelter and safety, stretching back into the past. An overwhelming feeling of peace flooded through her. She didn't know what exactly had triggered it. The feeling moved into her chest, beginning to grow, and she found herself on the verge of tears. Being here felt like coming home. It felt like being in the right place. Julia wasn't sure what she was going to do. But after the news of the morning and the feelings of the day, she definitely wasn't going to ignore it.

26

Lights in the Darkness

Stefano remembered the first time they met. She had stepped into the hostel and the world had shifted slightly. He had been patiently explaining something to a young traveler who was staying at the hostel. When she finally stepped aside, Julia had stepped forward, and told him not to worry, she could read the information on the noticeboard behind him. He had smiled back at her, feeling slightly foolish. Not normally lost for words, he felt as though his mouth could no longer form the words he needed to say. They looked at each other and the room, the noise, the people seemed to blur. As though someone had shone a light on them. On her.

She had debated over whether to stay in the rooms or the garden. He had stamped the cards for her. He wanted to tell her something then. Something about beauty and grace. Something about subtlety and uniqueness. But he didn't know how to frame it in English. Every now and again he would catch her eye as she wandered through the reception where he was working. He saw her friend nudge her; he was looking at her again. Julia turned and smiled at him. It was like a blow to the stomach. His legs felt weak and he knew he must speak to her.

She had once asked him how he remembered their time had been like together. They had been young, free. Well, she had been free, him not so much. She had asked him what it was between them.

He had thought for a while, then said that love was too simple a word to explain it, it was beyond what was commonly understood as love. Something primal, before words, outside of time. He didn't understand what it had been for her. She told him, being together had taught her so much about love. Lessons that reverberated through her life. What had it been for him? He knew he had broken her heart. Perhaps she had broken his too.

His mind went back to the first time he realized he might be falling in love with her. He had invited her and her friend to come to the lake for an ice cream, a spontaneous, perfect summer evening. They had gone in a group of four.

She was funny, opinionated, she laughed a lot, and she was so sexy. There was something about her smile that made him want to pull her close, kiss her and take her to bed. When he was with her the air seemed charged with electricity. Everything was brighter and sweeter.

He had not really understood the essence of love until then, and maybe not even then. Perhaps it had taken three decades, three chances, to realize that what he saw in her, what he felt from her was a kind of love that one does not often find in life.

She sometimes said he had saved her. That the memory of him had been a light in the darkness, anchoring her to life during a difficult time in her life, much later. He wasn't sure what she meant by that. Perhaps he couldn't see himself in the person she described.

He had told her last year that he had found the website of the place where she worked. He had watched the video of her there many times. He wondered if she remembered. It felt like a confession of his inability to let her go, unwilling to let the memory of their year together fade away. She had always been there, in the corners of his mind.

Every now and then she would flame into his waking thoughts, until time allowed him to move her from his conscious mind. Though she was never far away.

What she didn't know was that she had given him a gift that had been both beautiful and a torture. She had given him a glimpse of what it would be like to be loved by her. And he had let her go, like water in his hands.

And now she was here. In his arms again. He could not let her go, but how could he ask her to stay?

CHAPTER

27

Like the Lake

Monday morning. Julia found herself awake before the alarm. He was coming today. There was a part of her that hugged herself with the joy of an unabashed teenager. Delighted at the opportunity to see his face. Another part of her held a more philosophical view. This was the part she was trying to hold onto. Trying to wield it as some sort of shield against the effervescent joy that was running through her veins like a drug.

She dressed quickly, in her new dress. It just might be the pathway from talking to touch, if he wanted to touch her. Julia knew she wanted him, whatever the cost. To have him touch her. To feel her body come alive under his fingers. To feel his call and respond. Like instruments in an orchestra or voices in a choir. There was a sense of the sacred in what might be about to happen. That in taking this step, the opportunity of another road would unfurl in front of them.

She had asked him last night what it was that he thought she wanted. He had responded with a simple answer. Me. And that was true. She did want him. But not just his body. Confident he knew that too. That she wanted all of him. It wasn't about possession or ownership. Julia would choose him every day. She'd choose to wake up by his side. Walk through the streets. Take a coffee. Share a pizza together. Share the small and large thoughts of everyday being. Choose to come to bed with him. She would choose him every day.

And Stefano? What did he want? He said he didn't want to change his life. Yet here he was. Messages every night. Last year he had called Julia at the end of every work day and told her how much he longed for her. He had told her he couldn't make love to her. Yet here he was. In the apartment. Again. Longing. Longing for her.

A third meeting was beyond simple politeness. It was beyond the need to be forgiven for leading her on. The plans for meeting in Verona. Where they knew they would fall onto that bed. Should she ask him?

Then she remembered her journey to Sirmione on the ferry. The majesty of the mountains and the tranquillity of the lake. The lake doesn't ask the mountain to fall into her. He shines on her rippled reflections. And slowly. Slowly. He falls into her. A process that takes eons and yet is inevitable. A merging that lifts her up, full of him.

No, that question was not yet ready to be asked.

She wondered how he would be when he arrived today. The streets were full of market stalls and she hoped it hadn't held him up too much. He would be here soon.

It was the dress that brought him undone. Julia had known it would. He confessed as much as he left. But she was getting ahead of herself. She watched him arrive. Leaning out of the window. She saw him walk down the street toward her. His phone in hand as he let her know he was there.

She was waiting for him as he came upstairs. A quick grin broke across his face as her saw her leaning against the wall.

"Ciao."

"Ciao amore." He watched as she straightened up and in that moment all his resolve fell away. All the thoughts of betrayal and fears of the consequences, everything dissolved in this longing.

He stepped inside the apartment and took her in his arms. She came willingly, bringing her mouth to his. Before, he had kept his mouth closed. Trying to hold back the feelings. Knowing that if he opened his mouth, he would come undone.

This time he softened, his mouth seeking her tongue, asked a question, answering it with his own. He heard her make a small noise of pleasure. He could feel himself responding to her. He knew she could feel him through the thin material of the dress. He knew she also felt the line being crossed. He would not stop. She would not ask him if he were sure. It was as though a small spell had been woven around them. No words.

It had always been like this. A thought. A look. A smile and it was all he could do to not take her no matter where they were. Stefano felt Julia smile as he pressed himself to her forcefully. It was all the encouragement he needed. His hands slid down her back and pulled up the dress. Running his hands around her buttocks and between her legs.

Julia gasped, holding him tightly. His kissed her deeply and she pressed against him. He felt about to explode.

The coffee maker bubbled on the stove.

"Coffee?" Julia murmured as she leaned across and turned it off.

"Later," Stefano responded.

Leaning away he brought his hands up to caress her breasts. Impatient at the fabric that covered them, he tugged at the ties that held the dress together, pushing it from her shoulders. He groaned as he pulled her breast into his mouth. Her dress was hanging around her waist and he pushed it down. Feeling the softness of her skin under his hands as he moved them along her hips and across her stomach. He ran his fingers alongside the light lace of her panties. Her hands gripped his shoulders. Her eyes watching him.

They were still a little awkward. A dance they used to know so well; a few steps missed in the relearning. But he didn't care, all he could think about was touching her. Kissing her. Then she was kneeling before him, tugging at his belt. He pulled down his jeans. She looked up at him, smiling, his mind flying back and his heart nearly stopped.

He moved her to the sofa. He understood what she wanted. It was all he could offer. Pushing his jeans lower, he brought his hands under her and lifted her toward him. Julia gasped with pleasure as they moved together. Her head fell back on the sofa, her face flushed with desire. Her hands touching his. Stefano didn't know how long he could wait. How long before the pleasure would tip him over the edge.

Sensing how close he was, Julia stopped. Standing, she took his hand pulled him across the room toward the bed. He gazed at her body. He had only one thought. To be inside her again. Entering her was like coming home.

They began to move together. Rocking against him in search of her own release. She lifted her legs to wrap around him. A memory of her beneath him filled his mind. Taking her legs onto his shoulders, he pressed closer to her. It was too much. Too much memory, too much pleasure, too much waiting. She felt the waves of pleasure wash over her. It was as though the very source of her pleasure flowed from him.

Afterwards, Stefano laughed as he listed the places where there was pain. His knee, his shoulder. She laughed with him. It was to be expected, she told him. They weren't in their twenties any more. They lay there for a moment and then he sat up, with his back toward her. She heard him whisper as he shook his head.

"*Non dovevo.*" Julia knew what he meant; "I shouldn't have done that," but she also knew, deep in her core, that there had been no real choice. Some things were just bigger than the world. They sat wrapped together on the sofa. Talking softly of the past.

"I didn't really know," offered Julia, "I thought I was just, well you know what I thought." She was annoyed as the tears filled her eyes. She didn't want to cry now. But Stefano was like the mountain and the water of tears did not worry him.

"How could you not know? Every time we would be in touch since we met in Venice, and then you would disappear."

Julia nodded, trying to snuffle away her tears. "I just didn't know you thought of me."

Stefano looked at her. "But Julia, when we were together, it was something special. It is something." He felt lost for words. As though he had not really thought about it before beyond a deep knowing. Maybe he couldn't articulate it. It couldn't be spoken because it went beyond language.

"What happens now? What happens in two weeks?" she asked.

"You said we are fatalists," he responded.

"No! I said I was an incorrigible optimist, full of hope," Julia grinned at him. "But you understand that I don't just want you for this? There is much more here between us?"

Stefano nodded. "Yes, yes, I know."

Julia smiled at him.

She watched him as he prepared to leave.

"Wednesday," he said, "I'll try to come."

She nodded. Before she could stop herself, she asked him. "You said you would never change your life. Then a few days ago you said 'for now', and now this, this between us. I want you to know that I would change my life to be with you. I want to be really clear. So you know."

Not very lake like she thought to herself.

He looked at her. Her eyes were luminous against the soft blue scarf she wore. He nodded. He wanted to take her in his arms again. He wanted to take her away from everything. To take them away from everything. But things weren't that simple.

He had a lot to think about.

"Wednesday," he said. Julia nodded, her face lit up and he felt the love pour from her straight into him. He would find a way to come and see her.

Stepping onto the bike, he leaned in for one last kiss.

"*T'amo,*" Julia whispered softly as he maneuvered the bike to the road. "Me too," he thought, but he wasn't able to say those words. Not aloud. Not yet.

She watched him as he drove away. A long breath rounded her mouth as she let it go. She felt overwhelmingly happy. She couldn't think about what might or might not happen. Not yet. For a little while, she just wanted to hold onto that feeling of union.

Walking allowed the thoughts to flow, along with the tears. There was a spot by the willows dipping into the water, where Julia sat most days. Far enough from the centre of town to have some privacy. The emotions of the morning leaked out of her. In sobs and smiles and shakes of the head. Tiny waves licked the shore. The edges of the mountain. It was hot. Stripping to her underwear, she slipped into the water, gasping at the cold. Floating, the sun slipping in and out of the clouds, Julia felt her body soften and her mind grow calm.

Something had happened. The dam had been breached. There was no stepping back from what had been put in play. She knew it. And he knew it.

It would be a significant decision to unravel a life. As much as she wished it were easy for him to leave and come to her. As much as she wished he could simply pack a bag and be at her side. She hoped that he had been well loved and had loved well. She could not be so ungenerous as to wish misery on him. She hadn't asked him about how things were at home. He would not be at her door, he would not have spent so much time with her over the last year, if all was well at home.

How would she manage if he told her he could not leave the people he cared for, and supported. For her. For love. Would she walk away? Her mind said that if he couldn't commit to her then she should let him go. Leave him and walk away. Honoring herself, and the others involved. Her heart was not ready to listen. Her soul knew his and was sure that this is where she would be, if he left his life.

If he did, then she would have some significant choices to make. For both of them.

CHAPTER

28

I Don't Like Mondays

L ater that night, Julia was watching the sun set from the hotel bar that dominated the harbor. Outside, just beyond the portico, the extremely comfortable seats faced the water. She could get used to this life.

The light of the lake was an ethereal blue. Light whips of mist shrouded the mountains on the far side. She could feel the chill rising slowly from the water. Julia imagined what it would be like here in the winter. Shorter days and an ever-present sense that the lake was full of mystery. As she walked through the town back to her apartment, she was delighted to notice the small nods of greeting by some of the local people. It made her warm to think that she could return to Italy.

Back in her apartment, her sanctuary, she smiled remembering all that had happened there this morning. It was 8 p.m. by the time she sat down at her table. Good, she could send him a heart to say welcome to work. Julia didn't expect a response immediately. She busied herself until 10 p.m. It was weird she hadn't heard anything from him. Especially after such a significant morning. She sent a quick message, *"Is everything okay?"* Still nothing. She felt stupid. Was he not going to talk to her tonight of all nights? Taking her courage in her hands she sent a longer message.

Julia— *"You have never left me alone until this time of night. I can only imagine what happened between us this morning has made you unhappy. I am sorry if you feel bad. I understand that it is no small thing. For you or for us. I hope you will at least let me know how you are feeling?"*

11:11. She sent a prayer out to the universe that he would respond. That he would reassure her. That all would be well and it was just something at work that had pulled him away.

Then she began to worry. Had he left his phone at home? No, maybe it was just in his jacket pocket. She was pretty confident there was no computer at home, linked to his WhatsApp. Julia began to feel despondent. Had she actually been played?

Her phone pinged.

Stefano— *"I am not working tonight, it's Monday."*

Julia put her head in her hands. If nothing else this was evidence that she was bad at the whole mistress thing. She hadn't even remembered it was Monday, his day off work, so he would be at home. Lost in the afterglow of feeling his body on hers. She didn't reply. She was not sure whether to be embarrassed at her mistake or angry that she even had to think about it. "Idiot," she said to herself in the mirror. But she wasn't sure what sort of idiocy she was referring to.

He had said he was the one at fault as they drank their coffee yesterday. Leaning against the kitchen bench, she had been standing in front of him.

"No, my love," Julia had said. "It's not just you. I have also done the wrong thing."

He had looked at her quizzically, shaking his head. Bringing their heads closer, kissing each other with soft lips and a knowledge that they would do it again. And again. And again. As often as they could until she left.

Julia thought she should feel worse than she did. Mimi and Stella called her from a hotel bar as they sipped martinis. They were on a tour of the wineries in the Hunter Valley and a long lunch had dissolved into dinner. Their faces crowded the small screen, and Julia had to listen carefully as they spoke over each other.

Julia confessed that she had made love with Stefano. Confessed that she would do it again. And confessed that she knew now for certain, there was someone else in the picture. Julia could feel the words fall out of her mouth into their silence. Mimi came straight from the heart. "Oh God," she said, "Are you okay? Are you going to be okay?"

Julia felt the tears prickling behind her eyes as she nodded, desperate to hold them back. Stella was her sanguine self as usual. "It was the wrap dress, wasn't it?" she asked. "I told you that would do the trick. One pull and baby there you are." Julia could see Mimi look at Stella, shaking her head and laughing at the same time. Classic Stella, always direct, blunt. Graphic, even. She went to ask for details when Mimi reminded her they were in a public place. A few cocktails in to their evening, Stella was not to be stopped. "A public bar is exactly where we should be talking about this. People need to know! I thought I was deprived after two years without sex. Then Julia told me she had been without it for seven years. I don't know how she survived, quite frankly. We need to warn people, it's our duty. They should not live without love, or at least without sex!"

They all laughed. Though Julia was quietly glad she didn't have to see the faces of anyone around them.

"I mean look all around us, Mimi," Stella continued, "look at all these lovely men, just waiting for us to speak with them."

Stella was getting louder and Mimi was trying desperately to shush her. Returning her attention to Julia. "This really is Lars's worse nightmare come true," said Mimi. "Imagine if he saw you with Stefano! His face!"

Stella threw her head back and laughed. Half choking, still laughing, she nodded emphatically. "That's what you can say. It's not your fault. It was Lars for pushing you to go to Italy."

"Oh God, I forgot to tell you!" The events of yesterday had pushed Lars out of her mind. "Lars called me a day or so ago. He kept ringing and leaving messages. I didn't pick up but he suspects I'm here."

"How does he suspect you're there? If you didn't answer?" Stella looked confused. "Surely you can just ignore him and his stupid messages."

"The phone ring tone is different when you're in Europe. It sounds different from the way it rings in Australia. Of course I didn't answer, but he knows I'm in Europe and he suspects I'm here in Italy."

"If he only knew!" chortled Mimi. "Yes!" followed Stella, "If he only knew what exactly you were up to with The Italian!"

"That's not funny!" said Julia, though her grin said otherwise. She felt lighter for the confessions. "Perhaps Lars was a catalyst. But I'm not here because he told me I was still in love with Stefano. People come into our lives to teach us something or to remind us of things that are important that we may have forgotten. I had forgotten part of myself. Lars spent way too much energy trying to dig that part of me up, but only because he was hell bent on destroying it."

Julia didn't want to go on. She knew what she felt, but she wasn't ready to admit it. She felt as though she had come home, home to herself. And she knew she would do just about anything to come back here. To be here. Where her soul felt free. Where he was.

But it was also true that Julia had broken the sisterhood code that she had held so firmly all her life. While Stella and Mimi had emphatically said that men don't think they are cheating if it's online, Julia wasn't so sure she agreed. She certainly didn't feel that way herself. Julia knew exactly what was happening every time her phone rang last year and his gorgeous smiling face would appear. That feeling that bubbled from inside out, spilling onto her face as she beamed back at him. She knew he went somewhere on his days off, and despite all the quiet suspicions that he wouldn't be a man who lived completely alone, she had known not to ask him outright. She hadn't cared about that enough to stop was happening between them, the slow inevitable seduction. It hadn't stopped her from coming here. Taking a leap of faith that he would be at the other end to catch her. And he had. Almost.

She had broken it for him.

Knowing she would make love with him again every time he came to see her. But she didn't say all that to the girls. She wasn't quite ready for that level vulnerability with herself. It was not a comfortable place to be.

CHAPTER

29

Let Me See Your Beauty

On Tuesday, she had sent a stream of sorry messages as soon as he was at work.

"*Idiota,*" she had texted. "*Sorry.*"

"*It's fine,*" he responded, "*Don't worry about it, nothing happened.*"

Julia breathed a sigh of relief. She wasn't really surprised. His reaction to mistakes was generally philosophical. She let him know she was out with friends. When she got home, she sent him a message.

Julia—"*I am home. How are you?*"

He responded quickly.

Stefano—"*Where were you? Did you eat with friends?*"

Julia—"*We went out for an aperitif here and then a pizza.*"

She wished he was there.

Julia—"*I miss you, are you coming tomorrow? I hope so.*"

Stefano—"*Yes. If it doesn't rain.*"

Julia hugged herself with pleasure. Tomorrow. She kept him company through the night shift. She had been at the market and bought a gadget that would do amazing things to vegetables. She could hear his laughter. She told him about all the stalls, she had found souvenirs that would always be a reminder of this time. Something she could hold that would bring him back to her.

Julia could see the minute Stefano arrived that he was not in the same head space as Monday. He was tired. His situation was complicated and the reality of her being here, standing in front of him, had tipped his sense of balance.

Opening his arms, Julia's body melted onto his and he was amazed again at how she could make him feel. Monday had been unexpected. Impulsive. He shook his head and moved away from her.

"Shall I make the coffee?" he offered.

Julia nodded and waved him to the kitchen. She sat on the sofa, watching him as he poured water, carefully adding the coffee to the cafetiere spoonful by spoonful. Placing it on the stove, Stefano looked across at her and grinned.

Her face, she knew, would be looking back at him full of feelings. All of them. Love was there. Lust. Mmmm definitely. Longing, and close behind that, hope. Hope that he would take her in his arms and make love to her. But it was deeper than that. It was hope that he would step forward in so many ways.

She knew that he understood exactly how she felt. What she wasn't sure of was how he was feeling. He was coming here to see her as often as he could. But it was still only stolen moments. Perhaps Verona will be the tipping point, she thought. Perhaps walking the streets of Verona will give him . . . What? Julia thought. What does he need? Faith. Courage. "Maybe he doesn't want more than this." Julia felt rather than heard that small voice worm across her mind.

Sitting beside him on the sofa, Julia rested her hand on his chest. There was a vibe in the air and it was making her feel jumpy, when she was trying to be calm.

Be the lake. Be the lake and all will be well.

The coffee bubbled and she laughed as Stefano cocked his head on one side waiting for the perfect bubble. He smiled back at her and it was as though the sun had come out.

Standing at the small bench space, she placed two cups in front of him. "You pour yours first," she said. "I'll have the rest."

He obliged, stopping as hers was half filled.

"That's enough," he laughed.

"Don't you drink much coffee anymore?" Julia asked curiously, "You said something about your heart. Do you take tablets?"

"God is this what we have come to," she thought. "We are getting old."

Stefano shook his head, "No, but I have to be mindful of hypertension," his smile was a little abashed.

Julia remembered his father had died of a heart attack. Young. She was pleased to know Stefano was taking better care of himself, despite the fact that he still smoked. At that her face tightened.

There was an awkwardness between them, as though Monday hadn't happened. Julia knew it wasn't because she had accidentally messaged him. But he was not relaxed. As though he were balancing two swords or holding the reins of two horses that, if he took his eyes off them, would go in different directions. She didn't want to ask him about his feelings or rather she did want to ask but she didn't really want to know the answer.

Be the lake, she kept telling herself.

It was hard not to touch him. Especially after Monday. Julia resigned herself to the reality that today might just be coffee.

She sat forward on the sofa. Suddenly she felt his hand run along her back and then across her buttocks.

"What underwear have you on?" his voice was husky. His hand firm.

She was surprised. A trickle of desire ran through her. She didn't answer him in words, she looked over her shoulder at him, her eyebrows raised. She stood up. Still facing away from him. Careful not to break the spell that he was weaving around them.

"Check," she offered in a quiet voice. He pulled her skirt up, running his hands around the tops of her thighs, across her buttocks, between her legs. Julia was surprised at his sudden shift but she was definitely not about to question it. There would be time for that later. Right now all she felt was the energy that flowed between them.

He pulled her onto his lap. She could feel his desire building and knew there would be no stepping back. Reaching down she opened his belt and jeans. He was quick to help her, to free himself. His hands returned to caressing her. His breathing got faster as he began to rock them back and forward, feeling the movement building her pleasure. Then she slowly stood up, moved to face him and held out her hands. He took them and she guided him toward the bed.

"What do you want?" she whispered. Making sure the spell still moved around them.

Wanting to please her, to pleasure her. To touch her and watch her. It filled him with something, desire yes, but something else as well.

She gasped as he touched her. Catching small sips of breath. He felt the waves crash over her. God he was so hard. "What do you want?" she whispered. "This?"

They had spoken these words, these scenes. This was one, she knew, he had dreamt about. Stefano nodded, suddenly speechless. She heard him sigh his release.

They lay there, curled around. His head resting on her thigh. There was a contentment. A quiet. An intimacy. As though step by step they had begun to find their way back. Not just through words, not just though touch, into that space where they could feel each other. She could have stayed like that for ever.

"Bimba, sorry I have to go. I am already late." He was agitated as he moved into the bathroom. Julia lay there for a moment. The lovemaking was intoxicating. The minute she saw him, the moment he stepped into her apartment, a sweetness began to permeate the air. Something too strong to resist, something that would find a way. Julia wasn't sure who was the siren. She supposed she was since he kept returning.

It was clear that he was troubled, but it was not enough to hold him from coming to her, from beginning the slow journey of reconnection. Because that's what was happening.

At the beginning it had felt as though they were standing in the dark. Unexpected and devastating to both of them. But every time he came, every time they stood in the presence of one another, Julia could feel the flame begin to grow, the light begin to expand, to illuminate what might be possible. She knew he was as acutely aware of it as she was.

More than a siren song thought Julia. More like a call from soul. A call that could not be ignored. It would never be forgotten.

CHAPTER

30

The First Goodbye

Dressing quickly, Julia accompanied him out to the street to where he had left the Vespa. As Stefano prepared to leave, Julia handed him a small polished stone.

"I wanted to give you a gift. Something you can have in your pocket and when you touch it, you think of me." Looking up at him, she smiled.

Stefano took it. Blue like her eyes. He smiled and slipped it in his pocket. Julia hesitated. "I also bought this for you," a small heart shaped rose quartz was in her hand, "But maybe it's too—" she trailed off.

Stefano looked at the heart and something cracked inside him. "Give it to me when we are in Verona," he said huskily.

It was then that she knew Verona would be the turning point. If there were to be one.

Verona. Julia wanted to run there right now. Not take the train to Milan tomorrow or spend the weekend in Dublin. She wanted to run to Verona and find him there.

Stefano leaned forward, kissing her mouth with longing and promise.

"We'll speak in the meantime, but we'll see each in Verona."

Julia nodded and stepped back. Four days until she would see him.

The brightness in her eyes was unmistakable. His hand reached to caress her face before turning on the bike.

Stefano could no longer deny how he was feeling. He could no longer pretend that this was just something fleeting. A memory, a beautiful chapter of his life that he was re-reading.

As he rode away he could see her standing there, watching him go. He realized that he no longer wanted to drive away from her. He never wanted to drive away again.

These four days would be difficult. He could feel it in his stomach. Her return had set in motion feelings that he had long denied. Thoughts he had dismissed. Seeing her returned him to the place where anything was possible. He knew he would count the hours until she returned.

Verona. The city of love. The city where he had first loved her. Where they had first known what love was.

PART
THREE

Verona The City of Love

CHAPTER

31

Time Travel

L anding at Venice airport, the late morning was bright and sunny. Julia was suddenly reminded of something the fortune teller at the stall in the market had said to her. "Is it hot where you are going? I feel hot, like we are looking at each other and we're hot."

It was hot. Julia could feel the rivulets of water trickling down her spine. Julia began to wonder what else of that prediction might come true.

The train raced through the countryside toward Verona, city of Romeo and Juliet, the most famous of star-crossed lovers. Julia could feel the sense of excitement building as they approached the station. There was a sense of returning. Returning to herself. Reconnecting. Every day she spent in Italy brought her a sense of peace and satisfaction.

Julia didn't want to think about returning to her life in Australia, but unless Stefano was willing to step forward into sharing a life with her, she would go back.

She knew she would be different. Changed in some way or perhaps stripped back to where she had been, with everything yet to become.

Pulling into the station, Julia did a quick mental map of the city. A bus or a taxi would have been faster and more convenient but she wanted to savor the moment, walking the creamy pink slabs of marble underfoot. Watching the clock tower slowly come into focus and Verona's main square Piazza Bra open out behind it. The Arena amphitheatre, peeking out from the trees as she walked under the gates. Spring in Italy was beautiful, so much beauty everywhere she looked, bringing up memory after memory, that she was in danger of crying.

It was hot and she was sweltering in her travel clothes. Her jacket was slung over her arm, along with a jumper and a scarf she had needed in Dublin. No matter how carefully she packed her suitcase, there was always something that ended up in her hands. She couldn't wait to drop them off and change.

There was something deeply satisfying about navigating a different city. The day was drawing to a close as she found her way to the address where she was staying. The view across the rooftops from the balcony was breathtaking. It was as beautiful as the photos. She could picture herself sipping a glass of wine on the balcony, sharing a drink with Stefano. If he came.

Julia pushed that thought firmly out of her mind. She would be like the lake. That was all she could do. Sighing, Julia made some quick arrangements with Marco. She had left her heavier suitcase with him. He would bring the rest of her things over to her around 5 p.m. The road system was complicated around the old parts of the city centre, it would be difficult to get very close. Still Porta

Borsari was nearby and she could meet him there and bring her suitcase along the road. Thankfully, there was a lift this time.

Nestled in the rooftops, she could see the edge of the Arena, Verona's own Roman amphitheatre. It was still early spring, before the opera season was in full swing. Thirty years ago, anyone could walk in and sit on the stone steps, on the same stone steps where people had sat for thousands of years. Now it was controlled. Preserving something took effort.

This feeling of connection to those who had come before was something she loved most about being here. Memories flooded back as she looked out over the city rooftops. Seeing Romeo and Juliet in the Teatro Romano, another ancient Roman performance space on the other side of the river. It had been magical. Outside, in the dark. And a perfect place to watch Shakespeare.

Sitting on the balcony, Julia sipped a glass of water. She would go for a walk later, she decided, past Tre Santi, the small bistro where she and Stefano used to go for a drink. She smiled. They were often out bar hopping around their local area.

Julia shook her head at the absolute ignorance of youth. Even if you weren't that confident, there was something about being young and open to possibility, open to exploring all things new. It seemed strange to remember herself like that. So many different things had happened in the intervening years.

Walking across the city, her feet took her to the street where they used to live. She stopped across the road, looking up at the windows with their green shutters, framed by the soft yellow stucco. Julia wasn't sure who she was in search of anymore.

It had been a time of great love, she thought. Of so much fun and freedom. She had sung loudly, written poetry, dabbled with sketching. All the while blissfully in love with Stefano, in love with love and in love with life. She smiled to herself. Proud of the courage and the confidence that had opened her life to something more than she had ever thought possible. There were no regrets about that time. Except the ending. The leaving.

Julia wondered now how deep that wound had been. She wondered if she should have stayed and fought for love. Shaking her head, she turned, her feet following a familiar path. Love wasn't something to be won, fought for like a battle. Love was a gift. To be given freely or not at all.

Turning the corner, the familiar canvas awning of a local bakery came into sight. She would come here in the morning for freshly baked bread and the occasional treat. Her stomach rumbled at the memory. Pushing open the door, her eyes and nose were met by the rich colors and smells. Julia breathed deeply as she looked for a familiar face. There. Her back was turned as she spoke to a man buying fresh bread. Julia waited until the woman turned to face her. A polite blankness quickly turned to delight.

"Julia! Welcome! Welcome! How lovely to see you. When did you come, how long are you staying?" Julia laughed and leaned in as they kissed cheeks and hugged.

"It's so lovely to see you Chiara. I wasn't sure if you would still be here."

"I am always here," Chiara shrugged. "Have you got a minute? Let me just do a couple of things and then we can go for a coffee?"

Julia nodded, "I can wait. I have time."

Julia knew Stella would roll her eyes and say the feeling of excitement was because she was on vacation. But that wasn't entirely true. She had lived here. It was that sensation that pulled at her now. Could she be part of the city again. Would it be possible to work here, maybe even remotely? It would be a very fine thing if she could keep her job in Australia and work from here. It was something to think about. Something to consider. Maybe something she could plan.

32

Tre Santi

After coffee with Chiara and a promise of lunch in a few days, Julia walked on to Tre Santi. It was easy enough to find, although the name had changed. A young woman in her early twenties was behind the bar.

"Good evening, could you tell me if this place used to be called Tre Santi?"

"*Buena sera,*" the young woman had responded, "yes it was."

"And is the owner still a man called Lorenzo?

"Yes, but he is retired now. He is my grandfather."

Julia felt those words hit her. Retired. Lorenzo, retired. They were all getting old.

"Could you say hello to him from me and a friend of mine. May I leave a note for him?"

The young woman looked at her as though she was a little

crazy. "Sure," she said, "my mother is just through there. And my grandmother."

Julia suddenly felt wrong. She didn't know why. Her time in Verona was before this girl's family history had begun. The girl didn't know how Julia fitted into it, and she could sense that the girl was not all that comfortable about it.

"I didn't know your grandmother. I never met her. Lorenzo was our friend before that," she said as she quickly wrote a note, 'our friend' making sure she added her name with Stefano's to avoid any awkward misunderstandings. Handing it to Lorenzo's granddaughter, Julia wondered if it would just end up in the bin. Thanking her, she left the bar and once she was out on the street, she breathed a sigh of relief.

The memories of that time were easy enough to access. The memory of the small street that led between Tre Santi and Gorky's. The memory of Stefano's touch and his kiss. Julia could feel them again.

"*Signora!* Signora!" A voice called from behind. Julia stopped and turned. A man was walking toward her.

"Julia?"

"Yes?"

"Lorenzo."

Julia had already recognized him. Already transported back to the times when he had poured drinks and laughed with them. When the noise and bustle of the bar had been no contest to the energy that surrounded her and Stefano.

She shook her head.

"Ciao! Ciao, Lorenzo. Yes, I am Julia." He held out his arm as though to shake hands, then pulled her close for a quick kiss to each cheek, taking her arm, directing her back toward the bar.

"How are you?" he asked. "You look exactly the same."

Julia laughed at that. "That's very kind of you to say. Though you are a terrible liar!"

"No, no, not at all," Lorenzo protested. "I remember you well. Perhaps you are even more beautiful now."

"Flatterer!" retorted Julia. If nothing else, Italy and Italian men were appreciative of the female form. In another context it might seem insincere. Here it was just celebratory.

"I haven't seen Stefano for ages. I was upstairs when Lucia, my granddaughter, gave me your note."

"I'm sorry," said Julia quickly. "I didn't mean to disturb you. I saw Stefano recently when I was staying at Lake Garda. He knew I was coming to Verona and wanted me to see if you still owned Tre Santi after you sold Gorky's. We have such great memories of those times," Julia let the words fall to her feet.

"They were great times. You and Stefano were always fun to have at Gorky's."

Julia smiled at his enthusiasm. It was easy to see why he had been successful. Charismatic, welcoming. The necessary ingredients for an owner of a bar.

Lorenzo, oblivious, went on, "So you've seen Stefano. How is he? What is he doing? Last I heard he was in Venice. It's been a difficult time for all of us in the past couple of years."

"Yes, I've just been at the Lakes. I saw him. He left Venice late last year, he's working in Sirmione, in a hotel."

"Oh, I wondered what had happened . . . I saw him every now and then in Venice. He liked the lifestyle although I think he was a bit lonely. Not that he was keen to head home all the time. Did you meet . . ." Lorenzo stopped realizing that his next question might not be welcome.

Julia smiled weakly.

Taking her elbow, Lorenzo steered her to an empty table.

"Let me get you something to drink. Leave it to me," he added with a flash of the grin that had often been followed by some creation he wanted them to try.

"What have you brought me?" Julia sniffed the liquor suspiciously, though the smile on her face dispelled any real objections. He laughed.

"It was always a pleasure to have you at the bar. You were both so full of a brightness that it was like the sun had stepped inside." Lorenzo smiled at her. It must have been hard for her to leave, he thought, suddenly struck by what he had said. Perhaps those memories were not ones she kept. He looked quickly at her. Julia had picked up the glass and used it to hide her face while she composed herself. Looking up she smiled at him, but he could see her eyes were shining.

"Excuse me, Julia, I didn't want to bring up things that might make you feel sad."

"No," Julia protested, "they are treasured memories. I loved every night we spent at Gorky's. It was fun. I was young, foolish and in love. You can't ask for more than that!"

Lorenzo smiled, feeling relieved. He knew Stefano had taken it badly when she left. "I never understood why you left," he started. "You were both so in love with each other. It was like a story that you read about in books. I was sad when you left. Sad for you. Sad for Stefano." And sad for myself, he thought. Sad to have lost the light they had brought into the bar. Into his life.

"Was Stefano sad?" Julia asked. She didn't expect an answer.

Stefano had once said he should have had more courage. He should have made a different choice. He would have made a different choice if he had been free. But he hadn't been free and he hadn't made a different choice.

"Yes, he was sad," Lorenzo was emphatic. "Even if he didn't say much or show it much at the time. I could tell. But whether he said a word or not, I knew. How could he not be sad? How could he not miss you and all you were together?" Lorenzo coughed to cover up the awkwardness of what he had just said, if he had said too much.

"Thank you."

Lorenzo could see the love was still there, all these years on. It was not glowing like it had been all those years ago, perhaps, but it was still there. Steady. Shining. Constant.

He felt it again. That sadness that he remembered feeling sometimes when they had entered Gorky's. No sadness was not the right word. Lorenzo bit his lip as he thought. Melancholia. That was closer. The sense that in all joy there is also sadness. In all love there is also loss.

"Can I ask you something?" Julia found her mouth dry. Lorenzo nodded. "When you saw him, in Venice. Was he alone? Or was there someone there? I mean, clearly, I don't have any right to imagine that he lived like a monk. I guess I want to know the extent of how things are." Do I, she thought? But the words had been spoken.

Lorenzo had been Stefano's friend, not hers, despite what Stefano had said to her when they were together at the lake. Lorenzo had known Stefano before her and after her. But how had his life been in the between time. That was what she was asking now. Having that information that might help her find solid ground.

Lorenzo leaned back in his chair. His eyes held her gaze. "Julia, do you miss him?" He was surprising himself by the questions. Julia, too, was taken aback.

"I'm sorry. I shouldn't have asked you that," he looked down at his hands. "He was different with you, and if I am honest, he never was like that again." Lorenzo was quiet now.

"Yes, I do miss him," her voice was quiet. "But I think it's impossible."

Impossible to do what, thought Lorenzo. Though this time he kept the words to himself. Was she going to say it's impossible to be with Stefano? Impossible to stay in Italy? Impossible to return to the love of the past? He looked at her again. No, he thought. It is not impossible.

"I don't know where things are or what things are like for him right now," Lorenzo faltered. "If that is what you really think, that it's impossible, then perhaps it is. But I am not so sure. And I don't think you are either." Lorenzo stood up as he finished speaking. The bar was getting busy and he needed to lend a hand. Julia stood up too and he took her hand, kissing her gently on both cheeks. "I know you have courage," he said. "Perhaps you just need to have a little faith too?"

A smile tilted the corners of her mouth. "Perhaps I need to have a little faith. But courage, I don't think I'm the one in need of that."

Lorenzo squeezed her hand. "Then he is an idiot. I've always been one so I recognize one when I find them. If I see him, I'll tell him so."

Heading back along the river, the evening sky was gently beginning to darken. Julia turned toward Piazza Bra and decided to treat herself to an evening drink, to sit and watch the world go by for a while.

The conversation with Lorenzo had been revealing and a little unsettling. Julia needed a break from the intensity of the thoughts of Stefano that filled her mind.

Determined to refocus, she found herself watching the world go by from a table outside in the square. Thirty years ago, it would have been out of reach to sit here in that prime spot. The price difference between the main square and all the other places they usually went to was too much to be ignored. Now things were different and sitting here with a Campari spritz was well within her means.

She was not remotely unhappy that she had come. The future was always uncertain. It may all come to nothing. Stefano may not ever change his mind and leave the life he had, for this love. She would just have to accept whatever came. And know she had done all she could to offer the possibility.

33

Complications

"Julia!" She was shocked out of her reverie.

"Julia!" There was a sense of satisfaction in the voice as a tall lean man pulled out the other chair. "I found you. I knew I would."

"Lars! What the . . ." she stopped, "What are you doing here? You can't be here." Her heart was thumping in her chest. She had not forgotten the onslaught of his rages. Her body reacted. She tensed, ready to move.

"Julia, I couldn't let you do something stupid. I couldn't permit you to go back to him. You know he's just some Italian gigolo and . . ." Lars bit off the rest of the sentence. If nothing else he had realized that line of argument was a dead end. "But I see you are alone. Perhaps I am wrong. Perhaps I misunderstood."

Julia opened her mouth to tell him that actually he had understood, when he held up his hand to stop her.

"Can we walk?" he said, "I need to tell you something, ask you something."

Julia looked at his face. It wasn't in her nature to be cruel, and she knew only too well that any information about Stefano would be difficult. She heard Stella's voice in her head,

"And none of his damn business."

"Okay." Pushing back her chair, she stood up and stepped away from the table. They moved off, away from the crowds and toward the old castle and the river. Running through her head was a combination of What does he want? Why is he here? and equally the determination to not speak first and to definitely not get dragged into whatever drama he had planned. Resolved, she straightened herself up. Her mind calmed and she waited. They crossed onto the castle bridge when he stopped and took her hands. Taken by surprise, she let him.

"Julia," he began, "when I called you it was to tell you something. No. To ask you something. Something I have been thinking about since I left Australia."

Julia started to pull her hands away but he gripped them a little harder.

"I know you wanted more from me. More than I could give you at the time. But since I've been gone, I've had a lot of time to think."

She felt her hands, still in his, get a little hot. Clammy. Her thoughts, which had momentarily quietened, started to swirl again. "Oh God", she thought, "he's not going to, is he? No surely not. Oh God! What if he does. Shit Shit Shit."

"Julia I can't stop thinking about you. I haven't been able to stop thinking about you. I called you to ask you if, if you wanted to come to Germany. To see me. Or if you wanted me to come back. I wanted to ask you . . ."

Ripping her hands from his grasp, Julia instinctively covered his mouth with a hand. As she covered her own. Shaking her head to stop him, it was all she could do to keep breathing.

"Don't," she whispered. "Don't say it." Inhaling she let her hands drop to her sides. "It's too late to ask me anything. There is nothing that can change things between us. I'm sorry, Lars. I'm truly sorry, but nothing has changed for me since we last saw each other."

Well nothing in relation to you, she thought, though again she bit back those words.

She watched his face fall and then harden slightly. Julia has seen this pattern before and she was not about to bear witness to it here.

"I have to go. Lars, I'm sorry, but you should go home. Go back to Germany. There is nothing for you here. I don't want to see you, not now, not here, and not anywhere else."

Turning, she walked swiftly back along the bridge, willing herself not to break into a run. Lars was not use to being thwarted. She turned a corner before she dared look over her shoulder. Julia did not want to see him looking at her. She remembered too well the expression on his face that had sealed the fate of their relationship. It had chilled her then and it did the same now. Taking a longer route home, she checked to see if he had followed her. Slipping in her apartment, she closed the door. Only then realizing how full of tension she had been as she slid to the floor. The sense of relief flooding her.

CHAPTER

34

What Are We?

The station was busy and they missed each other in the crowd. Stefano was waiting outside as she skipped up to him. Courage and faith, determined to hold them close. He seemed distant.

"What's up?" she asked.

"Nothing, there are just some people who know me on the train. Let's walk." His reply terse.

Julia suddenly felt flat. The anticipated reunion in Verona had not started well. First the unexpected and disturbing meeting with Lars and now this. As they walked toward the Porta Nuova, the entrance to Piazza Bra, Stefano took a few steps back. Julia looked at him quizzically.

"Just walk on," he had said, "I know people around here."

She felt bad and the edges of her mind felt tinged with shame. But at least now it was clear. It was impossible. She was a secret, something that could put his life, his home life, at risk. She turned to face him, to tell him that she wasn't prepared to be a secret, that this was crazy and they couldn't make the same mistake again. As she stepped toward him, determined to tell him that this was not ok, someone brushed past her.

"Stefano! What are you doing here? I thought you were working in Sirmione. How are things?" A man in a blue shirt was standing between them, with his back toward her. Julia she saw a brief look of something? Anguish? She wasn't sure, in Stefano's eyes as he turned his attention to the man.

Turning on her heel, she fled. What had she been thinking? Perhaps she was just a momentary fling. An enjoyable, a seductive, sensual walk down memory lane. Sure, one with a story, with history. But it was a love that had to remain a secret. The reality of her position starkly drawn.

Walking swiftly through Piazza Bra, she sought refuge in the crowds. Conversations with Mimi, Stella and Hermione filled her mind, where they had dissected the situation. With a lot of love for her, and sprinkle of justification for her actions, they had not pulled punches. Hermione laid it on the line when Julia called her from Italy.

"We have to face it. He's married," she said. "It's clear now. He's married and that's why he went quiet. It's the reason why he's been so unavailable." There was a long silence on the line. "Not judging you for loving him," she reassured her friend, "but we have to face facts, even though it is so hurtful to do so. We can't just ignore what we know to be true. As true friends, we have to be truthful to each other. That Venus placement in the twelfth house in Scorpio in his chart is a hint that he likes to have a secret love, and you my lovely friend, are the secret love. You're a secret love he has had all his life, even when you were seeing each other openly when you lived here, he had someone back home. Perhaps you are the love of his life, but you're still a secret and he's keeping it that way for a reason."

"I don't want to just be his lover, and definitely not just a secret one," Julia had said, refusing to hear it. Julia couldn't imagine choosing a life as a secret lover, a mistress. That was not going to work for her. Never. "I want all of him." There she had said it. It was a clear call out to the universe if nothing else.

"So then, if you are going to make it real, and be with him as a life partner, not just stolen moments as a secret lover, it sounds as if he is going to need to make some very big changes in his life first." Hermione was clear. "And," thought Julia as she slipped down the slide street toward her apartment building, "right as usual."

She turned the key and pushed open the main door. Another hand, larger, familiar, covered her own.

"May I?" stepping past her.

Julia followed Stefano into the entrance. Though what permission he was asking for, possibly required a more thoughtful and less automatic response. She wasn't sure what to say or do. The situation in the street had thrown her. They went up in the elevator in silence. His face tense and hers, Julia hazarded a quick glance at her reflection, hers was white, as though her soul had left her body and she was left empty.

She turned to face him. "Who was he?"

Stefano looked uncomfortable, but he answered, "Manola's cousin."

Manola. She had not known her name. Julia realized she didn't want to know her name. She didn't want this other woman to become any more real. Knowing her name meant she was a real person, his partner. It was one thing to not be chosen, in an abstract way, another thing altogether to put flesh on the bones of the woman they were both betraying.

"I think you should go." The words stripping the skin from her tongue.

He was beside her. Taking her hands, he pulled her to him. Her body moulded against his as though it was a piece of a puzzle, finding the right place.

"Julia, you don't want me to go. I know you don't. And I don't want to go. Please. I can stay until tomorrow morning." It was an offering, small. Perhaps an apology.

Julia sighed as she softened in his arms. There was nothing to be done. When he was here, it was all she could care about.

Julia pulled away her face away from his. "And then?"

"Then I have to go, I have to go home."

There he had said it. Though the words fell flat on the floor between them. He watched as a shadow crossed her face.

Incorrigible optimist, her words echoed in his mind.

"Julia, I know you want more. But I can't change the way things are for me right now," his face twisted as he shrugged. "I wish things were different, but they are what they are. And I can't . . ." He stopped speaking, his voice was cracking.

Julia nodded. "I know. I can't either. I can't stay in this place for long. It is a space I really shouldn't be in at all."

They sat in miserable silence. "But I can't change the way I feel. There is something between us." It was her turn to grimace. "I can't stop that feeling, even if I wanted to. I think it's something that almost doesn't belong to us."

Stefano looked at her. He couldn't speak. There was a truth in her words that he felt in his bones. There was nothing he could say to make this any better. Stefano moved his hands to hold her face. He wanted to kiss her.

Tilting it upwards as he brought his lips to touch her forehead, her eyelids, her nose. Her mouth curved upwards as he ran his tongue across her lips. Parting her lips, he felt her sweet soft breath mingle with his. There was something so enticing about her. He couldn't imagine life where she wasn't present in his mind and his body and in his heart. It wasn't something he wanted to face. He knew he loved her and he had loved her for all this time, across all that distance.

He also knew that there would be no resolution talking about what happened, what might happen. No matter where the conversation went. No matter how it unfolded. He was unable to imagine a future without her, and equally unable to think how to make the changes to his life to create space to be with her.

To give her all of himself the way she wanted. The way she deserved.

They sat on the balcony, sipping coffee. A silence had surrounded them since her words. It was not uncomfortable. It was space to let thoughts linger, to feel them. It was peaceful sitting here in her presence, he thought. Suspended from life's responsibilities. Stretching his legs out, his foot nudged hers.

She reached out her hand. He took it, looking at her. "We haven't finished this conversation," he said.

Nodding, she reached over and touched her lips to his. The sweetness of it flooded him with feelings that he had trouble holding, his throat tightened. "We may never finish it."

"Come with me," she instructed.

Julia reached into the bedside table and drew out a bottle of oil. She moved to sit across his back, ever so lightly resting her own bottom on the hill of his. Tipping some oil into her hands, the light citrusy scent of the oil filled her senses.

Julia felt a lightness. They were together in this moment, maybe only ever this one, and that was all that mattered.

Was that how love worked? Not just love that began with a flame and then burned all around it to ash. Like the one she had experienced briefly with Lars. No, this was different in a way that she couldn't put words to yet felt inscribed on her bones. Love that had an openness, an acceptance, a generosity of spirit which allowed it to remain across time and space. It wasn't consciously chosen, it simply was there when two souls recognized each other, it became present, existing between them. That's what it felt like.

Julia began to stroke the muscles across his shoulders. Kneading and stretching out the knots and tiredness, he slowly began to relax into her touch. She felt him giving up to her hands. Julia loved this view of him, stretched out beneath her. The heat from her hands warmed the oil and her fingers began to hone in on the places which held the tribulations of the day. The rise and fall of his back began to lengthen in rhythm.

It was curious to her that people didn't think about the breath of the back, they were so focused on the front of their body that they forgot about the very thing that held them upright, enabled them to walk, to embrace. The energy of the back of the body is always more peaceful than the front, she thought as her hands moved along the sides of his spine, as they stretched and pulled the muscles. The muscles had their own story to share, unraveling under the heels of her palms, firmly pressing and kneading them like dough.

His body felt heavier under her hands and every now and then his breathing roughened. Turning her attention to one side of his lower back, then the other, she felt him slip deeper into sleep.

The liminal world between waking and dreaming was where he was right now. Where there are no boundaries between realities, spaces, time and thoughts, no custom or structure, the mind roaming, perhaps connecting to the deeper wisdom of the soul. The twilight and the dawn, as the light gives way to the dark and the dark to the light in an endless cycle of shift between what is known and what is real, where desires and dreams can take form and it is up to each of us to choose what they will bring and give form.

Slowly she eased herself from her place on his buttocks, and slid alongside him, pulling the covers over them both as she did so. His face was turned toward her, his eyes closed, relaxed. It was the first time she'd had a chance to properly look at him. Whenever he was awake, the sparkle of his eyes and the upward tilt of his mouth were too distracting. Now, as he slept, she could take her time.

She remembered he had told her that he had watched the video of her on her work website a thousand times, maybe more. If there had been a video of him, something she could watch that animated him, would she have watched it? Yes. She listened to music they had shared, wine they had tasted, food they ate. All reminders of the time they were together.

Those memories were a place of refuge as well as one of hope. Places where the soul can rest before it returns to the world. She had rested many times in the refuge of that music, the tastes and smells, seeking refuge in the memory of their love.

Something had held her steady as the maelstrom that turned her life inside out crashed around her. The light was not yet leaking in, it was still the earliest soft glow which would herald a dawn.

She remembered now. A concert under the stars, in the grounds of the winery, when the moon was full. Leonard singing in his gravelly baritone of love, loss, and the bittersweet seduction of life. Mimi and Stella dancing with her on the grass. That's when the untethering from her present began. She could see that now. She could feel the moment when those lines had cracked open. Letting in the light. Letting him in.

At the time she hadn't known that he still thought of her. She thought he had moved on years ago and that there had been many others, some who may have captured his heart the way she thought she had. Now as she looked at him, she realized none of that really mattered, because what was here now was something beyond all that they knew. There was an uncertainty, but not an ambiguity.

"Would we speak of it?" she wondered, "Would we breathe air, life, hope into it and allow it to forge a new path for us?" If there were any possibilities to have these conversations, then Verona was the place to give them voice.

35

Afternoon

She noticed his breathing change rhythm. His hand began to slide along her side, pushing the covers free to trace all the way down and over her hip. She turned slightly onto her back. His hand now finding itself on the flat of her stomach, traveled toward her breasts. One quick brush across her nipples and they were hard and tender to touch. Her fingers slowly moving along his shoulder, slipping under his returning arm to trace her own mapping of his body. He shifted slightly, dislodging her hand from where it had been sliding along his upper thigh. Julia fingers finding themselves very close to the top of his legs, entangled in soft curls. He leaned over, bringing his mouth closer. Julia reached up and gently took his lower lip between her teeth. Feeling him draw in a sharp breath, she let go and ran her tongue along it.

"Give me your tongue," she whispered.

With very gentle, featherlike movements, she ran her fingertips up and down his body.

"How old are you? Surely you must be much younger. Time has not passed at all." She wanted to turn back time.

"Yes," he agreed, "When I am with you, it's as if I am still young. As if I have all life in front of me. I have in my arms some sort of witch who cast a spell that has taken away the years and reinvigorated my longing of life."

Julia was silent. Reaching up, she wrapped her arms around his neck, pulling his face closer. "Kiss me, take me now. I want to feel you inside me."

He slid his hand down along her stomach, running his fingers through the hair that framed her core. He could sense the heat and his hand soon felt the slippery softness. Keeping his mouth on hers, he shifted his body. His thighs were heavy as she moved her legs to bring him closer. Julia's hands ran down from his shoulders to the place where his back curved into his buttocks. He looked at her and she held his gaze as he slowly eased closer, deeper. Her pelvis moving in small slow circles.

"Julia," his voice was soft, husky, "how you do it? When we are together, it's as though I find myself."

Already dissolving in the sensations, his words swirled around her thoughts and she could see with absolute clarity the truth of them. When they made love. Even in the moments when they would come together fast and hard, almost thoughtless in their need for each other, there was the sense that they were home.

Julia's hands moved along his back in a rhythm that followed his pace. She could feel herself pushing against him, breathing faster. He heard her breathing start to get choppy and increased the speed of his thrusts as his desire mounted. His mouth moved down along her neck, as she arched against him, her breasts rubbing his chest. Her hands on his hips, encouraging, imploring with every thrust.

She squeezed him tightly, as the sensation flowed through her, as though to hold herself in place, in one piece. And he fell apart.

Some time passed before her grip softened and he slowly, carefully lifted himself and fell back onto the bed at her side. His arm was curled around his head and the hand of his other arm rested on the top of her thigh. His eyes were closed. His head was tilted slightly back, his breathing deliberate with a soft sigh as he exhaled. She rolled her head slightly to the right so she could see his face, her left arm reaching across to rest on his chest.

A sense of peace, of wellbeing, settled over them. There was no need for words. This was something that asked them to dive in deeply. It was not just his body that called for hers. Nothing so simple or fleeting. It was an essence of each of them that called across time and distance each to the other. A yearning to know one other, on the inside and the outside. To explore how they saw the world, to take time to see things through their lens, from their perspective. It was not just physical; it was something elemental that found its expression in their bodies. "If we are made of star dust," she thought, "when he is near, it's as though we merged in some sort of cosmic union."

The sheet was draped over her body, the cool of the evening air flowing in through the open window. Noises from the street drifted upwards, enticing rather than disturbing. She felt his gaze on her. Turning to look at him, she blushed slightly. A cool hand cupped her warm cheek.

"So Bimba, how are you?"

Her lips curled up at the corners, "Good, and you?"

"Yes, I feel good. I have not felt this good since, I don't know when."

"Me too, but I am a little hungry. Shall we eat?"

He nodded, "Let's go out to eat, then I'll eat you for dessert."

Julia's breath caught in her throat and her pulse began to race again. He felt the shift in the air between them.

"Or," he said, "Or I could eat you right now."

"Yes," she replied, "Or I could eat you. Given that I am hungry."

All thoughts of going out faded as he pulled her toward him.

CHAPTER

36

Collision

"Do you remember the night we went out? Maybe the second night we went out together? You took me to a bar on the river, near Ponte Pietra, the bridge of stones, our bridge. I don't remember who was with us but it was an enchanted evening."

"Of course I remember, that's why we're here," he said leading her inside. The room was cavernous, softly lit with small tables dotted around.

"Oh!" Julia hadn't consciously been watching where they were going.

"Yes," Stefano looked at her, "I remember it well."

He guided her through the tables, out onto the terrace, overlooking the water. Speaking to the waiter, he ordered drinks and food. He looked to see her watching him with a raised eyebrow.

"What?"

"How do you know what I want to eat or drink?"

He reached out, cupping her face with his hand.

"Bimba, gin tonic, and some snacks. Okay?"

It was hard to even pretend to be mad at him, but she tried a little longer.

"Perhaps I would have preferred a spritz."

"Perhaps," he agreed, "but tonight you'll have a gin tonic okay?

"Ok," she laughed, "chauvinist!"

He pinched her wrist, "Quiet Bimba, otherwise I'll have to . . . hmmm what shall I do to you? Discipline you somehow?"

"Promises, promises," she teased.

Leaning forward, he brought his mouth close to her ear. "Si, I promise, if you behave yourself."

Tilting back slightly, his mouth close to hers, the energy began to crackle between them. His hand resting lightly on her thigh suddenly felt like it was burning. A cough broke the spell. The waiter set their drinks and some small plates of food in front of them. She looked at the droplets forming on the glass, composing herself.

"Cheers, to your health," he raised his glass to hers. "It is a great pleasure to be here in Verona, to see you after all this time."

"It is wonderful to see you again," Julia agreed.

They seemed so formal, but underneath the words was something else. Stefano's hand reached over, covering hers. Julia turned her palm upwards to hold his. The energy between their palms pulsed. It made Julia think of reiki, the way energy can be transferred between one another. "Is that what happened?" she thought. "Did emotions gather a life of their own and flare into being?"

Julia began to ask him questions about his life, about the time that had intervened. Sometimes she would forget to concentrate and get lost looking at his face. He ordered more drinks. Her slightly raised eyebrow causing them both to laugh. The music volume was louder and people began to arrive.

It felt wonderful to be outside in the early summer, writing a chapter in their story. Julia paused for a moment and reminded herself to look around and capture the moment, to store it away. She was here with him, after all these years.

"Just one moment, I'll be back," she kissed her fingers and touched his lips. She excused herself from the table and wended her way around tables to the restroom.

Returning from the bathroom, she stood in the door way to the terrace. There was someone in her seat. Slivers of ice seemed to have lodged somewhere in her heart. A man. No not just any man. She recognized the blue shirt from the morning. Damn it, what should she do? It was obvious Stefano hadn't been there alone. Her half empty glass of gin and tonic, and the plate of antipasto told their own story. The man looked up from his conversation, his eyes moving around as if searching for the recent occupant of the chair.

Julia smiled weakly as his eyes found hers. She took a step forward. Here was her opportunity to step out of the shadows. She would not play the role of a secret lover. This was not some tawdry affair. There was so much more here than some illicit affair.

"If it were done . . . then well it were done quickly," she thought, not daring to look at Stefano. Not knowing if what she was about to do was right or wrong.

"Julia! Julia!" Hands reached out and grabbed her around the waist, spinning her to face inwards. "What are you doing here?" "Great to see you!" She was caught up in a flurry of kisses and embraces. "Come eat with us, Ally and Vittorio will be here soon too. We came by your place to get you but you were out, obviously! We were going to text you when we got here, but now we don't need to."

She had never felt more relieved to see some friendly faces. The momentary reprieve had brought her back to her senses. There would be no honor from a confrontation. Nothing good would come from that.

Marco headed out onto the terrace to find a table. Francesca squeezed her hand, sensing that something wasn't right. Julia looked at her and shook her head. "Not now," she whispered. "Not now." Francesca nodded, keeping hold of her hand as they followed Marco through the tables. Of course, there was only one free. Of course, it was right next to the one she had just left.

Surreptitiously she slipped her bag from the back of the chair next to her and moved it to the one she was now sitting at. Her eyes glanced across at Stefano. His face was blank, expressionless as he leaned toward the man in the blue shirt.

Vittorio, Marco's brother and his partner Alessandra, arrived at the table. Julia had met them both when she visited Marco in Rome some years ago. Greetings, exclamations and more kisses caused a disturbance that drew attention.

Julia studiously avoided looking at Stefano, but she could feel his eyes on her. "Oh God," she thought, "what will the waiter say?"

She soon found out that discretion was a requirement of the job. The waiter took her order for a gin and tonic with studied politeness. A slight tilt of his head betraying his confusion. Their table was noisy and while Julia joined in the laughter, she was constantly aware of the table beside her. She could feel them, discordant and unsettling.

She heard the blue shirted man ask Stefano who he was with and leaned back to hear his response. "Just a friend, who had to go. I was about to go myself when you walked in."

The man looked at him. "Oh" she heard him say. "Well good, have you time for another?"

"Ahh . . . sure." The man continued talking, now he speaking about plans for the weekend, a family gathering. Was Stefano coming?

Julia felt hollow. If she needed proof that Stefano had a life with a family and all the connections that went with that, then here it was. Proof in the physical form of a man in a blue shirt.

A thought quickly followed, "What if the blue shirted man was meeting people here? Oh God." She thought, What if . . . She felt her heart pounding in her chest, her skin clammy. What would she do if the other woman arrived? The woman he lived with, had a family with, shared his life with. What would Stefano do?

Her attention was broken by Francesca nudging her. "There is someone at the door looking at you? Do you know them?"

Julia turned, just in time to see Lars striding across the terrace toward them. "Oh shit, could this evening get any worse?" she muttered. Francesca looked at her in surprise. Julia realized her mistake. "Sorry. I'll explain later."

"Julia!" Lars was at the table. "I found you." The satisfaction in his voice annoyed her. "We haven't finished our conversation. Can we talk, Please."

Julia was acutely aware of the eyes looking at her. All of them. Marco and Vittorio looked like they were about to stand up. Julia didn't dare look at Stefano.

"It's okay, please don't get up," she held up a hand to her friends. "This is, ummm, an old friend." Marco's raised eyebrows and look of concern suggested he knew very well there was something lacking in that description.

"Would you like to join us?" there was no invitation in Marco's voice.

"Yes I will do." Lars needed no invitation.

For a moment Julia was frozen. "No. No," Julia stood up and pushed past Lars, nearly falling in her haste. "I'll speak to you outside."

"I'll be back in a minute," she said to her friends, loud enough to be heard beyond her table. Out of the corner of her eye, she saw Stefano begin to stand.

"Oh God, please don't say anything, Not now, not here," she pleaded silently. Trying to communicate all that in a single glance, before she turned on her heel and moved toward the exit.

Standing outside the bar, her anxiety had turned to anger. "Lars you have to stop following me."

"Come with me Julia," he began, as though she hadn't said a word. "Say goodbye to your friends and come with me. I'll take care of you and I won't ever speak of Italy again. I love you."

Julia looked at him. She had spent three years waiting to hear that sentence. Waiting for him to call it what it was. But it was too late and what he felt was not love, not really. He wanted to possess her, not to love her. Obedience and compliance. Julia waited for the hurt and anger to give shape to her words. To send barbs toward him in return for all of his words that were intended to maim and wound. But they wouldn't come because it was not anger she felt, just indifference.

"No," her voice was clear rather than sharp. "I'm sorry, Lars. I know you think you love me. And maybe you do. In your way. But love is only real when it is offered freely with no conditions. And that is something you weren't ever able to offer me. And it's not what you are offering me now." She looked at him. "I'm not coming with you, Lars, you have to go now."

He went to protest, but Julia was no longer listening. Stefano had stepped outside the bar. Lighting a cigarette, he moved to stand beside her. There was a roaring in her ears.

"Is everything okay, Signora?" his voice was soft but there was no mistaking the threat.

Lars took a step toward him. "Everything is fine here. Mind your own business."

"The lady is asking you to go. I think she has made that clear."

Lars looked at Julia and then back at Stefano. "It's him isn't it?" he hissed. "I should have known. I should have known you'd go running to him the minute you could. I was right, you were always his. We never had a chance."

The desire to protest died on Julia's lips. Let him think what he liked. All she wanted was for Lars to go away. For Stefano to take her in his arms and for this evening to be over. But right now she would settle for Lars leaving. She no longer cared what he thought of her. That would never change, she realized, he would always find a way to think the worst of her.

It was always right there, just below the surface. Well now he has his proof, she realized. She looked at Lars and shrugged. "It doesn't matter what you think. I no longer have the energy to explain myself. But if you want to know," she knew there was danger in what she was about to say, but it was the only way to convince him. He would go away filled with righteous justification and she would be free. "You were right. There was never a choice. It's always been him."

"Julia?" Francesca's voice reached out from the doorway. She had watched the scene playing out, these two men and Julia. Clearly all three of them knew each other in some way.

"Are you okay? Shall I call for Marco?"

Julia turned and shook her head. Touching Stefano's arm, his hand covered hers briefly before he nodded toward the door. "Go inside. I'll talk with you later."

Reaching Francesca, Julia took her hand, realizing she didn't have to say anything. Curious she might be, Francesca would keep her own counsel about all that had transpired.

The two men stood looking at each other. As Lars curled his lip and opened his mouth, Stefano put up his hand, "You can think what you like. But anything you say will do you no honor." Stefano smiled, "Julia deserves more than you or I can give her." Crushing his cigarette on the ground, he turned and walked back into the bar. Passing by Julia's chair, his hand briefly touched her shoulder, and they exchanged a quick tight smile.

More drinks and pizza had appeared on the table while she had been gone. Looking at the food, she wondered if she could eat. Her stomach still roiling, as her senses stretched out beside her. A quiet conversation was in progress. Hearing the chair scrape backwards, she was bumped by the man as he stood.

"Ah excuse me, Signora," his quick smile turned puzzled as he looked at her carefully. Had he recognized her from the morning? It was clear from the earlier welcomes that she had been an unexpected addition to the table beside him. The man looked at Stefano and back at Julia. His mouth tightened. Leaning across the table he clasped Stefano's hand and said something she couldn't hear. Stefano shrugged. She received another hard stare before they both walked from the terrace.

Now there was a dilemma, how could she extricate herself from the group without causing offense.

Francesca was there to rescue her. "Oh I am tired!" she yawned. "Marco kept me up all night with his snoring." They all laughed as Marco expressed mock horror. "Francesca! How can you say that! It's not my fault if you cook so well and I eat too much! And anyway, if you are going to say I kept you up all night can you please tell a different story. I don't mind if you embellish it a little."

Taking her cue from Francesca, Julia yawned as well. "Me too, it's been fantastic to see you. But I think it's time for me to head home." With promises to see each other soon, maybe in Australia too, Julia left the restaurant and stepped out into the amber lit street.

Half an hour had passed since Stefano had left. Not sure where he might be, she began to retrace her steps. Passing a large doorway, a hand reached out to take her arm. Twirling around, she found herself pulled into a tight embrace.

"I didn't know what to do," his voice muffled in her hair. "When Gino stepped onto that terrace, I panicked. God, Julia," running his hands through his hair. "And then that guy, I couldn't leave you out there alone. Not with what you'd said about him. I couldn't bear it, no matter what might have happened, I want to have you by me. I want you. What am I going to do?" he trailed off.

"I can't answer that question for you. When we are together, we are one person, one soul. But I can't be part of this story if there are other people in it. I can't."

The scene at the restaurant had shaken her, but now she was sure of one thing. She had to live by her own words of freedom and love. She knew that now. No matter the whispers from her heart as it tried to find a way through the waves that threatened to drown her.

There was no question or doubt in her voice or her words. He wondered what it might be like to fall into it, to let go and let it carry him away. He knew it would turn his life upside down. He was as unable to step away as he was to move toward her.

Coming back to the moment, she was watching him, a soft smile on her lips, and sadness in her eyes. Raising her hand to his lips he kissed it, then turning it over, placed his lips in the centre of her palm. The kiss softer, longer, she moved her hand so her fingers could slip into his mouth. He bit them gently, watching her eyes lose focus for just a moment, as his tongue swirled around her fingertips. Letting them go, he took her hand and tucked it into the crook of his arm.

"Gelato?" he ventured, trying to bring the evening back to some sort of balance.

Julia looked up, her nose wrinkling with delight, willingly stepping into the feeling he was trying to create. "Well it is impossible to say no to ice cream!"

"Come with me, Bimba, let's get a gelato and then I will take you to bed."

Her heart took a little skip as she walked beside him. Determined to drink in each moment, burn each kiss into her heart. His laugh echoed in the street. The tension of the evening receded. Her enthusiasm for life was infectious and he found himself wondering if all she promised really was possible. They walked slowly back to the apartment. The sweetness of the ice cream in their mouths. He liked how there could be an easy silence between them and then words would flow, and hours would pass.

He remembered the long car drive they had taken when they were first together, when she had needed to leave the country to have her visa renewed. His stomach tightened at the thought of losing her, of losing her again. Back then it had seemed only logical to drive for hours and have lunch at some tiny restaurant in the mountains of Switzerland.

Blueberry gnocchi, they had eaten for lunch. Then on the drive back she had leant across the car and unzipped his pants. The memory of it stirred him. This constant level of instant reaction could cause him some issues.

As though sensing his thought, she reached for his gelato and stuck out her tongue, taking a long lick. He lent forward to create space in his jeans which had suddenly begun to feel too tight. Closing his eyes, he shook his head and blew out through his nostrils.

"What's up?" Julia's blue eyes bright. "What are you thinking about?" Dropping her gaze lower and raising her eyebrows a little as she noticed his discomfort. "Oh!" came the soft exclamation. She grinned at him. Composing her face. "How far away are we?"

Throwing their ice creams in the nearest bin, Stefano pulled her into a narrow side street that was quiet. Holding her fast against him, his kisses were hard and hot. She was startled at first, though her body's reaction was well ahead of her thoughts. It was instant, instinctual, and immediate. His mouth on hers was making her knees tremble and any coherent thought fell away.

Turning her so her back was against the wall, his hand slid down her side, moving around to slip under her dress, seeking the soft warmth between her legs. Julia felt with aching certainty every move of his fingers as they found the lace of her underwear and began to stroke her through the flimsy fabric. Her body arched against him, as she felt the warmth begin to flood through her.

"My God, I want to take you here," Stefano groaned, bending his head to the neckline of her dress. Pushing aside the material, allowing his mouth to meet the soft cup of her bra. Julia pushed her breast toward his mouth, aching for the feel of his mouth. His fingers began to move in slow circles, pressing through the fabric. He could feel the desire heating. Holding his head to her breast, it was all she could do to not dissolve right there.

The banging of a door further down the alleyway brought them to an abrupt halt. Stefano stepped back, and she nearly fell over. Taking her arm, he steadied her and steered her back out to the street. He wondered what would have happened if they had not been disturbed. Whatever it was between them at times felt almost dangerous, as though it had no interest in social niceties. They were not in their twenties anymore and yet here they were.

The morning sun had just begun to peek its way over the edge of the horizon. Julia stretched languorously on the bed. Long fingers of golden light lay across her body, still half in shadow.

The sense of lightness from the evening before was there still. Along with another feeling, of being in a space that was not quite of this world, a world between worlds. What was it about Italy that made her feel as though the rest of the world didn't exist, didn't matter. She didn't have that feeling anywhere else, only here. Stealing a few moments before he woke to study his face, an idea began to curl around her thoughts.

Closing her eyes, she took a deep breath, not wanting to give it time to become more than a whisper. She was not ready to entertain that thought. She wasn't quite sure what would happen next, but she was fairly certain that to live beyond this moment was folly. Julia wondered if it was like this for others, other women in particular. Was it the stuff that sent them flying to Greece like Shirley Valentine or heading to Bali and finding love?

Moments in life when you went hunting in the past for a map, a way, a rehearsal, a sign of how things might be. How one was. Especially when there were not just storms but cyclones or when life felt like a prison and time like a sentence. Clues from the past for the way forward, even just the next step or to sip another breath, and then another, because those memories offered, if not a well-lit, well-traveled road, then at least a path from one place to another. Perhaps that's why she was here. With another deep breath, she opened her eyes, this time to find him looking at her.

"Good morning *cara mia*," he said.

"Good morning," she stretched her arms.

"How did you sleep?"

"Very well, you?"

The corners of his eyes crinkled slightly, matching his lips. He nodded. There was a hooded sleepiness to his gaze that was just so intoxicating, as if every moment was somehow an invitation to lean in closer.

"Julia, I have to go. What will you do?"

Shifting slightly to face him, she slipped her hands under her cheek. "I don't know. I didn't really have an itinerary. I just came to see you."

That wasn't what he had asked. Not really. It wasn't the day to day that required a response. But she couldn't give him what he wanted. She couldn't give him permission to go with grace. He ran the tip of his finger along the ridge above her eye, following her cheek bone and down to her lips. Julia opened them slightly and he felt a tightening in his lower belly and a tingling that settled a little further south. She pulled his finger into her mouth and took it gently between her teeth, trapping it, then her tongue began to very slowly swirl around the tip.

It was so erotic that he immediately felt himself respond. Julia watched as his eyes deepened like dark pools of liquid and the desire ran across his face.

"Julia," he said, "What are you doing to me?"

She let the corners of her mouth tilt upwards in a response, never letting go of his finger. Very slowly she began to suck on it, bringing his finger further into her mouth.

He groaned, unable to stop the aching need that rose in him, that was always there when he thought of her. He moved closer to her, capturing her mouth with his as she released his finger, his tongue pushing deeper in search of hers. Every now and then she would capture it and suck at it. It was ridiculous how she could make him lose all sense of time and reason. His hand slid down her side, following the line of her breasts, then the curve of her waist and around the swelling of her hip.

She pushed against him. As his fingers moved toward the place between her thighs, he could tell why. The sensation was intense and he kissed her not wanting her to stop. She shifted slightly, pushing him onto his back. Ever so slowly she slid down onto him. She held him tight for what seemed like forever, but it was only a moment before her hips began to rock slowly back and forward. Her breath coming short and sharp as she moved herself along him. He grabbed hold of her hips, guiding the rhythm and trying to hold on to the growing sensation. His breath joined her ragged breathing as she moved faster, pushing against him. He felt her more than he heard her, feeling her tighten around him as she called out, as he followed her, shuddering against her as they both dissolved into the bliss.

As she went to move, his arms tightened. "Don't move." His eyes still closed. She kissed his nose, then his cheeks, nipping at his chin. His hands tightened on her waist and then he ran his fingertips lightly, tickling her. She squirmed and laughed, not able to decide whether to come closer or pull away.

"I had forgotten how ticklish you are," he said through his own soft laughter. "Okay I'll stop, I'll leave you in peace."

She turned her face up to look at him.

"There will never be peace."

His breath caught in his throat. There was something in her face that made him feel as though time was some sort of construct that didn't belong to them. That maybe they had known each other before, in a different time and place. His mind slipped away from that thought. He usually didn't find himself here, but her presence made him fanciful, it made him feel as though dreams were possible and that the life he had imagined for himself might also still be possible.

The buzzing sound emanating from his jacket brought him back into the present and pushed him toward the very near future. He slid out of the bed and pulled on his trousers.

Pulling back the sheet, he ran his hand along her side, marvelling at the curves and shapes that seemed so familiar to him, though it had been decades since he'd done this. He felt the sharp intake of breath, her body remembering this touch as much as his hand had reached to do it.

Then he was gone.

37

Fear to Tread

After he left, she felt agitated.

What had the Healing Hare said? "Why are you going back into the past?" She had mentioned love, loss, pain, and incredible hope. That's pretty much what shaped this story, thought Julia.

Unable to stay in the apartment, she walked to Ponte Pietra. The bridge had been blown up by the retreating Germans during the Second World War.

The Veronese people painstaking collected the stones from the river Adige and rebuilt it.

Like this story with Stefano, thought Julia. It had been blown up, perhaps she could collect stones from the river of sadness that threatened to engulf her.

No. Julia had to stop thinking like that. Despite the fact that Hermione had pulled the card Patience from the tarot deck in that seaside cottage. Patience for what? Patience was a distraction. She had to face facts. She had to struggle against the flame of hope that it quietly sparked. She wouldn't give herself the luxury of waiting. No matter what the cards said. No matter what advice the Healing Hare had offered. Julia knew she would be foolish to hang on to something that clearly was never going to be enough. Her conversation with Hermione early that afternoon had unfolded in much the same way.

Julia couldn't decide who was the biggest idiot.

"He clearly is!" Hermione shouted, loyally, through the screen. "There's no doubt about that!"

Julia smiled. There is also no doubt that the unconditional support of friends is something to be treasured.

"No seriously," Hermione continued, "You're not making a fool of yourself. You, my lovely friend, have traveled across the world for love. You have opened yourself up to love. You have been so incredibly courageous. You set out on this journey, even knowing that it may not take you where you think you want it to go. But I can assure you, whatever happens, this has to have been worth it. Look!" she said waving a card, "The Fool. This is the beginning of a journey for you. I don't know if Stefano is waiting for you at the end of the journey or if he is the catalyst. Maybe he has the role of making you realize that love is truly worth the adventure. You had to believe in this love to set out on this journey, to bring yourself back into the centre of your life. You've followed your heart, after so many years doing it all on your own. And this one," she continued, "Patience. The journey has begun and time is all it needs to unfold."

Hermione was willing her friend all the strength and courage she could muster to face any disappointment. Julia smiled at the support pouring through the screen.

Hermione was right. It had been worth it. Even if heartbreak was at the end of it, it was right to have taken the risk and come. It was right for her heart, it was right for her soul. Whatever the outcome.

She tried to explain this to Hermione. "I can't afford patience. I can't afford the hope. I just can't," Julia's eyes had filled with tears. "I can't hope." Breathing slowly and carefully, she said, "It's hopeless and I just have to accept that. I know I want him. I want things to be different. But they aren't. We both know it." She trailed off, her chest lifting with the breath.

She knew it would take some time to create that alchemy where sorrow, no matter how bitter, would arrive, eventually, at something piercingly sweet. The delicate dance where love and pain, joy and sorrow, beauty, and brutality coexist. It was there.

She felt it every time she walked the streets of this city that she loved. A lifeline that would pull her from the bitter to where it would meld with the sweet. Even though right now she wasn't quite ready.

"Let's remember, I came here not knowing if I would even see him. I just knew I had to come. This whole trip has been about something else as well as him." Julia shrugged, "I know it would be easy to place the success or failure of this trip on whether I even saw him. Let alone . . ." Julia waved her hand. She wasn't talking to Stella who'd go into all the raunchy details of the close encounter, this was Hermione. "But I have to focus on the reality that's in front of me."

"You know," said Hermione, "some people have relationships like that, that are secret."

Julia nodded, "Yes I said to him, that I was kept in his secret drawer. That I had been there his whole life. He knows I am always there . . ."

"Do you want to stay there?" Hermione wondered, "Marriage is not all romance. You know what it's like living with someone day in day out. It's not all excitement and passion. There are people who only want the romance and passion but not the arguments over who left the dirty dishes in the sink and day-to-day decisions. Some people are happy to be a lover." She was trying to make it sound reasonable.

Momentarily it seemed less apocalyptic than losing him forever, even somewhat tempting, but they both knew deep down that it would never be right.

Julia sighed. "I can't do that. I couldn't do it thirty years ago. And I can't now, I am not willing to live like that. I mean, let's be honest. It's not as if I didn't know. I guess I just didn't realize how much he was unwilling to change things." Julia paused because this was the part that cut her deeply. "I suppose I justified seeing him and making love with him because I thought that maybe it would be enough to remind him of what we had together." Julia felt the tears slipping down her cheeks. "I didn't expect him to leave his life on the basis of a video call with someone on the other side of the world. But I guess I hoped when he saw me it would remind him of what we can be together. But it wasn't enough. I wasn't enough." Her cheeks puffed out as the breath left them.

"Don't let this heartbreak break your belief in yourself," Hermione urged her friend. "You are enough. You are more than enough. Look at you. You're smart. Accomplished. You have looked after your family for years; you have built a career around supporting them. You have deep lifelong friendships." She breathed confidence back into her friend with all her will. "Maybe Stefano is the catalyst to make you believe in love enough to leave your life and come back to Italy. Maybe Stefano is a way to remind you what love can be even if he can't offer it himself."

"Thank you for not letting us be anything but honest with each other. And thank you for letting me dream." But Julia sounded deflated.

"Dream! You are the most optimistic and hope filled person I know. I don't want you to get too caught up in the sadness. He isn't free to be with you. Deep down, we knew that all along. But we had to make space for that dream take shape. The dream of building a life in Italy with this man you love. To see if it were possible."

"There is the longing for him, to be with him. But there is also a longing that brings me back to myself as I was before the bigger things of life began to take over," Julia said through tears. "My youth, my freedom, before children, careers, marriage, deaths. You know. All the fun stuff," Julia smiled through her tears and Hermione smiled back sympathetically.

"The sadness is what makes us make art. You know. It's how the light gets in."

They spoke the same language. Julia could appreciate her friend's intention to offer her hope in a hopeless situation. To bring some light through the cracks of her broken heart.

Had she been wrong to let him go the first time? Had she been wrong to leave, all those years ago? Julia remembered boarding the plane, tears streaming down her face. Sobbing as though her heart was breaking. It did break. Shattered into a thousand tiny shards. Perhaps she had come back to collect those pieces. To put herself back together like the Japanese art Kintsugi in the hope that the lines of gold would be made of love. A sense of loss ripped at her. She was not ready to place Stefano in the role of catalyst for a life without him. Not ready to let go of the possibility of having this love.

All through the stolen moments spent with Stefano in the past week, when he had spoken about the people they had known, she had been filled with a sense of regret. Regret that she hadn't believed in love enough to stay. She felt an ache for the time they had missed. For what might have been.

As Julia began the longer descent from the castle on the hilltop, the tears began to quietly slip down her face until they became a river. Stepping through the streets, she came across the old building of the Youth Hostel. Leaning against the locked gates, she could see the terrace that led to the garden. She was on the outside looking in. Knowing that just out of sight were the stairs where he had asked her to come with him into the garden.

Julia was right to have left the first time and she would be right to leave again. She was not going to be someone's secret lover. But it hurt so much that she held herself tightly. Part of her wondered at the force of the feelings, another part held no surprise. This was what it meant to be human. To take risks and to love with all our heart.

"Why can't it be simple," she thought. "Peace and quiet are dead people's goals, remember." Julia's face shifted into a wry smile, though the tears kept falling. She didn't want dead people's goals. But right now, they seemed a safer choice than the one she had made.

She didn't want to leave, but she had to. "For now," whispered the tiny voice inside. "For now."

CHAPTER

38

Despair and Deception

The bells pushed her out of bed. Julia had planned lunch with Chiara, which was probably better than wallowing in her misery. Their friendship had begun in the bakery, laughing together at Julia's attempts to speak Italian and Chiara's even more basic English.

They met at a restaurant overlooking Ponte Pietra, Marco's suggestion. But the menu was full of fish and offal.

"I think we chose the wrong restaurant," said Julia, looking at the menu, wrinkling her nose. "Will we look bad if we leave?"

Chiara nodding, looked at her. "To hell with it," she said. "We can do what we want."

Chiara made some comment about having made a mistake with the location after receiving a phone call. The waiter had nodded. Clearly not very interested in the needs and wants of two women in their midlife. He had waved away their offer to pay for the water that was already on the table. They stepped out onto the street and burst out laughing. They ducked into the bar a few doors down. Julia inhaled sharply. The same one as before. She had a photo of herself standing on this terrace overlooking the water, wrapped in Stefano's arms. Without him by her side, it felt wrong, all the emotions from the night before swelled up and her eyes filled. Blinking rapidly, she looked at the menu. They ordered some food and Chiara suggested a beer. It was hot.

"So what's been going on?" Julia smiled. "Only thirty years to catch up on."

Chiara had recently decided to leave her husband. They had been together for eighteen years and she had grown fed up with his unwillingness to take her wishes into account. His refusal to travel, to change, to grow. "And," Chiara said, "the fact he was a dickhead." Julia snorted her drink as she laughed. It seemed the problems between people were the same the world over.

"You have already made the hardest decision," Julia said encouragingly. "I know everything seems hard now. That you are juggling too many things. These difficulties will pass. I promise you."

Chiara nodded, though Julia could see she was only partly convinced.

"So. Did you see Stefano while you were here?"

Julia sighed. She knew it was a question that would come up at some point. Chiara had an idea that Julia had always held something in her heart for him. She had always wondered why Julia had left.

"He already has a life with someone else." Julia said flatly. "Like the time when we first met. It was the reason I left." Julia looked at Chiara, "Different woman, same story." She shrugged. "I think I have always loved him. But I won't be a second choice or a side. A mistress. I can't live like that."

Chiara screwed her face up and hesitated for a moment. Then she shared that she had a similar issue. When she younger, she had been in love with a boy. They had been together for two years but then he left her. "Since then, I have always thought about him."

Julia found herself wondering if there was always a story, in everyone's past. A story of love so great that it could never be forgotten, and yet could never be.

Chiara continued. "He even called me on my wedding day to wish me well. I cried because I didn't want to get married, I wanted to be with him," Chiara confessed. "We have had a friendship all these years. But I want to be with him. I want him to be mine. But he is married. They have children who are still at school. He won't leave them. He won't break up the family. I told him I loved him. That I'd always loved him. I'm glad I did."

Her eyes filled with tears and Julia's welled up too.

"Did you tell Stefano you loved him? That you would come to Italy for him?"

Julia nodded. "Yes, I told him and even though it didn't make any difference, I do feel sure that it was important to say the things like that. Because no one knows what might happen in life from one day to the next. You have to live it. Not just exist. No matter the risks."

Chiara was nodding her head emphatically. "Exactly Julia. *Brava!* We must live this way. There is no other way. Love is all we have, it's all we are."

When they got up to leave, Chiara said, "You are the only one that knows, Julia. Not even my friends here know."

"Don't worry Chiara. I won't say anything."

"I don't talk about it to anyone, for the respect I must show to his family."

"So, I am assuming you are seeing each other?"

Chiara nodded. "Yes. Whenever we can. It's not enough. But it's all I have right now."

Julia could feel that comment slide in between her ribs and take her breath.

"But Julia, why did you leave the first time? If you had stayed, maybe he would have left his girlfriend. He did eventually leave her, didn't he?"

Julia nodded. And the feeling of nausea rose up in her. She felt sick about it. It was a loss she could not fix. She had been feeling sick for days.

But she had to put these thoughts to one side. To think like that would take her to the edge of madness. She couldn't regret all the beautiful things in her life. People she would have never known. The friendships she would never have had. Her children would never have been born. Those thoughts about whether she should have stayed were of no use to her.

"Chiara, you know, I can't rewrite the past. As much as it may be one of my greatest regrets. I can't regret my life. The people and the places I have known are because of the life I have had. And my children, the most beautiful gifts of life's longing for itself. Like you and your son. I know you wouldn't change having him for the world. We can't go back in time. We can't live our lives forever with the what ifs. The only thing we can do now is in the present. We can only be courageous and let things unfold. Sometimes it's hard to speak the truth. Especially when you know it will hurt other people. But we have only one life to live."

Chiara was nodding again, "Yes, you're right of course. We have only one life and that is why the day I woke up and looked at myself in the mirror and asked myself if I was truly deeply happy, that was the day I knew I needed to leave my marriage."

Julia reached out and squeezed her hand. "See, you have already made the hardest decision. You've already done the most difficult thing. The rest is simply logistics. And you will get through them. Bit by bit. I know you will."

Her head down, Chiara glanced up at Julia through her lashes. "You really think so?"

Julia nodded. "Yes, I promise. You will be okay because you know life is precious. You have chosen life over just existing. Sure, it's going to take some time and it will require some strength. But you will be okay. And I will be there on the other end of the phone when it's late at night and you don't have anyone to speak to. I'll be there." Julia resolved to stay in touch.

After lunch, Julia found her way to Piazza delle Erbe. Sitting a bar outside, she twirled her glass, watching the fading sunlight shine through the stands in the marketplace. The stall in front of her was closing. The women were chatting as they packed up. There was something about the way they interacted. Julia was reminded of time stretching backwards. Women had always worked together, taking care of others; children, partners, family. She could see the satisfaction in their faces. There was a sense of personal accomplishment in the way they moved around the stand.

Home. It was a strange word. It no longer held any meaning for her if it ever had. Perhaps Julia felt it more keenly because she was on her own. Maybe couples who created a family home together keep that sense of it when their children leave. Her parents had divorced when she was eleven and from that time neither parent had successfully created a place that held the archetypal energy of home.

She wasn't sure if she had missed something important. A way to be grounded, centred in one place. She shivered at the thought. Perhaps the lack of roots had freed her to roam the world. Freed her to find an internal sense of home. It was an interesting thought that she began to turn over in her mind. It made a lot of sense.

The longest time in one place before now was London, where she had lived with Hugh, where her girls had been born. There had been a sense of community in the street. Julia remembered the parties, especially at Christmas, when every neighbor would host a gathering from Christmas Eve to the New Year as the dark days of winter stretched ahead.

Perhaps that had been the time and place where home had meant something recognizable. But even that had come to an end. Just as this time would. She could feel it within her. The need to return to Europe. She would prefer to live in Italy but perhaps England would do. If Stefano never . . .

That was a thought she couldn't follow right now. It might take longer than a year. But she would begin to make plans for possibilities and slowly begin this shift to whatever life awaited her next.

Julia was pretty sure why her mind had run down that path. She could feel herself shifting and sifting through what was important. Adjustments in her mind and her heart. Whatever happened or didn't with Stefano, Julia yearned to be in Italy. Her heart and soul belonged here. If she couldn't be with him, then being here would be her solace.

Her flight was leaving the day after tomorrow. What would he come for? Another goodbye. No, it was better to slip away. Less fuss. Goodbyes were usually full of fuss. She hated fuss. No. It would be better this way. Sunday morning, early, she would be on her way. Home.

Marco and Francesca came by to take her for one last pizza. It was a beautiful evening. The lights of Castello Vecchio, the old castle, had just come on and the air wrapped around them like a soft blanket. Julia's phoned pinged as the pizzas arrived at the table.

Stefano—*"Ciao"*

Marco looked sideways as she pulled out her phone. She threw him a quick smile before typing a short response.

Julia—*"Ciao"*

Stefano—*"Are you out?"*

Julia—*"Yes, pizza with friends. Are you coming tomorrow?"*

Stefano—*"If you would like me to."*

Julia—*"Yes."*

Putting her phone away, Julia looked up to see Marco watching her. Before Marco could say anything, Francesca cut across him. "A woman is entitled to her secrets."

Julia grinned at her in gratitude as Marco rolled his eyes. "Fine. As long as it's not that guy from before." Which guy might be more accurate. Marco would not like either option. Julia grimaced. She laughed a bit louder to cover her reaction and she picked up her glass.

Francesca had wondered. Her mind went back to the previous night. Julia had not been there by chance. There had been someone there. The man, the one who had been staring. The one who had followed her out of the bar and then returned after she came back in. Julia knew Francesca had noticed it all and understood. Intuited, as women do. She shook her head to warn her. It was received with an equally imperceptible nod.

Stefano—*"Are you home safely?"*

Julia—*"Yes."*

Stefano—*"I'm coming by scooter tomorrow. Let's meet somewhere."*

"Oh," thought Julia, "so you don't even want to make love to me again." Somewhere public. Somewhere safe. Somewhere that will let us be civilised. Friendly. False.

Stefano—*"Let's see each other somewhere that's not right in the centre. It's difficult. If we could see each other, let's say at Castel San Pietro. That would be faster and easier for me."*

"Difficult for you," she thought but she typed something different.

Julia—*"Right at the top? At the Castle?"*

Stefano—*"Yes! Let's do that."*

Julia—*"Okay let's meet there. Where we used to go."*

Stefano—*"You can take the stairs near the Roman theatre."*

Julia knew how to get there. She had already retraced the steps of the past several times this week.

Julia—*"Yes I can. The funicular doesn't start until 10 a.m. Damn it!"*

Stefano—*"There's a funicular? I didn't know about it."*

Julia—*"It is more convenient than the stairs!"*

Stefano—*"Exercise!"*

Julia—*"What are you saying! That I need exercise :)"*

Stefano—*"We all do!"*

Julia—*"Diplomat!"*

Stefano—*"Eh Yes."*

Julia could see he was trying to make the conversation lighter. Playful. Playful in a very different way to how he used to. How they used to be.

He was careful not to take things in a direction that he could not go. He knew it would take only a moment for him to fall into the desire that simmered just below the surface. It was more important than ever that she thought he didn't want her. So she could let go.

He pictured her sitting outside on her balcony where they had drunk coffee. Listening to the sounds of life in the city. She was texting him about the moon.

Julia—*"The moon has always held power in our lives. She represents emotions, feelings and, usually, women."*

Stefano—*"But can we understand what happens on the dark side of the moon, or in women?"*

Julia—*"I would say the moon has the power to reflect the dreams of humanity. And woman hold the secrets of life. So, the moon, like a woman, holds the dreams and secrets which we have hidden. Perhaps even from ourselves. Let me know when you leave tomorrow."*

Stefano—*"Okay."*

Julia put down her phone. Filled with rage at the unfairness of love and the lies of hope, she turned off the lights. Sleep came blessedly quickly. Though with it came the dawn. Her last full day and the last time she would see him.

CHAPTER

39

To the Castle

The streets of Verona were cool in the quiet of the early morning. The sun was up and the tops of the buildings glowed with the promise of heat. At the bottom of the steps was a small bar. Stepping inside she ordered a coffee macchiato. A few sips and she was done.

The steps leading up to the castle were quiet. Julia took her time, wanting to arrive looking presentable, rather than flustered. She stopped to gaze at the view. Of all the places she knew in Italy, Verona was her favorite. A psychologist would probably call that year in Verona a formative experience, and they would be right. Italy had found its way into her heart. Perhaps it had been a key. A way of finding herself or part of herself. Her studies. Her work. Her thoughts about the world. Italian, her second language. And him.

Verona was where he had opened her heart. And then crushed it, she reminded herself. Just like he was doing right now. Perhaps she should be raging at him for deceiving her. For wooing her back into love with him all through the last year. For making her feel things for him that she had put away in that box of old memories. But the anger wouldn't come. She could feel the numbness hovering around the edges of her consciousness.

Protective. Comfortable. She had pulled it around her when Hugh died. When things were difficult with the children, it had helped her find a space to meet their rage with a semblance of calm. She had used it as a guard when she needed to push Lars away. Julia could feel it now, calling her heart like a siren. Resistance was all she could do now. This trip had been about dispelling that numbness. Stepping out into the world and risking feeling. Risking love. She did not want to live a life where she retreated into that space again. She wanted love. To love and to be loved. "Maybe a lake," she said to herself. "But not numb."

The sound of a scooter behind her made her turn. There he was. And there was no rage, no anger, no numbness. Only love.

Stefano thought it would be safer to see her in public. He would try not to touch her, try not to take her in his arms and make love to her again. Because he couldn't give her what she wanted. To make love with her again would just be selfish. It would be wrong. He knew it would take all his willpower, but it was all he could do. For her. For himself and for the people in their lives that depended on them. But he had not taken into account the memories that overwhelmed him as he took the road up past the old hostel. They flooded his mind as he rounded the corner and saw her standing there. silhouetted against the morning light. He remembered a night; she had come up to the hostel toward the end of the day. They would eat together, a group of them. Drinking wine and laughing, planning which bar they would go to. Often there was music. That night they had all stayed at the hostel longer than usual. He remembered, he had walked past her and made some comment.

She had looked at him with a smile that pierced straight to his heart. He took her hand, excusing her from the group. Telling them he had something he needed her for. And he did. He pulled her into the kitchen and locked the door. She had held him tightly as their breathing returned to normal. His face buried in her neck where he had tried to muffle his voice. They left the kitchen, Julia's hair falling around her shoulders. Dishevelled would be the right way to describe them. As they stepped back into the common room, it was probably clear to everyone what he had needed her for. A small smile had played on Julia's lips as they walked through to the reception area and out into the night. He would want her again before the dawn came. Unable to leave her alone no matter how hard he tried.

It was a memory that did not help him now.

They stood together as he pointed out the roof tops of various places and pieced together the movements of the past they had shared. He seemed so reserved. As though he was holding himself. As if a sudden movement might startle him. Startle him into what? Julia wondered.

The bittersweet feeling of this meeting threatened to overwhelm her at times. She was fighting down tears and trying to bite back words. Questions she already knew the answers to. Answers that made her feel despair. Sick. But she would hold it together because there was no other way. But she allowed herself to lean into him. To touch him. Trying to bring all her senses to bear. To remember this.

They sat for a while on the wall, warmed from the sun. It was there. He could feel it. The crackle of longing that flowed between them. Julia beside him, angled toward him. Running her fingers through his hair.

"They are not like before," he said.

Julia smiled at the translation, "No but they are still beautiful."

He tried not to think about that time in the kitchen where she had tangled her fingers in his hair. He spoke about an issue he had with his leg. Trying to think of something to distract himself from her hands. Her nearness. Trying to find ways to help her turn her face from him. She moved and then she was standing in front of him, cupping her hands around his face and bringing her mouth to his. Sympathy in her kiss. Maybe some sadness. She pointed to the scar that encircled her neck.

"This scar," she said, "is from thyroid cancer. I have to take medicine every day to keep me alive."

"What does the thyroid do?" he asked.

"Metabolism. Keeps everything working in the body. I have to take the hormones that I can no longer make for my metabolism and something to keep any rogue cells dormant." She laughed to make light of it. "I have to take a little more than I need. It should mean I can eat more chocolate! But it doesn't really."

They were both quiet for a moment. It was something to know the fallibility that came with age. When they met, they were young, there had been no room for that. Now it was different. Stefano looked at Julia. He saw in her face that it made no difference to her. That she would be there for him, no matter what happened. His heart felt full. He knew it was no small offering she made. Unspoken though it was. She had faced death already. Her own and someone she loved.

"This is what love feels like," he thought. "To be totally wrapped in love." His hands instinctively went to her hips, and he pulled her forward. She leaned her forehead against his.

They stood there for a moment. Knowing that there was another person on the earth, who would be there for them, no matter the circumstances. Love, in its purest form, that inexplicable combination of being blind as well as being acutely aware of the humanity of the other.

Stefano felt his eyes dampen. He blinked rapidly and he looked down, becoming aware of her breasts. Soft and close through the satin fabric of her top. It was all he could do to not bury his face in them. He gently pushed her away. Feeling rather than hearing her sigh as he did so. "The café should be open now," he said, not daring to look at her.

Julia took a step back away from him. Taking his arm, she moved beside him as they began to slowly cross the square toward the bar. He could feel her breast pressing into his arm. He knew it was deliberate. He wanted to pull her into his arms and kiss her until they could no longer breathe. He closed his eyes.

A few steps and they were in the cafe. Music was playing and Julia shimmied her shoulders and then her hips in appreciation of the song. Stefano laughed. He loved the way she moved. The way she would slip into some playful act, as though the years hadn't passed, as though they were still young, together. Full of possibility.

They sat at a small table overlooking the river. There was an ease between them, despite the moment. It would be easy to imagine they had been together always. That they could be together this way. Every now and then, a charge zapped through them, and their words or laughter would stop. The sun was bright and Stefano was glad she kept her sunglasses on. It was difficult to sit there and not touch her. Hard not imagine making love to her. He could feel the desire in his bones, his senses were attuned to every move she made. It was an aching that he now realized would never end. And yet. He couldn't. Somewhere within him there was a hard stone of sadness, of regret, of loss.

His sudden movement startled her. He reached out a hand, "I have to go now."

He had made it through this morning without falling to his knees and begging her to stay. He stepped onto the bike and pulled her in for one last kiss. Filling it with as much longing as he dared. And she was there, matching his longing with her own.

"We'll see each other soon."

Julia shrugged. Fighting back tears. "Sure," but she didn't know for sure. She didn't know if she could see him again.

She watched as he rode away. He looked back and waved as he turned the corner.

Julia felt her legs move her toward the wall. Stumbling, she reached out her hand to find the stone seat, tears blinding her.

CHAPTER

40

Unexpected Visitor

She had packed everything the night before and planned the journey to Milan Malpensa airport. Sitting on her balcony with a cup of coffee in hand, Julia found herself counting her breaths and she breathed in and out. It kept the panic at the edges and stopped her from fragmenting. She was leaving later that morning. Time enough to get ready before Marco was meeting her for breakfast in the piazza.

Her phone pinged. Perhaps Marco had changed the plans. Reaching for her phone, Julia flipped open the case.

"Ciao Julia. I'm here."

The message was not from Marco. Julia felt a flood of longing begin at her heart and spread until it reached the tips of her toes and fingers. She felt hot and shivery at the same time. Stefano. Stefano was here. Now.

Stefano—*"Can you let me in?"*

She pushed the door lock, hearing it open in the corridor below. Julia listened as his feet came up the stairs.

"Ciao, Julia."

"Ciao," she felt tongue tied. He had come. She knew she had been right.

"But why?" She stopped herself. Shut up Julia. Be the lake. "I was just about to have a shower. Give me five minutes? Help yourself to coffee. I won't be long, I promise."

Trying to calm her heartbeat and slow her racing thoughts. Why had he come? Why had he come? They had said everything that needed to be said the day before. He had reiterated that his life was his life and there would be no change. But here he was. Again.

Julia knew she had been right to come. No matter what happened now. She knew that something in him, something elemental, essential, eternal, longed for her. No matter what happened next, whether they ever met again, it was almost enough to know that.

She felt a slight change in the air. All of a sudden two hands slipped around her hips and she was pulled against a hard chest.

"Julia," he said into her ear, "I . . . I couldn't let you leave without seeing you one more time."

Her heart, already startled at the intrusion, started to race. He had not said something like that before, stepping into the space between them. After their last meeting, what she thought had been their last meeting, she had felt resigned, despairing that she would not see him again.

Julia knew she would have to step back. She would have to wrap him up again and tuck him into the cupboard in her memory that was for lazy afternoons and rainy days. But for now, he was here, and she felt she might completely unravel. It took a moment. A millisecond of his presence and the longing returned at full force.

Turning to face him, she slipped her arms around his neck and pulled his face to hers.

"Si," she sighed, "but now you're here."

Their kiss was long and deep, as though they were drawing energy from each other. She could feel her insides begin to melt and heat up. It would always be like this between them. His response was clear. His need was as obvious as hers.

"Mmmm," she said. The water made his curls darken and tighten around his head. She tilted her face up to look at him.

"It is always like this, enough just to see you, enough to touch you, and—"

He took her bottom lip in his teeth and gently pulled, then kissed her again. It was some minutes before either of them could speak again.

"All I know is when you are close to me, when I can see you, touch you, that becomes everything and I can't think of anything else. What am I meant to do, Julia?" Stefano's voice was strained, as though he was holding tightly to reality.

Julia looked up at him, the shower raining on her face. "I want you," was all she could say. "I want you always, but this has to stop. It's too much."

Stefano looked at her, the water had plastered her hair around her face. She looked fresh faced and young, as though the years between had never happened.

"It's as though all is well with the world and I am exactly where I should be," she continued. "But I'm not, am I? I mean you have made it really clear. You don't want to change your life. And unless something changes then this is all we will have. It's all we can have."

She stopped, trying to control her breathing. Stopping herself from changing what she needed to say. "I can't do it this way." She shook her head. "It's too hard for me. When I am with you it's as if the sun comes out and I feel wrapped up in warmth and possibility. But to know that in a few moments you will walk out the door and the sun will go behind a cloud. I can't live with that day in day out. I just can't."

Tears pricked her eyes again. Julia went to brush them away. But then she stopped herself. Let them fall. She thought. Let them fall. Things are what they are and will be what they will be.

CHAPTER

41

Risk Another Goodbye

Dressed now, they sat at the small table on the balcony, coffee cups in hand. Julia's tears had stopped except for an occasional tear that escaped. She could still feel the salt lines on her cheeks.

"Sometimes these arrangements work for people. But not for me. It is what it is."

Her tone was soft, colored with despair and longing. Stefano had said that the guilt of betrayal lay with him. But she knew it was hers to own too. Especially knowing he was not free, and he was not prepared to change his life. She sighed. What was left to do but say goodbye. Julia knew it would be impossible to put a fence around her feelings. But she had let them quietly sink below the surface of her conscious mind, once before, and she could do it again. It just felt sadder this time because time had taken a different form and love had become something as precious as breathing.

"Just go now," Julia whispered. "Just go and leave me. If you won't change your life, then this is too hard."

"I don't want to leave you like this," his voice was anguished, "Julia I can't do what you want. I can't change things, and I can't leave you like this."

His face dropped into his hands. It took everything in her to not reach out for him. Her knuckles were white with the strain of holding herself still.

"You have to go. Because there is no other option. I have to go to Milan and get on a plane. You have to go to work," she had nearly said home, but the word stuck her throat.

She was right. But he couldn't be brave. He couldn't let her go like last time. There would have to be a way to hold her in his life. He needed to know she was there. That there was someone in the world who thought of him. It felt selfish. But he didn't care. He felt if he didn't have that then life would have little color. That there would be nothing to hope for other than slipping away into oblivion.

There was no joy in her flight from Milan to Melbourne. She spent most of the time staring at nothing. Pushing the food around the small airplane tray. Declining the wine. Knowing that would be a bad idea.

PART
FOUR

Things Have Changed

CHAPTER

42

When He's Gone

The mornings were dark. The first fingers of dawn just shifting the night to a gloomy grey. Julia walked briskly to the gym. Hands in her pockets, scarf tight around her neck, shivering slightly. The cold she felt was as much internal as it was the weather.

It was hard to ignore his messages. They could have spent their whole life together. She had been ready to change her life, come what may. Even if it failed miserably. She would have gone to the other side of the world to be with him. But not like this, not as things were now.

He had done nothing to suggest he would make any changes in his life. He had done nothing aside from messaging her every day.

She realized he may never go quite as far away as before. She knew she would need to tell him to leave her alone. Leave her to make some space where he had been. Julia shrugged on her winter coat and left the gym, letting the door swing shift behind her as gasped in the cold air. As she stepped onto the sand, Julia felt an ache in her chest.

"But not yet. Not just yet," whispered her heart.

Closing her eyes, she filled her lungs with the early morning air, cold and slightly salty. "But soon," cautioned her mind. "Soon."

The cold wet sand crunched under her feet as she made her way for a morning walk along the shoreline. The sea was calm. The tide was out. Winter sunlight dazzled on the water. Even in this state of loss and longing, the sea brought a sense of time and peace. It was always there. Every morning. Sometimes calm and sweet like this, as though there was nothing but goodness, fun, pleasure. Other times wild and raging. Full of anger and disturbances that made it scary, dangerous, powerful.

Perspective and space. At least to her mind and, occasionally, to her heart. Let him dissolve back to where he was safe. Because otherwise he may just message her forever.

She had wondered as much to Hermione, whose reply she didn't want to hear. Hermione had remarked that it must be confusing that Stefano's language was steady and persistent, "As though you haven't said anything you've said . . . or with his fingers in his ears as if he hasn't wanted to hear you say it. But from where he is sitting, isn't that what works well for him," she suggested.

Julia thought she was the one wanting to put her fingers in her ears, knowing what was coming.

"He doesn't need to change his life. It was perfect for him. He thinks lovely thoughts of lovely you, he says lovely things and has moments for delicious conversations. You come to Italy; you book a love nest. He visits you in the lovely apartment. A quick visit, to fit around his work. Then he leaves again. He doesn't need to change anything about his life to do this. Anything more would mean drastic change. And until you wanted so much more of a possible life together to materialize, just seeing him was a blessing."

Hermione's version of their love story sounded more one-sided than it had felt. But Julia had to admit there was some truth in that.

Love was something to be offered freely. To be held lightly. Knowing that every day there was a choice to love. A choice to be true to another. Love was an offering and she had offered hers to him freely. She had done all she could. And he had done what he needed to do. It would never feel right unless he chose her for himself. Chose her because he couldn't live without her. Chose her because he loved her. Chose her because he knew it was the only thing to choose in this life.

She wasn't waiting for him. She had never waited for him. That was not how things were between them. They simply were. Whenever the thought of the other became conscious then it was as if they were together.

"But if you won't choose me. Then I must choose myself."

She had said to him that last morning. When was she going to start?

CHAPTER

43

Come on Back to the War

Stefano looked at his phone. It would be a reasonable hour in the morning there. His fingers opened the app. He could message her. But a wave of guilt stopped him. What was he doing? What did he have to offer her? He couldn't give her what she wanted. He couldn't take what he wanted from her. He knew it was wrong to try to hold to on to her when she could be free and he was not. Stepping outside, he lit a cigarette.

He remembered the castle above the hostel. He had made up some nonsense about meeting out of the centre of town, knowing if he had the chance to touch her, to make love to her, then he could not stop himself.

Even then, even in that open space, it had been hard not to take her in his arms. To say things to her that he was not free to say. No matter how much he might feel them. Rounding the corner, he had seen her standing there backlit by the sun. Pulling up beside her he had leaned toward her for a kiss, immediately realizing his mistake. Stepping off the bike, he had pulled out a cigarette to buy some time and create some space. She stood beside him as they looked out over the city, leaning against the wall. Lighting it, he glanced to the side, as she turned to look at him.

"Can I?" she'd said reaching for his cigarette.

"You'll feel sick," he'd warned.

"Maybe," she'd replied.

He could feel her body close to his as their fingers touched. His mind took him there again. Taking back the cigarette, he had smiled at the face she'd pulled. He probably should give them up too. He found himself talking about a health issue, with his leg. Julia standing between his knees. So close. She had stroked his face. A light curve of her lips and a softness in her eyes.

He realized that she didn't care that his body was not as it used to be. She didn't care that his hair was grey. She didn't care that his life was full of complications. She didn't care that he smoked. She didn't care about any of it, and he understood that now. He could feel it.

She didn't care, because it was love. Love wasn't interested in the mind. Love wasn't interested in logic or reasonableness. Love just was. Eternal.

He knew to his core that she would have stayed if he had asked her to stay. That she would open her life to him if he was willing to step forward. Whatever the risk. In sickness and in health. For richer. For poorer. For better. For worse. To have and to hold. All those words suddenly felt as if they held meaning. He knew she would love him until they were no longer.

And how did he feel? He had opened his arms and pulled her toward him. Feeling her body soften. Moulding herself to him. He had buried his face in her shoulder. Because he couldn't let the thought take root in his mind.

Stefano exhaled, the smoke clouding his vision, excusing his tears. Letting the memory dissolve. He couldn't fall into that feeling. There was nothing he could do. He couldn't just abandon his life. He knew where he was. It was safe. Secure. There was kindness. Affection. And he was needed.

This woman who had roamed the corridors of his mind for thirty years. Who he still reached for in his dreams. Her need was different.

That he loved Julia was not even a question. The longing that consumed him and the sadness that overwhelmed him.

He put his phone back in his pocket.

44

Winter AGM

This year their AGM was in the mountains, Winter Rose cottage. Julia picked up Mimi, winding their way through the roads with music blaring. This time the roof was on and the windows up against the cold. It might be nearly spring but the cold lingered.

Stella would arrive later; she had work commitments in the city.

So much had changed since they last met. Stella's new house. Mimi's growing business. There were long discussions to be had, wine to be drunk and food to be eaten.

Julia looked across at Mimi, who was filling the car with music. They had had a big scare this year. A suspected cancer return that had worried them through the winter while they waited for results. Mimi caught her eye and smiled. Knowing what she was thinking. "I'm fine now, what are you being all soft about?"

"Fine now! Yes, thank goodness you are fine. And I am deeply thankful for that you know what's on my mind."

Julia switched back to watching the road.

"Remember the friends of your mum coming to visit her, to take her out on drives even though by that stage she could barely string a sentence together and hardly knew herself let alone anyone else. And her lover. The man who had loved her for years, coming to hold her hand and walk her along the road."

"Not that you mean to be morbid," Mimi laughed.

"No! It's just that there is something about friendship. Remember when my Dad died, my brother and I realized the greatest loss would be felt by his best friend. A man he had spent every day with for five decades, he saw him every day for fifty years."

Mimi closed her eyes and nodded, "Yes, my mum's friends, your dad's mate. We will do that for each other."

Julia reached over and squeezed her hand. "But not for a long time, ok! Not for a very long time."

"No, not for a long time," Mimi promised. "Don't worry." She tried to be reassuring but neither of them liked this topic. "So how are you really?"

Julia shrugged, "I'm okay." She glanced across at Mimi, a small smile, before turning back to watch the road.

Mimi watched her friend's face tighten and close. There was some work to do there, she thought to herself. She patted her bag. Ever prepared, Mimi had brought along some things she knew would help them relax.

The gravel crunched under the tyres as Julia swung the car onto the cottage driveway.

Julia dumped the luggage in the living room as Mimi took the bags of food and drink through to the kitchen, calling behind her, "Can you light a fire?" It didn't take long before there was a fire crackling in the grate. Mimi handed her a glass of wine.

"We may as well begin. Stella will be ages. We'll get a chance to talk properly before she comes to take the stage."

Julia raised her glass before taking a sip of prosecco. Mimi waggled a joint in front of her face. "Come on. Shall we go outside?"

The sky beginning to darken. "Full Moon tonight."

Mimi nodded. "Full moon in Pisces. Dissolving, emotions, merging, love."

"Nearly spring equinox too. I'm looking forward to the days getting longer. I'm tired of the cold, it's time for the sun to come out."

"And you? Are you coming out to play too?"

Julia shrugged. "I don't know. Soon I'm sure."

The joint was beginning to take effect. A small tear slipped down her face.

"Oh babe," Mimi put an arm around her shoulders.

Julia ducked her head and wiped her face.

"I've tried. I have been on a few dates. It's just, I don't know. I don't think I'm in the right head space for it. It's not their fault. They just aren't, they just aren't . . ."

"They aren't him." It wasn't a question.

"No. They aren't him," Julia looked across at her friend, a wry smile on her face.

"Maybe I don't get another chance at love this time round."

They were sitting on the outdoor chairs wrapped in blankets. She looked up at the sky again, dark enough now to see the stars.

"Maybe it's enough to know that a love like that is real. Is possible. To have felt it and to have experienced it and to know that someone else in the world feels it too."

They were quiet for a while.

"Is he still messaging you?"

Julia nodded. "Yes. But I try not to answer. At least not every time. You know. Like weaning myself off a drug."

Looking at what her hand was holding, she laughed, "Well we know how well that works. The right time, in the right company, it's hard to resist." Julia wasn't talking just about now, and Mimi knew that too.

Stella's noisy arrival shifted the conversation and Julia was glad of the reprieve. Curled up near the sofa, the prosecco and the spliff had messed with her head, rather than dancing and laughing, she was happy to let the conversation ebb and flow around her.

She was glad that Stella had drawn Mimi's attention away from her though it didn't last for long. Stella plopped beside her on the sofa.

"What's up with you? What's been happening? Have you been out on any dates?" Her rapid-fire questions filling the air.

"Oh, I'm good, just tired. It's been a long week and a long drive to get here. Then Mimi with her temptations," Julia smiled over at Mimi, who winked back at her.

Stella looked at her speculatively. "You're not still mooning about over that Italian are you? You have to get out there! Another man is just what you need to get over a broken heart. Just use one to forget about the Italian."

"I'm sure you're right. When the right one comes along, I'll be sure to be ready." Julia said to divert her.

"You can't wait forever," chimed in Mimi.

Julia looked at her sharply, not wanting Stella to know all the details of their earlier conversation.

"You could give one of them a chance. Even if you're not sure at first. You never know, they might grow on you. They might help you forget."

"It's true," Mimi nodded, "you can always find a reason not to, but maybe you need to find a reason to like them."

Julia nodded her head slowly. "I'm sure you're right," she said. Though she knew they weren't.

Love wasn't something that you willed into existence. At least not the sort of love she had experienced with Stefano. It was there, like alchemy. Coming into existence with no effort or thought or will on the part of those involved.

They were right, though. Julia knew it was time to step out of herself. But she felt sick at the thought. She would have to go slowly. Carefully. It was the right thing to do. Even if it felt all wrong. She would try.

* * *

CHAPTER

45

The days were longer now, and the sun was already up, despite the early hour. Julia undid her shoelaces and felt the sand, already warm, under her feet.

Facing west, the sun warmed her back as the waves washed in over her feet. The summer break was not too far away. Julia was looking forward to a few weeks of quiet. The opportunity to take some time to reflect on the past twelve months and where things had landed. Her heart felt heavy, but there was a sense of peace. The morning sun helped, she thought, turning her face to feel its light.

It had been months since Stefano had messaged her and she had resisted contacting him, hoping it would eventually occur to him that she couldn't risk another goodbye. She would never forget he existed, but perhaps the day would come when the thought of him would not fill her day. And then maybe another day. And another.

She stood on the shoreline, then rolling up her chinos, she moved toward the sand banks, feeling the waves swirling up toward her knees. The sun was glinting on the water. Bright and sparkling, heralding the even warmer day to come. It was almost warm enough to swim. Maybe tomorrow.

Her phone pinged. Pulling it out of her pocket, Julia flipped open the cover.

It was a message from Stefano.

"What's the water like?"

Julia looked at the phone stupidly. How did he know she was standing in the water right now? Her heart began to race. There was the sound of someone walking out. Turning into the sun, all she could see was an outline moving toward her. But she didn't have to see his face to know it was him. Reaching her he pulled her into his arms, as his mouth found hers, he murmured, "Things have changed."

About the Author

As a twenty something, Amanda spent a year living and studying in Verona, and like Julia in the novel, she left part of her heart in Italy. She likes nothing more than spending time with friends, talking about life, love, and what adventure—internal or external—may be on the cards. Amanda considers herself an accidental explorer and an occasional philosopher. She has lived in London, England, and Melbourne, Australia, where she resides with her three amazing children, three cats, a dog, several fish, and a horse. She is working on her next book and has another story bubbling in the background.